SEVERED

Kate Watterson

TOR

A TOM DOHERTY ASSOCIATES BOOK • NEW YORK

This is a work of fiction. All of the characters, organizations, and events portrayed in this novel are either products of the author's imagination or are used fictitiously.

SEVERED

A Tor Book
Published by Tom Doherty Associates
175 Fifth Avenue
New York, NY 10010

www.tor-forge.com

Tor® is a registered trademark of Macmillan Publishing Group, LLC.

ISBN 978-0-7653-9298-5

Our books may be purchased in bulk for promotional, educational, or business use. Please contact your local bookseller or the Macmillan Corporate and Premium Sales Department at 1-800-221-7945, extension 5442, or by email at MacmillanSpecialMarkets@macmillan.com.

First Edition: October 2018

Printed in the United States of America

0 9 8 7 6 5 4 3 2 1

For Mark and Bobbie Jo Monahan.

ACKNOWLEDGMENTS

Many thanks to Jody McMahel and Elissa Morris for all you do.

SEVERED

Chapter 1

He was in trouble.

That ongoing theme had been part of his life since adolescence. He didn't conform because it wasn't in him. There had been some forgiveness when he was younger, but that seemed to have gone away.

"I've been arrested. I need a lawyer." It was the second time Randy said it.

His father said, "Then I suggest you get one."

"This happens to be my only phone call and—"

The line went dead. He shut his eyes and dropped his head, the phone clammy in his hand. He couldn't swallow, could barely breathe, and his whole body was shaking.

It wasn't like this was smoking some weed, or a speeding ticket. This was for murder.

Jason Santiago had just gotten out of his truck before the glowering Wisconsin skies decided to open up and let loose. He ran for it, barely made it into the courthouse before he was thoroughly drenched, and had to duck into the men's restroom on the first floor to try and repair the worst of it with a paper towel. Why was it every single time he was due to testify in court he spilled mustard on his tie, or in this case, ended up soaking wet?

He was in luck, because the presiding judge was a good old boy who didn't care about his appearance all that much but only wanted to hear what he had to say when he was called to the stand. They had certainly interacted before, and that helped. "Go ahead, Detective Santiago."

"Well, the defendant had been sexually harassing the victim at work, got fired for it, and when we obtained a warrant after she wound up dead in front of the office building, we found a gun under the mattress of his bed. It proved to be the weapon used to kill her, so I believe arresting him on the spot was not a bad decision."

The defending attorney stood, but Judge Tate said, "Sit down, Counselor. If you even try to argue wrongful arrest on the basis they couldn't know it was the murder weapon, it will irritate me and I'll have to remind you they were exactly right. It *was* the murder weapon. I'll take care of this."

She sat down.

The judge did level Jason with a stare. "What made you think it was the gun used to kill the victim?"

"I've seen my share of gunshot wounds, so thought it was probably the right caliber. There was exactly the correct amount of bullets missing from the chamber if it had been fully loaded at the time of the murder. May I point out to the court the defendant had violated a restraining order previously. It wasn't brilliant detective work, since he'd vowed revenge in front of witnesses. It seemed he'd followed through and we arrested him."

Tate nodded. "Thank you, Detective. You are dismissed."

When it came to court, "dismissed" was his favorite word. Jason couldn't wait to get out of there. He went down the steps of the courthouse thankful the deluge was over at least temporarily, and jerked to loosen his tie. He slid into his vehicle and immediately called his partner in Milwaukee Homicide, Detective Ellie MacIntosh. "That bastard will burn in hell," he told her. "Or at least live life in it if prison counts as hell, and it really sounds to me, if all the rumors are true, it fits the description. I didn't stay for the sentencing, but I read Tate pretty well. That judge will toss max at him. He'll definitely get murder one, since it was premeditated."

Ellie was at her desk because lucky her, Tate preferred to grill male police officers and had a special soft spot for pretty blondes. She hadn't been summoned to testify. "He's a woman's worst nightmare."

She meant the man they'd arrested, not Tate. He agreed. "Hers, yes. I'm hoping the victim will haunt him. I'd buy a white sheet and do it myself, but I doubt security would let me near his cell, and floating around saying boo isn't in my skill set."

"A lot of things aren't. We have an interesting new problem."

That wasn't exactly what he needed. He had a pregnant girlfriend who didn't want to discuss marriage, parents he barely knew and he'd just had to do something he despised and go to court. Plus he was soaking wet. What he wanted was a cold beer, or even a lukewarm one, and to sit on his old couch in just sweatpants and watch a baseball game, preferably involving the Brewers handing some other pro team their ass.

"Like what?" He groaned. "Dammit, I don't like the tone of your voice. How big is this 'new problem'?"

"Medium to large. I'll tell you all about it when you get here."

It was raining again, indicating that sitting at his desk in wet clothes was still in his future. He just wasn't a believer in umbrellas. When it was sunny it never even occurred to him to pick one up, and when it was coming down in buckets it was a little too late. Besides, they always seemed to be so ungainly to manage, so he just toughed it out. After parking the truck he sprinted toward the doorway, trying to ignore the trickle of water down the back of his neck. He passed another detective named Rays in the hall, who started laughing. "Well, look at the bright side, Santiago. At least you won't have to take a bath tonight."

"Yeah, thanks. I could use some sunshine like you on a day like today."

Rays grinned. "What are friends for?"

Ellie was wearing a pink top over white Capri pants and dainty gold sandals when he arrived at her desk. She looked nothing like the no-nonsense homicide detective, with her smooth blond hair loose and a hint of glossy pink on her lips, but then again he knew she was heading off to meet her sister for dinner. Jody and her husband were in town for some sort of business meeting through his work, hadn't brought the kids but enlisted a friend for baby-sitting duty, and since her brother-in-law had a late meeting, Ellie had suggested a girls' night out. She and her sister were definitely the best of friends.

He had a feeling he might be a major topic of conversation, but definitely was not invited. Fine, he wasn't a female, so didn't qualify for a spot at the table, but he'd love to hear that discussion.

Of course Ellie took one look at him and asked in open amusement, "Do you ever check the forecast?"

Why lie? He couldn't change it, so no, he didn't look. "No. So what's up?"

"Don't drip on my desk."

"I'll do my best if you will just answer my question."

"Metzger wants to see us."

Oh, just what he needed. A trip to the chief's office? The last time he'd gotten that order, he'd been suspended from duty. Jason had been cleared of all charges, but it wasn't all that long ago. "Why?"

"There's a special case that's cross jurisdiction. There has been a specific request for us to assist."

That was good news anyway. He wasn't in trouble for a change. "Who asked?"

"Aren't you full of questions? So am I for that matter. The chief has a way of being pretty clear. I guess let's go and find out."

She stood, and he assessed her appearance and wondered how many people might have guessed that long, flowing feminine top was to conceal the changes to her figure. She wasn't showing too much yet, but she *was* showing. He asked softly so no one would overhear, "How's our baby today?"

Ellie was adamant they didn't talk at all about their private life at work, especially the upcoming baby, and Jason Santiago had been pretty good about it, considering he was definitely a man who went his own way. Occasionally, he leaned in too close or put his hand on her waist or the small of her back in what might be construed—correctly—as too much familiarity. However, she could cut him some slack because she had every intention of just going ahead and telling their boss after the official part of their meeting. She had a slim build and suspected very soon it would be an easy guess anyway. Half her clothes didn't fit already.

"Fine." She kept her tone brisk. "Let's hope he or she can hear classical music, but not discussions about murder while in the cocoon."

"The cocoon?" He had intensely blue eyes and they were amused. He was also soaking wet, his blond hair in damp curls. How anyone could look attractive while absolutely drenched was a mystery to her, but he pulled it off pretty well. If she faced the truth, she was puzzled by the attraction in the first place. He was hardly the boy next door.

"I'm quoting my sister." Ellie was really looking forward to seeing Jody, who knew pretty much everything about motherhood. Well, no one did, at a guess, but her sister at least had some experience in the form of three healthy, if a little exuberant, children.

"I can't wait to hold the baby, him or her. No preference." He held her gaze a shade too long, and that was yet another reason to just tell Metzger she was pregnant. Anyone paying attention had already noticed Santiago's romantic interest, and that was everyone they worked with. The janitors would probably come to the conclusion this baby was his, and thanks to a stalker case they'd worked recently, Metzger already knew they had a physical relationship.

Great.

The chief was not going to be happy about the unexpected development.

They walked down the hall to the chief's office and met his harried secretary just before they got there. She waved them on. "Go in. He's about done with a call."

Chief Metzger was a big, square man with a very limited sense of humor who took his job seriously and was good at it. Ellie liked his Spartan and direct approach, and she respected how he handled his authority. He still was on the call and simply motioned for them to take a seat. He ended the call abruptly with the words, "I'll make sure this is handled well and quickly."

The chief had a steely gaze and knew how to use it. He first looked at Ellie, and then at Santiago in a deliberate sweep, and pointed at an envelope on his desk. "When you leave, take that with you. Those are crime scene photographs from a few days ago. We have a situation that needs to be addressed, and you two have been especially requested to help in the addressing of said situation. I'm hoping for results that reflect well on the MPD. Got it?"

Santiago predictably replied, "Not yet. What situation?"

"We have a murdered daughter of a district attorney. Her boyfriend has been arrested, but the young man is swearing his innocence."

"If he was arrested," Santiago pointed out, "there must have been probable cause."

"Sure is. An eyewitness. Well, two of them apparently. Also physical evidence." Metzger perpetually drank coffee and picked up his mug before going on. "Cut and dried. Or so it seems."

Ellie had to admit she was confused. "So why exactly are we here? What does 'or so it seems' mean in this case?"

"Because it isn't that simple. He comes from a prominent family, but is a bit of a black sheep and they have nothing to do with him any longer. There's plenty of evidence to take to a grand jury, but here's where it gets dicey. His family's accounting firm has been under a covert investigation for possible ties to embezzling and corporate fraud, and their tentacles are elsewhere too. His father works there, both his brothers work there, and his uncle is a partner. Everyone is involved, which includes the FBI and forensic accountants from the IRS; even the DEA. At more than one level people are wondering if the killing wasn't just a warning to back off. Complicated investigation, lots of parties doing different things, and what they want from you is to find out if this young man really did kill her or if it was a hit and they just set him up for the fall since he's estranged from his family. The various agencies will handle the rest, but you will assist them by determining if this is a legitimate arrest or if he's telling the truth. It *looked* cut and dried at the scene, but the officers who arrested him aren't homicide and they aren't you."

Ellie started to say, "Surely the FBI—"

"Are undercover. They can't ask questions, but you can. You *are* expected by the family, due to Randy's arrest, to show up for a few interviews, so they won't be surprised. You are homicide detectives and this is definitely a homicide."

That made sense.

He went on. "Plus, you've handled a case like this before. We deal with people who view the law as an option they can ignore. These people have money and don't care how they get it apparently. That's not our problem. Our problem is one victim who can't speak for herself because she's dead and a young man who deserves a fair shake if he's telling the truth. I have people in high places telling me he really might have been set up."

"By his family?" Santiago didn't look aghast, he was just asking. His unusual childhood and his stint in the military, not to mention his current occupation, made it almost impossible to surprise him. Ellie had found that out in the course of working with him for several years now.

"Or whoever controls them and knows they won't step forward to help him out. Randy is still sitting in jail. These are people who have cocktails with judges at fancy parties and the money to meet almost any bail, but they aren't interested in lifting a finger on his behalf. Why not?"

If the young man was guilty, she didn't feel sorry for him, but if he wasn't . . .

Jason was never shy. "He's the fall guy."

She agreed. Instantly.

Metzger spread his hands. "Once again, that's not our problem. Your job is to find out what really happened between our suspect and Janet Locke. If the system chooses to prosecute because of what you find out, then hopefully that's justice. If they choose to hit the family and their suspicious friends with both barrels because Randy Lane is considered disposable and framing him for murder is a crime, then that is the decision of people who have a lot more at stake in this than we do."

"*Locke* is a U.S. district attorney and a hard-ass. Well, shit," Santiago muttered. "You've got to be kidding me. I think I've pissed him off more than once. This is a federal case."

"It happened right here in our jurisdiction, and there is no indication that it was more than a lover's quarrel gone bad. If there is, I expect you to find out."

"Can we see the arrest report, sir?" Ellie wasn't thrilled with this assignment either.

"Here it is." He handed over a piece of paper. "No emails on this one, and that order doesn't come from me but from above me. Before the murder, they'd been working on this for months and aren't happy to involve us, but don't have much choice. It would be absolutely a red flag if the MPD didn't look into it as deeply as possible, and you have gotten enough press that they are hoping maybe that if she *was* murdered as a message, it will stir things up a bit just in case you two can figure out who really did it if it wasn't Randy Lane."

"It sounds dangerous." Santiago looked as bland as much as he could pull off, but it wasn't a very good performance. "Maybe I should work this with Grasso."

Both Ellie and Metzger looked at him like he'd lost his mind. The chief leaned back. "Where the hell did that come from? I believe you of all people understand MacIntosh can handle herself because she's saved your sorry ass a time or two. I have always been under the impression that if I assigned you a different partner on a case you'd be extremely unhappy."

"I normally would be."

She knew exactly where it was coming from, and this was not necessarily how she wanted to do this, but then again, she didn't want to do this at all. She said quietly, "He's worried because I'm pregnant."

There, it was over. Bandage ripped off and tossed away.

Metzger shut his eyes and leaned back in his chair and blew out a breath. It took him a long moment. "There's only one reason I can think of *he'd* be so worried. What? Did you both skip health class in high school? For two people I consider some of best detectives I've ever had, you both just slay me."

Chapter 2

There was no sense to it.

He'd tried so hard to figure it out and came up with . . . nothing.

Randy understood his world had been shattered, maimed, devastated. But it was an abstract concept, like he'd always felt about other universes out there into infinity. Tomorrow he would go before a judge who might decide how he would spend the rest of his life.

He lay on his thin mattress and stared up into . . . nothing.

At this point that was his life. It was nothing.

"You might have mentioned you were going to do that." Jason wasn't truly upset with Ellie because that was an inevitable conversation, but he might have wanted some fair warning.

She slanted a look at him out of those striking hazel eyes that were the first thing he'd noticed about her. "Oh, right. You're the one that made him start wondering on the spot why you'd ever request another partner. Besides, everyone is going to figure it out soon enough and probably him first of all. He could be the most observant person I know."

She had a point. Metzger didn't miss a thing.

He still wanted to argue it. "I don't think you should work a case if it involves a professional hit. That's what's bothering me. It isn't like you haven't worked multiple murder cases and you aren't smart and intuitive and everything else—I hate to admit it, but you are probably a better detective than I am—but please get my position in that this isn't all about you any longer. I'm involved."

"I have to make all the concessions?" She was more than ready to argue right back.

"It sounds like what I'm saying, but—"

"But what?" she interrupted. "I'm not crippled, I'm having a baby. So different."

From day one they'd clashed. Obviously not all the time, but he couldn't help himself from saying, "That happens to be my child also. I'm not just worrying about you."

He could see her eyes glistening even as she turned to stare at him again.

Maybe it was not stated as diplomatically as it could have been. God, he was really bad at this relationship thing. "Don't cry or anything. Fine, we'll work the case together. Metzger never said we couldn't. He just asked us to not tell anyone else."

"Hormones," she told him, and turned her back to stalk off. "I'm not crying because of you. You aren't working it with Grasso. You are working with me."

Oh, he'd handled that perfectly. Yes, she was tearing up.

Detective Ellie MacIntosh was usually cool and calm. He followed her, baffled about how to handle the situation. She didn't want to talk about marrying him. He'd offered and been shut down. She didn't want to talk about buying a house and living together; that was another brick wall. But the idea of him working a case with someone else got to her.

He wasn't sure how to feel about it.

Maybe Metzger was right, they were both idiots. If he really wanted to be an idiot, he'd point out he'd been more concerned about birth control than she had, so a part of him wondered if in her subconscious mind she'd *wanted* to get pregnant. She was in her thirties. Not all women desired children, but he thought most did, and she certainly loved her nieces and nephew. He couldn't be happier, and he truly thought she was too, but yes, it was going to impact their working relationship. Jason had a feeling the only reason Metzger hadn't assigned someone else to this case immediately was because he was convinced that as a team they had the best chance of handling this sticky situation.

She sat down at her desk and he stood next to it, deciding to keep it all business. "You read the report and I'll look at the crime scene photographs. Then we'll switch and compare notes. When you go to dinner, I'll go visit Randy in the lockup and do an initial interview while you are eating tapas, whatever the hell that is. Damn, I hate the jail. It makes me avoid a life of crime even though crime probably pays more than what I see on my paycheck each week."

Ellie had recovered. "I wasn't aware you were considering that option, and tapas, for your information, are small plates of different dishes like marinated olives and fried sardines."

"I'm too delicate for jail, so I've decided to toss out the idea of breaking the law. Just give me a burger and I'll skip tapas. I like lots of ketchup and a side of fries, but fried sardines? I've never had them, but I'm already not a fan. They have eyes. No. And that's a firm no."

She laughed and he was glad to hear it. "Delicate, yes, that's you."

He always had the ability to ruin the moment, but somehow refrained. "I do refuse to eat anything that looks back at me. I hope you and Jody have a good time. I'm going to take these photos to my desk. If anything stands out, I'll let you know."

That was a really good call. He sat down, opened the envelope, and understood at once why Lane had been arrested.

They were brutal. At the top end of brutal with a toe in the pool of sadistic.

The victim had been beaten badly, there was crusted blood under her nose and under one eye, and her throat was nothing more than a gaping wound. There were defense wounds on her forearms, and . . .

He'd seen it all in his career, but he had to sit back and take a moment. It shook him, and he wasn't shaken easily.

Yes, Locke was a hard-ass in court, but no one deserved this. Jason closed his eyes, raked his hand through his hair, and tried to regroup.

First impression? It didn't look like a professional hit. Strike that.

It looked like a crime of passion where violent anger was at the forefront. But maybe that was intended just to sink Randy Lane.

There was no way he was going to share these pictures with Ellie before her fun dinner out with her sister.

When she came over and handed him the arrest report, he casually covered the pictures with a report from another case. "I'll take a look at it, but I got a call, so

I'm not done with the pictures yet. We can talk it over tomorrow."

Ellie was too astute to fool. "If your obvious effort to protect me from seeing them is any indication, they must be bad."

"Obvious?" He pretended affront. "I thought it was pretty good." Those pictures would ruin anyone's relaxing evening out, and he knew she was really looking forward to seeing Jody.

She folded her arms. "Transparent comes to mind. Fine, I'll look at them tomorrow after you talk to Randy Lane. Let me guess, frozen pizza for you tonight?"

"I'm one hell of a cook, but yeah, I was thinking along those lines maybe. I have a can of ravioli that's been languishing on the shelf for about a week, so I might shake it up and go for that."

She shook her head. "I won't be late. Want me to bring you something else?"

It was an olive branch. It also meant she was willing to come to his apartment. He took it. "Sure. You pick. Who knows how long the interview will last, if he'll even talk to me without an attorney present. It is a little late for that."

"I get the impression a public defender is going to be the best he can do. During the initial interview that's what he asked for. Not that there aren't a lot of good ones, but his family could get him a high-powered attorney with lots of experience in profile cases of this caliber. They aren't on board with it. I think he's on his own here, and he's a college student. His single bank account is low, and it's his only personal asset besides an old used car."

"I'm guessing they'll have to move his trial to another part of the state. His arrest has already been made public so it's been on the news. Given who the victim is, and what family he's from, there will be lots of coverage on this one."

"He won't be offered bail either. He has a pilot's license and the family has a plane, so I'm guessing the judge will consider him a flight risk in the truest sense of the phrase. If there is bail, it will be very high. Without backing from someone, he simply doesn't have it."

"The system has flaws. What happened to innocent until proven guilty?" Jason said somberly, because the pictures were still bothering him. "If I were him and he's innocent, that's what I would do. Get my hands on a plane and head for somewhere without extradition."

"And if you were guilty?"

"I wouldn't be guilty of that." He pointed at the stack of photographs still covered by a sheet of paper. "Not in one million years, so I can't say."

She was curious, but refrained. "I'm going to just agree with your decision to not show them to me right now. I'm supposed to pick up Jody at the hotel in fifteen minutes. I'll see you later."

She left and he watched her go, admiring the slight sway of her hips. He wasn't the only one either as a uniformed cop passed her and glanced back, which annoyed him, but he needed to not be all sensitive about it and let it go. This was a police department and there were women, yes, but certainly more men, and in his opinion Ellie was more than worth that backward glance. He was guilty of doing it himself.

He wrapped up a few things quickly and went out to his truck. He didn't want to, but he drove to the county lockup and checked in. Patted down, weapon secured, and the inevitable wait.

Randy, he found, was more than happy to talk to him, even if it was the dreaded police. He wasn't what Jason expected, in that he was solidly built and clean cut enough with dark short hair. It was hard to judge someone's appearance when they were wearing the lockup uniform and leg shackles, because they already looked guilty. Jason sat down and they assessed each other for a minute. He said, "I'm Detective Santiago of the Milwaukee Police Department. If you care to talk, let's do it. If you want to lawyer up, we can do this tomorrow instead when we will be interrupted at every turn. Let me say this: I'm your best friend if you didn't do it, since I'm investigating this case, otherwise we won't get along so well. If you killed her, I'll bury you."

Randy leaned forward. "Let's talk. But first, I really need you to do me a favor."

Jody ordered the sardines and the olives, added marinated beef on skewers, spiced shrimp, and some sort of spinach rolled up in pastry with a sharp Spanish cheese. Ellie had to ask as the food was delivered, "Do they grow spinach in Spain?"

"If we can grow it in Wisconsin, I'd guess so. It doesn't matter, it's delicious." Her sister nibbled away. "You look fabulous, by the way. How's the junior detective in the cocoon?"

"I want you to know I'm so sorry I ever told you." Ellie agreed, those spinach things were to die for, the table elegant, and the restaurant not too loud. "How did I know you would joke about it the entire nine months?"

"I didn't know for the first few months, so seven months tops. Don't exaggerate. Besides, what are big sisters for?" Jody didn't skip a beat, but she never did. She also looked fabulous with her chic haircut that swung at her jawline, and her makeup was as always understated but flawless. "It's probably inevitable. Born

to detect. I expect this baby will arrive with a magnify-
ing glass and be examining a crime scene the minute he
can crawl. I'm thinking Sherlock for a name."

"Even if it's a girl?" Ellie had to admit her sister was
outrageous but fairly funny.

"You could call her Sherl."

"I'll take it under consideration. You know, I could
live without those kinds of suggestions." Ellie said contemplatively, "Santiago and I have a new case. It's really
complicated and I suspect he's dealing with someone
right now who is either a ruthless killer, or has been
framed for a heinous crime."

"Only when I have dinner with you do I hear ruthless and heinous as part of the conversation. My girl-
friends usually discuss the cute sweater they found on
sale at a divine price. The word 'adorable' might be
bandied about now and then if someone gets daring.
Go on."

"I have my own unique style." Ellie said it wryly.
"And I can't go on until we really get the investigation
under way. Young man supposedly murdered his girlfriend. There was enough to arrest him. Santiago
wouldn't even let me see the pictures, so I'm going to
guess it was bad."

"Good for Santiago. That's awful."

"*If* this guy did it. He says he didn't. We'll know more
when Santiago gives me his impressions of his face-to-
face interview."

"Santiago. Do you call him by his last name in private?" Jody looked amused as she snapped up the last
spinach wrap and shamelessly ate it. "I'm your sister,
so I'm allowed to ask a personal question like that. I
swear I don't even know his first name, but I admit he's
nice to look at. Santiago. That's all I know."

Ellie felt a faint blush touch her face. And why she'd

do that escaped her. She wasn't sixteen. Blushing? Really? "His first name is Jason."

In retaliation for the wrap thing, she ate the last shrimp. They were now even.

"You two should come to the zoo for the weekend to visit us." Jody made a face. "I know I jokingly call our house that, but it really is a zoo. The little heathens are forever fighting over a toy, tattling on someone else, or requiring a bandage for a scraped knee because this one pushed that one. And that big goofy dog Doug wanted jumps right into the middle of it. I settle more disputes than a diplomat in a war-torn country. Your Jason might run for the hills."

Ellie didn't think so. "He actually seems to really love kids, which is either odd because of his less-than-perfect childhood, or maybe predictable because of it. His mother left him when he was five with a man who wasn't really his father. My impression is neither of them were happy with the arrangement. As a bachelor— and a homicide detective—he still chooses to live in a building full of noisy families. He claims it's because it has a laundry hookup in the apartment and he hates going to the Laundromat, but I'm guessing he likes all the laughter and children running around."

"Well, he'll love the zoo then. Come on up to see us. I'll make something gourmet like my famous spaghetti casserole. Don't scoff, they will all eat that one. A rare event. Anything else and at least one of them will turn up their nose and sulk. I can slave over the stove for hours and it doesn't matter. If mushrooms are involved, forget it. A can of sauce, some cooked noodles and pre-shredded cheese, and they get along for five minutes while their mouths are full. I can even get a few bites of salad down them if I make it."

Ellie laughed. "To tell you the truth, Santiago would

probably like it just as much as they do. The man lives on frozen pizza and takeout as far as I can tell."

"Bachelor." Jody didn't look surprised. "If we weren't married, Doug would just eat potato chips and brag he was a vegetarian. When are you going to tell Mom about the baby?"

That was Jody. Right down to brass tacks.

It was also a valid question.

"I wanted to wait for the second trimester." Ellie had tried to figure out how to tell her mother, but hadn't resolved that yet. "Metzger sure wasn't too happy."

"I imagine he wasn't. Are you both in trouble?"

"He'll reassign us."

"If he does it will still be worth it." Jody stood firm. "The heathens drive me nuts, but you know I wouldn't trade those monsters in for anything."

"I thought they were heathens."

"Heathen monsters. Brace yourself. The other day Ethan announced he was a boy. I agreed, yes, he was a boy. Then he informed me Daddy was a boy. I knew that, believe it or not, and then he told me Mommy is a boy. Well, I argued that point and lost. He thought it over and told me very definitely that Mommy is a *boy*. By the way, Aunt Ellie and Grandma are both boys too. He's a toddler. His mind is made up. Then he asked for more applesauce and fed most of it to the dog, but used the same spoon to eat some of it himself before I caught him. Now tell me, does that qualify as a heathen monster?"

"It might." Ellie was really laughing. "Balancing my life is going to be interesting."

"Marriage isn't on the table?"

Ellie looked at her sister and said with reluctant honesty, "He's asked."

"But the answer is no?"

"The answer is very much I *don't* know. He's emotionally hard to understand. Bryce wasn't all that available in that arena either. Maybe it is just me."

"You do seem to like complicated men. The author and the rogue homicide detective."

"I don't think I like them all that much," Ellie muttered. "I just get involved somehow with them."

"So not true. You do like them. If all they were about was driving a delivery truck and playing poker with the boys on Saturday night, you wouldn't even give them a chance no matter how nice they might be. You prefer your men off the grid."

Ellie was afraid her sister just might be right. Santiago was certainly not the norm.

"I don't know exactly what I want." It was a quiet admission. "He's talked about buying a house on his own but us living together. He wants us to start looking around."

"What's wrong with that?"

Well, about a thousand things.

Ellie sighed. "Maybe I'll consider it. He's just such a wild card. One minute I'm going to a dinner at the governor's mansion with him and the next he's falling out of a speeding car after being attacked by a murderer. I don't want my life to be an action movie. At least Bryce would be home making roasted chicken or something similar, and watching the evening news."

"Life would not be boring with Jason Santiago, but consider this undeniable fact." Jody rested her chin on her fist, her gaze as direct as ever. "You will have to share this child with him. You owe it to your child to have a father. So he's a bit of a bad boy, that's fine, you certainly seem to respect him as a police officer, and you must like him at least a little or you wouldn't be in your current pickle. My darling sister, you do realize that at least this particular man won't blink an eye over what you do for a living. I know several men who are nice, good-looking, and successful enough that I've thought about dabbling in some matchmaking . . . but figure they'd pass out over dating a homicide detective. I really don't think *your* baby daddy will be bothered a bit. I forget, which one of you shot a person last?"

"Very funny." Ellie really wished she could have a glass of wine instead of sparkling water, but she was reserving that indulgence for very limited occasions. Her doctor had said one glass now and then was just fine, but she had a feeling Jason would be counting every sip. "Please never say 'baby daddy' in front of me again. I beg you."

Jody grinned. "I knew it would bug you. Here's my advice if you want it."

She was going to get it anyway. She knew Jody. Ellie rolled her eyes. "Oh, don't hold back. That would be unlike you."

Jody let the caustic tone just slide off. "I never hold back because what's the point of it? Anyway, get a big backyard, not just for the kid, but for you so you can sit on the deck and watch him run around. No pool because you don't want to have to worry about that, and let's face it, this isn't Florida, and I don't picture you floating around on a raft. Relaxation doesn't appear to be part of your makeup. Otherwise, just don't choose a remodeling project because you don't have the time for it, and opt for a quiet street. You'll be fine."

"I have no idea what I'll do."

"Honey, you moved into Bryce's house, and he was a different kind of man altogether. There's no harm in helping Santiago pick something out. If nothing else you'll have some say over where the baby is when it's with him."

That was a valid argument. If she chose to not live with him, he'd still have custody rights. "I'm not sure yet I want to play house. He is not a halfway sort of person. I've directly experienced watching him leap into a lake and cling to a speeding boat with a gunshot wound in his arm. I'm also positive the kid's first words will involve profanity of some sort."

"Well, don't fault him too much for that," her sister said dryly. "I dropped a glass on the floor the other day unloading the dishwasher and there's Kylie walking around barefoot with shattered glass everywhere. I believe she went around saying 'oh shit' for about three days because that came out of my mouth. I was such a proud mother over that one, but at least she didn't get hurt. I was petrified she was going to say it in front of one of her little friends. For all I know she has, but no one has said anything to me yet, so I'm keeping my fingers crossed."

"I'm not going to be good at this motherhood thing, am I?" Ellie was alternately elated and petrified over being pregnant. It was certainly unplanned, but it had happened. She was even happy overall, but she wasn't sure about her personal relationship with one Detective Jason Santiago. Professionally, they were normally on the same page, but the situation was *not* exactly normal.

As parents they could be the worst match ever.

"If you are half as good as I am," Jody said serenely, "you'll be great. Now then, you skipped the wine, so by default, you get to pick the dessert. What are we having?"

Her phone beeped. It was Jason, and she might have ignored anyone else, but . . . not him.

He said without any greeting, which was absolutely him, "It looks like we're dog sitting."

Chapter 3

It really was a version of waiting in hell.

Worse than any flight delay at an airport by far. Worse than when he was trapped in traffic six hours in LA by a monstrous accident and had to listen on the radio to the number of fatalities and then drive past the ambulances. Worse than sitting and waiting for news in a hospital about his grandfather's bypass surgery while his mother sat and cried.

It was the waiting.

Randy was actually grateful to have had the cop come see him because it was something to do, and if that wasn't messed up, he didn't know what was. He was practically climbing the walls. Plus, at least someone seemed to care about the truth. The guy hadn't been one of those old-school types with a paunch and a notebook either; he'd been very direct, but not accusatory, just interested. On the younger side, he'd been casually dressed, and with no notebook in sight. Tall and blond, no nonsense, Detective Santiago made Randy fairly sure if he dished out a lie this guy would sense it. Not old school maybe, but hard edged. He'd sat down like he was willing to listen, but not to bullshit.

It was difficult, especially with nothing to do, to not replay the conversation in his head. The first question especially.

"Well, let's get this out of the way. Did you kill Janet Locke?"

"No!"

"We have an eyewitness willing to testify in a court of law he heard screaming and saw you running out of her house with blood on your clothes."

"I was the one screaming. Wouldn't you? The blood is hers, yes. I have no idea why I thought there was something I could do to help her. I knelt in the blood, and I put my hands on her, and yes, I picked up the knife. I was truly in shock. I look back on it and regret making your job harder, but I remember it like a nightmare. I still can't believe it ever happened."

He wasn't even going to be allowed the closure of her funeral. It was so unfair if he thought about it he would really lose his mind, and he was halfway there already.

"Why did you run?"

"I know this sounds stupid, but my phone was dead and I needed to call 911. I mean, I saw all that blood, but what if someone could help her? I think I knew she was gone, but what if she wasn't and I didn't do something? I couldn't live with that."

Naturally, the cop looked skeptical. It sounded stupid to Randy too, or now it did anyway.

"You do know they will rip you into little tiny pieces for that story. The only thing that might help you is blood spatter evidence, and there is always the argument you changed clothes and staged the rest of it since you knew you'd be a suspect."

"I wasn't thinking about that. Keep in mind, Detective, I knew I didn't do it. I couldn't believe it. Jan was really a rock after my family turned away from me. I loved her. I'd just asked her to marry me, and just so you know, she'd said yes."

"Do you think you were put in a bad position on purpose?"

"I don't want to, but maybe."

It was emasculating, but he'd cried at that point before he shook it off. He wasn't a ten-year-old boy any longer, he was a man, and he had the feeling he'd be in for the fight of his life. It was more accurate to say the fight for his life to live outside bars and slamming cell doors.

His mother hadn't even been to see him. He'd added quietly, "I've known for some time I've been severed."

Then he'd asked the unthinkable of someone he didn't even know. "Can you watch my dog, or do you know someone who will? I'm . . . lost. I don't know where to turn. She's small and really even keeled, but someone needs to be humane and let her out, and I really can't contact anyone right now. I swear she's great. Please at least let the Humane Society know she's there. The idea she's locked in and that no one is feeding her is so wrong."

The detective had looked at him with remarkable equanimity. "I agree. How do I get in?"

Lieutenant Carl Grasso liked his coffee black. Stark black and strong, but from past experience, caution was in order.

He picked up his cup and took a sip, then decided it was enough to make an old-time Texas Ranger cringe even if he'd been in the saddle for two days chasing down notorious criminals and needed to stay awake. Santiago had made it.

The file was front and center. He took another sample of the toxic brew and put down the mug. Fergusson, the chief detective, looked troubled. "We have a district attorney asking for two particular detectives to look into his daughter's murder. We have a family being investigated for charges that could go back decades and involve millions of dollars and multiple arrests on a lot of levels. It is the tip of the iceberg, literally. We have federal agents involved on several fronts from different branches. Are MacIntosh and Santiago up for it? I want this clean and neat."

It wasn't doubt that made him think it over; it was more how to answer the question. Carl said carefully, "You know they're a good team. She is collected, and he's got more experience. One thing I will say for Santiago is he lets her talk. If the underlying question is will they mess this up, my answer is no. I think they will successfully investigate the murder and not blow the other investigation. That's the goal, right?"

"If you have a grieving prosecutor breathing down your neck, yes, right." Fergusson squared his thick shoulders. "I don't blame Locke one bit either. I have four daughters. I just can't imagine."

Carl didn't realize that. "Four?"

"Four. I've been last in line for the bathroom for years. And if someone even lifted a hand to one of them I'd rip his arm off, much less what happened to Locke's daughter. Santiago now has been suspended twice, though I will say Internal Affairs couldn't make anything stick either time. He's a straight cop, but he can be a loose cannon. Both times I basically agreed with his justifications, but maybe not his methods. If this department was the only one involved I wouldn't lose sleep over it, but it isn't."

It wasn't as if Carl hadn't had IA crawl all over him once. "I'd lay odds in Vegas they'll figure it out."

"Well, I don't want them to figure out too much. That's our real problem. We can't let this kid hang for something he didn't do—if he didn't. The information I have says it didn't look like a hit, but maybe that's intentional. Locke wants justice, plain and simple, so *he* can hang the perp high. Being in the middle of all this won't be easy. None of us get to know who is a good guy and who is a bad guy. Not me, not you, not Locke, and not Santiago and MacIntosh."

It sure didn't sound simple.

"And you will help them out. I want someone keeping tabs on how it's progressing. I'm going to tell the feds to contact you if there's any problem at all." Fergusson stood. "I'd handle it, but my wife and I are going on a cruise. Some sort of European river thing she planned with castles and polka music, and I am just going to sit around and drink beer and eat sauerkraut on anything that ends in 'wurst.' The timing is bad, but she's been planning this for two years. She'd better not mention the low-salt diet I'm supposed to be on. I hate polka music, but I love that kind of food. You are a lieutenant for a reason. You'll be in charge while I'm gone. Please tell me I didn't see a dog in here earlier, because I'm fairly sure I did. Take care of that problem too because this isn't a kennel."

He walked off and Grasso swore softly under his breath. Fergusson was not a subtle man, but as chief detective he was responsible for overseeing how the cases were handled.

The last time Grasso assisted in a case with Santiago

and MacIntosh the killer came after him and broke his
arm and his collarbone with a baseball bat. Not that
he blamed either of his colleagues for that particular
scenario, but they seemed to inherit the dangerous cases.
The other possibility was that the cases turned dangerous *because* they'd inherited them. When people who
held no value for human life became threatened, they
lashed out like animals. Luckily, that particular animal
was no longer loose in the wild if it was Lane.

But there was the dog.

He called MacIntosh on her cell. "The Locke case . . .
we apparently need a meeting. Where's Santiago and
where's that dog? It can't wander around here."

"The dog is an interesting problem. Lane asked him
during the initial interview if he would take care of it.
She's sweet, so if he's the murderer, we know he's kind
to his dog anyway. Santiago had no idea if it would
bark all day so he brought it with him to work. It's back
at his apartment now."

One thing already done, so that was good anyway.

MacIntosh said, "I wondered if you'd be invited to
this party. I haven't hosted one without you in quite
some time. Just met with Metzger?"

"Fergusson. Where are you?"

"We're at the murder scene." She gave him the street
name and number. "The crime scene has really been
gone over, so we are just looking around, trying to get
a feel for how it happened. You are welcome to wait
for us to get back, or else pay us a cheerful visit. If you
like the sight of bloodstains, you'll enjoy it."

He didn't, but it was part of his job. He sat and
thought about it, and since he always preferred the
actual investigation aspect to his desk, grabbed up his
suit coat and took off.

The house was in a small but increasingly stylish

neighborhood, and the address was growing in value probably by the day. Not too far from downtown, reasonable prices for now, and decent-sized yards. The loops of police tape told him he was in the right place.

He went up the steps and ducked under the tape. He didn't bother to knock since the owner wasn't home, she was in the morgue. He didn't like the thought of that at all. He had a tough skin after all these years, but still was capable of compassion, or at least he hoped so.

There were two small pots of daisies on the front porch and a whimsical garden gnome statue between them. It always surprised him when something like that hit him hard. It was a beautiful summer morning, too. Promises of blue skies. The person who'd loved that gnome statue would never see the sun shine again.

Every homicide was gruesome in some way, even with the quiet ones when you could tell the victim never saw it coming and just went out like a light with a burned-out bulb. The others were worse, when you knew they realized it was going to happen. He'd agonized for many years over whether or not his parents had realized the accident that killed them both was about to occur even for the split second before impact. He hoped not. In their case it hadn't been murder, but just plain bad luck.

He did his best not to visit that dark moment.

This moment was pretty dark as well and this had been murder.

Blood spatter was on the wall and there was a huge dark stain on the polished wood floor. She'd bled out, but he already knew that. He saw a small comfortable red couch with a remote control probably for the wall-mounted television, an open book, a coffee table. Plus a broken vase on the floor indicating a struggle. MacIntosh stood there, a faint furrow on her normally smooth brow, and glanced up as he walked in. Without a greeting, she said, "I just talked to Hammett. Her opinion is that the sex probably was consensual like he says, but they do have DNA from Randy Lane."

Carl studied the stain on the floor. Blood had seeped into a patterned rug as well. "So we have her blood on his clothes, his DNA on the victim, and an eyewitness seeing him leave the crime scene, correct?"

Santiago snapped off a pair of gloves and dropped them into a bag used for disposing of potentially infectious items. "Oh hell yes, that's right. He was *fleeing* the murder scene," he said, "according to the neighbors. Let's not forget his prints on the murder weapon. The neighbors are a young couple who were out watering their plants. They didn't see anyone else go into the house, but did say they hadn't been outside for very long before Randy Lane came out the door like a tornado on the Fourth of July." Then he said flatly, "I'm not buying he's the killer."

Carl took that in. "Why? Interview impression?"

Santiago contemplated. "I don't know why. He's convincing, but we've all been fooled at one time or another. Still, it doesn't feel right. He *seems* guilty from the evidence. 'Seems' is the operative word there. I think he's no angel in that he was a rebellious teen, but neither was I."

If Carl had never worked a case that way he'd disagree, but he had. "You for sure aren't an angel even now," he agreed. "Find out why you're buying his story. Fergusson has put me in charge of talking to Locke. If it was any other bereft and traumatized parent I'd still feel bad, but this is Locke. I know him pretty well. He'll rip this case apart if there is a single flaw. While Fergusson is putting on more pounds he doesn't need in Europe, this is my problem."

"We'll try to be fast." MacIntosh meant it, he could tell. "Santiago could be right and it always pains me to say that. She was surprised. I think with a lover's quarrel she would have maybe seen it coming. Certainly not Lane necessarily attacking her, but if I had to call it, she answered the door and was backed up to here at knifepoint"—she pointed—"and then was killed. You can see the nick in the wall where she was pinned by the knife. Someone hit her more than once with their fist. She landed facedown when they pulled out the knife. Lane is the one who rolled her over. He admits that. He knelt in her blood. He says he was in such shock he just picked up the knife."

"Could be to cover it up."

"Yeah, it could," Santiago agreed. "But I'm not convinced. That's the essential problem. I'm *not* convinced. He could also be telling the truth. He'd just proposed according to him, and she'd said yes. There seems to be a double motive. To take her out and to take him down? I think it seems too convenient. He says his family might be responsible for her death."

"Proof?"

"Just his word for it."

"All of it is from someone who has all the signs of a killer from fingerprints to leaving the scene, but it doesn't feel right." Ellie looked very unhappy. "You know how it goes. Every case has a *feel* to it."

"Exactly." Santiago wasn't fazed. "It's too easy. He went out to pick up dinner. He did pick it up; the team took it into evidence since he supposedly dropped it all over the floor when he walked through the door and saw the body. I can tell you are going to now argue he did that as a smokescreen as well. We visited the restaurant. He had to walk in to pick up the order. No one noticed blood on his clothes. That means he'd have had to kill her before, change his clothes, go pick up food, and then come back, drop it so it spilled, and then kneel in her blood. The blood on his clothes doesn't match the attack according to the spatter guys."

Carl said evenly, "It doesn't matter what I argue, it just matters what you can provide as evidence, either way. This isn't an average case. As we know full well, unfortunately, men and women in a relationship occasionally kill each other, hence the phrase 'crime of passion.' If that's the case, it has happened and we can't erase it. If it isn't the case, then this situation needs a whole new approach because it could smack of premeditation. Locke asked for you for a reason, and he got you."

This was a particularly savage crime from what he could see from the scene, and the photos of the body were enough to call for an extra scotch by the pool tonight so he could sleep.

"The confidence is flattering, but until we can dig up anything to indicate it wasn't Lane, it is all speculation." MacIntosh didn't look too pleased with the assignment. Her hazel eyes had a troubled look. "I understand Locke is a very determined man; we've all worked with him."

It was hard to argue. "See what you can do, and do it fast, please. With Fergusson gone, that means you get to give me reports on how this is going. Look at the bright side of it all, *you* don't have to talk to the angry father who wants immediate results because he's going off the deep end with grief, not to mention fear for the rest of his family."

It wasn't like both of them ever didn't put in a full effort—that's why Locke had asked for them. Quite frankly, the initial assignment of them as partners was a disaster in the making, or so he'd thought. Having a good partner was like a marriage. You had to work at it all the time. Overlook the shortcomings and concentrate on the good. They'd achieved a balance that surprised everyone except maybe Chief Metzger.

Santiago was a tough kid who had grown up mostly on his own, and MacIntosh looked like a high school cheerleader who was probably homecoming queen. Especially now when instead of her usual tailored look, she wore a feminine top with fluttery sleeves and a long lacy hem. The shoulder holster for her weapon looked incongruous next to her attire, but it was summer now and really warming up.

"Here's one weird thing, though, if Randy did it," MacIntosh said. "The fingerprint guys couldn't find a single one on the coffee table. They pointed it out. That makes no sense to me. Randy has every reason to have his prints all over this house. He and the victim were sleeping together. He was a regular visitor. The only logic I can see for anyone cleaning off the coffee table is that they touched it accidentally. Maybe it was knocked over and the vase breaking showed signs of a struggle. Maybe habit made them decide to right it, and then they realized what they'd done." She paused. "To my mind, Randy wouldn't have any reason to kill his girlfriend, get her blood all over him, and yet clean off her coffee table before he ran out of the house. The crime scene crew said it had just been polished. There's blood spray on the floor, on the couch, the wall, the rug, but none on the coffee table. Why? Someone was getting rid of a print."

This wasn't going to be music to Locke's ears, that was for sure. Carl couldn't disagree. It wasn't a phone call he was anxious to make. "Okay, I'm not going to be more specific until you dig deeper. Why is it I always want simple and never get it?"

Santiago said in his straightforward sardonic way,

"Welcome to my life. Simple is an abstract concept used to sell products like oven cleaner or new software for your computer. Don't let them fool you. It doesn't exist. My oven still looks like I roasted an ox in there and my computer deleted half my files when I installed a *simple* new program. We'll go around the neighborhood again when people start getting home from work. I'm sure most of them saw the broadcast on the news last night about the murder, and someone would have called in if they had information, but you never know." He grimaced. "Right now I have to chuck my manhood out the window and go walk a dog that could be carried around in a purse. The things I do for this department."

Chapter 4

The message was short and sweet.

Apparently the detective was a man of few words. *Have dog.*

Randy could at least get that off his long list of worries, he thought, as he looked at the piece of paper the deputy had handed him.

Jan had given him that dog as a valentine present. His apartment didn't allow any animals over a certain weight and she'd been an advocate of rescue dogs, volunteering at the shelter close to her house twice a month. She'd delivered the puppy with a red ribbon around its neck and a small bed. Randy had eyed it dubiously, but the truth was, he'd grown attached to it pretty fast.

She'd also loved children, planted an herb garden behind her small house, and visited her grandmother without fail every Sunday.

In short, she really had been such a good person to his mind, and in no way had deserved what had happened to her.

It was beyond frustrating that he was trapped, locked

up, and couldn't do a damned thing to turn back time and protect her.

"**Remember when you** told me a few months ago I should get a giant dog and name him Killer?" Ellie petted the animal nestled on her lap. "Is this what you had in mind?"

Louise was a Chihuahua/Boston terrier mix about the size of a cat. She was very sweet, but she trembled frequently and was only house trained on a moderate basis. Luckily it was Jason's apartment. So far he'd done the cleaning up with mostly patience, but he wasn't exactly a happy camper.

The dog had an immediate attachment to Ellie. Not a fan of Detective Jason Santiago.

"She growls at me," he said in affront.

Ellie offered up helpfully, "You're too tall. You scare her."

"What am I supposed to do, shrink? I rescued her sorry ass. A little gratitude would be nice. Just one wag of her tail and we'd be good."

"She likes *me*."

"Brag on." He pointed. "That is not a dog. It's like a rat or something. It's a rat dog."

"I'm not the one who went to a murder suspect's home and picked it up." She rubbed Louise's ears. "You're jealous because she likes me better, but that was really nice of you."

"Whether Lane is guilty or not, I'm hardly going let a dog suffer. Look at her. I know *she* didn't do it. Maybe she could kill a flea, but I doubt it. I'd put my money on the flea."

Louise growled. He glowered. "Look, rat dog—"

Ellie laughed softly. "She's sweet. Maybe she'll grow to love you. I hate to tell you this, but you are definitely not love at first introduction."

"I've gotten that impression a time or two." His smile was wry. "She's certainly motivation to get Randy Lane out of jail so he can have her back. Let's go talk to Janet's neighbors. They should be home from work by now."

She set Louise on the floor. "I'm in."

"She's going to piss in my apartment while we're gone, isn't she?"

"Probably." It was an educated guess.

He muttered something under his breath, but did check her water bowl before they went out the door, which was good of him. Ellie was the one who drove back to the address of the crime scene. The street certainly looked serene, but bad things could happen in nice places.

The house was typical, built a century or so ago, tidy and right next door to where Janet Locke had been attacked. They were expected, but Ellie doubted very welcome as visitors.

"I suppose we're technically living in sin." The young woman was obviously trying to make a joke, but her smile was wan. "We just bought this house. Our wedding is in two weeks. To have someone murdered right next door is not how I wanted our life together to start. I don't want to think about it."

Ellie sympathized, but this couple was the closest to witnesses available, and the fiancé worked second shift so he actually wasn't there. "Any information you can give us would be appreciated. I realize you've already spoken to the police, but it would be helpful if we could go over it again since we are assigned to this crime. I understand you were outside when Mr. Lane came out of the house."

"Yes." She pointed at the yard. "I was standing right there watering our new rosebush. David just bought it for me. Yellow like what's going to be in my bouquet."

There were two rocking chairs on the front porch and the future Mrs. Richards sank into one. She was a pretty brunette, probably in her midtwenties, and would make a lovely bride, but at the moment her expression was taut. "I heard someone screaming. Literally screaming, 'No, no, no,' just over and over. It was one of those moments when you just stand there and don't know what to do. I'd met her to the extent we'd waved at each other and said hi, but she was gone a lot. I saw on the news she was a student at Marquette. This is so . . . sad."

She had been pursuing a degree in English. Ellie also thought it sad that a young dream was extinguished. "I know," she said quietly. "It's very tragic. What else can you tell us? Recount again what happened when Mr. Lane got into his car."

"He started it but didn't go anywhere. He was covered in blood, I could see that much, and I couldn't move, but David was also outside and he called 911. We thought there had been an accident."

Jason spoke for the first time. "Did you see any other vehicles? Any strangers go to her door?"

"No. We are so new here I really don't know who is a resident and who isn't supposed to be here. I grew up in a small town. Everyone knew everyone. Milwaukee is different for me. I was also watching a show on home improvement as I fixed dinner before we went outside, so I wasn't paying attention. We want to redo the kitchen. I put the hot dish in the oven and we went out and that's when it happened."

Ellie took a moment. "Tell me how he seemed. Randy Lane. Just give me your impression. Was he acting or truly horrified? This isn't evidence, but I'd like to know how you viewed it in the moment."

No hesitation. "Horrified. He was crying and couldn't get his car door open in three tries. Once again, I absolutely didn't know what to do."

"Were you outside when he pulled up initially?"

"No. I heard a car door slam, that's all. We had the windows open. We went out a minute or two later."

"If you had to estimate it, how long before he ran out of the house was that?"

She shrugged helplessly. "I don't know. I wasn't paying attention. Why would I? There was nothing to indicate anything was wrong."

No doubt that she was justified in that statement.

"We agree, but are just looking for answers. Thank you for your time."

They left. It was one of those soft summer evenings and the air smelled like grass clippings. Jason said, "So, are we thinking the same thing?"

"I'm not as convinced as you yet. He could have been horrified at what he'd just done. An argument that went out of control is still possible."

"But you don't think so." He opened her door and held it. They'd had the discussion he didn't need to do that because she was perfectly capable of doing it herself, but she'd lost that one and finally given up.

No, she didn't think so. Ellie climbed into the vehicle, thinking hard. This was really early in the case. She wasn't convinced either way.

Except the lack of fingerprints on the coffee table was a problem. In many cases killers had tried to eradicate evidence by cleaning up bloodstains—which rarely worked—but she'd certainly never investigated one where they'd just chosen one spot.

Jason got in and started the truck. "Ellie, Randy didn't clean the coffee table. Someone else did it. We need to go talk to Locke anyway. I'm not faulting the arresting officers. I would have arrested him too. But that one thing stands out. Everything else, including screaming and tears, can be contributed to guilt. How many men have hit a spouse or girlfriend or child and been instantly contrite? For that matter, your gender isn't entirely innocent either. Plenty of women have killed their lovers."

She didn't want to even think about that. "He didn't just hit her. Whoever did it stabbed her and slit her throat."

"Out of control, I agree. What about the coffee table? And the blood spatter on his clothes doesn't match the time frame if they heard him shut his car door and went outside just a minute or two later, unless there was some serious planning involved. I don't know if it looks good or bad for him. If they got into it and he killed her, he'd have to have a very cool head to change his clothes, clean just the coffee table and hope we'd pick up on that, run out for the food, and come back and put on the act of a lifetime. In person, he's pretty convincing as someone who could never be that dispassionate."

She agreed with the entire argument. "He wouldn't just wipe off the coffee table, or at least we can't guess why he would. We also couldn't find a container of furniture polish, so whoever did it took it with them. It wasn't in his car and he didn't drive away after he supposedly found the body."

"Well, if he killed her first, he drove away. He could have dumped the polish anywhere."

That was true and possible. It made it all look worse for Randy. Ellie really wasn't sure what to think. "He just got into his car and used his phone charger so he could call 911 because his phone was dead. In his defense, he did do that, but maybe it was a diversion."

The blood in his car had granted the arresting officers an almost instant warrant to search it from a judge who usually wasn't all that amiable, but considering the identity of the victim gave the crime team anything they wanted.

"If he's smart enough to plan all that he's a pretty cold and crafty guy. He just didn't strike me that way."

"Let's call Grasso and see if wants us to talk to Locke face to face. We have to interview the family anyway."

"Shit. Can't I go get a cup of coffee or a beer and you can tell me how it went?"

He really hated that part of the job, she knew that. Ellie didn't like it either. "No. Necessary. At least he'll listen to us. Maybe we can do something to lower the bail for Randy Lane. I'm trying to picture something worse than being in jail for a crime you didn't commit and in the bargain losing a person you love. It sounds like pure hell. I'm not convinced he's innocent, but I'm not sure enough he isn't. If it was a crime of passion he isn't really a danger to anyone else necessarily, and if it was a hit, he doesn't deserve to be there."

"Ellie, I want you off this case." Santiago's profile was like a stone wall.

"Thanks for the vote of confidence. You have a much better chance of solving it if I work it with you."

"I wish that wasn't true. You have a much better chance of me buying you a suit of armor."

"Oh, that would be interesting down the line. Please order the impending whale size. I tell you what, let's just agree to figure this out quickly."

"You and I need to agree on a lot of things, and we need to do that quickly too. I want to go look at a house on Sunday."

He really *was* serious about it.

"I think I'm the one who should be intent on nesting."

"Hey, I'm in touch with my feminine side."

He was a football-watching-beer-drinking tall guy from Wisconsin. She'd seen him take a bullet—or two—and get in a serious fistfight that he'd won, plus she knew he'd been boots on the ground in countries that did not welcome American troops. There *was* no feminine side.

Dryly, she remarked, "I'm surprised you don't wear a feather boa all the time."

"I've thought about it. Pink, right? Will you go with me?"

She'd considered Jody's advice. Looking at a house? There was no harm in that, was there? "Well . . . okay."

"It has a big backyard for the bambino and the dog I've always wanted."

"You have a dog."

"Weren't you listening? I said the dog I always *wanted*. Right now we're baby-sitting the little rat dog. A big yard is important to me. I don't care too much about the rest."

Another Jody echo. "Sounds nice."

Then he turned typical Santiago. "Jesus, MacIntosh, can you show some enthusiasm? We are having a kid. Together. Me and you. I thought I was the worst person on this planet when it came to commitment, but I'm starting to think you give me a run for my money."

Defensively, she said, "My one attempt at living with someone didn't work out. Your one attempt at living with someone didn't work out. We're not exactly batting a thousand between the two of us, are we? I'm unexpectedly pregnant, not married, and was recently stalked by a serial killer who tried to strangle his wife right in front of me. Life has been more than a little interesting lately, and it wasn't all that ordinary before. Let's mention we just left a crime scene, we both know we'll be assigned different partners when this case is done, and in the meantime, someone out there doesn't play so nice. A big backyard sounds great, but I just don't know if I'm in an effusive mood right now."

He was much more intuitive than he let on. "Hey, I don't want to talk to Locke either."

"Good. I'll talk and you listen."

"That's a bargain I can live with."

Nathan Locke immediately answered the door to his sprawling midcentury Tudor-style house and said with his usual precise intonation Jason had heard in the courtroom, "We'll have this conversation outside. My family doesn't need to hear it. I've tried to spare them as many of the details as possible. It says a lot to me that they aren't asking more questions, not even my wife." His wife was also an attorney and a partner in a prominent firm.

Jason was happier with that anyway. He could deal with Locke; he certainly had before. A devastated family was a no, thank you. He was fairly sure all of a sudden both he and Ellie were getting a whole new perspective on what they did for a living. Introducing a child into this sometimes brutal world made him cold all over.

Case in point, Locke looked like shit. He was usually Mr. Suave, with impeccably neat dark hair, chiseled features, and expensive suits. He was not wearing his usual tailored attire, but instead wrinkled slacks and a shirt open at the neck. If he'd slept recently, Jason doubted it, his eyes were so bloodshot. Locke said succinctly, "You've been to see Randy and the crime scene. Talk to me."

They walked along the trim lawn as if having a casual conversation, when it was anything but casual.

Ellie was her usual composed cop persona. "Santiago doesn't think Randy Lane did it despite the evidence, and I'm really starting to agree. Crime scene evaluation shows inconsistencies that bother us both. Some can't be easily explained away by blaming Randy. I think both Detective Santiago and myself follow the policy that if something makes no sense, even something small, then perhaps there is a much different explanation to what seems on the surface to be the truth."

That was well put. Jason would have messed it up and said something like he was afraid there was some bullshit with the evidence. No wonder he got reminded in every single case to let her do the talking.

"Like what? I'm a district attorney. Convince me."

"Someone cleaned up evidence, but not how we think Randy would have done it." She explained about the coffee table. "There's no reason I can think of that he would bother unless to deflect us, and that takes some very level thinking if you are going to pretend you found the body. He isn't stupid, but still . . . he ran out of the house screaming and called the police."

"That was my grandmother's house. My wife and I decided rather than sell it, to let our daughter live in it rent free while she finished school. You have no idea how much I am second-guessing some of my decisions. It was supposed to be a safe neighborhood. Go on."

She did. "There was also no reason to hide he was there. Maybe he could have changed his clothes after the crime, but then why wipe down the coffee table and nothing else? His prints are all over the place. He could still claim exactly what he claims happened even in different clothes. As it stands, his story makes sense. Explain the coffee table to me. I suppose it could be argued he desperately started to try and clean up and realized it would be too difficult and chose a different approach, but the furniture polish is missing and was not in his car. Surely she had some. Crime scene said it seemed freshly done."

Locke's jaw hardened as he thought it over. "I would think she would have some. Okay. Keep talking."

Jason helped her out, since he could sense she didn't want to do it. He didn't either, but the man already knew the bitter truth and wanted the facts. "Then there's the food spilled all over. We think she opened the door and are wondering why. I'm finding it hard to believe that Randy first of all wouldn't just walk right in, and second of all, would go get food after killing her. I'm not saying he isn't that farsighted, but I *would* say most people aren't. I know if I was that angry with someone, I wouldn't keep my cool that way."

"A valid point. That has bothered me all along. Jan didn't say they were having problems." Locke looked away, his expression remote. "I never liked the tie to his family, but then again, I didn't get to make those decisions for her. They met up at a college bar and apparently hit it off. She was old enough to know her own mind. I'm starting to get convinced. I'm going to nail the bastards to a wall and light them on fire when you catch them. I didn't really believe Randy did it in the first place. His family is a different story. The more that comes to light, the more I think they had my daughter killed to intimidate me because my office launched an investigation in cooperation with several other agencies. I'm standing here telling you it is going to have exactly the opposite effect they wanted. I might have to send my family—the rest of my family—somewhere, but it'll be worth it."

Ellie said quietly, "I still have a house in northern Wisconsin. It's just sitting there. Send your family up there anytime if you like until we sort it all out. It's secluded. I can give you the county sheriff's number and he'll have deputies on patrol swing by. He's a great guy. He'll look out for them, but with no credit cards involved it would be really hard to trace them, unlike to a motel. Send them with cash for food. The closest grocery store is pretty far away. They couldn't be found."

Jason almost said she should go with them, but he wasn't winning any points with those suggestions. And it wasn't a bad idea for Locke's family.

At all.

It was clear Locke was worried enough, he considered it carefully. He said slowly, "I appreciate that offer more than you know, Detective MacIntosh. I don't want to put more people I care about at risk. I can handle most things, but this is . . . difficult. I was thinking passports and a foreign resort, but these people have a long reach."

"I'll drop off the key and directions tomorrow. Tell them not to use their GPS. I don't know exactly who we might be dealing with at this point. If I were you I'd rent them a car. That way there can't be a tracking device."

"Good suggestion . . . I'm not myself right now. The funeral . . . I'm not sure how I'll hold up." He turned away and stared remotely into the yard before he got it back together. He leveled a piercing look at them both. "I'm glad Metzger listened to me. I'm an attorney, but I'm a father and husband first. I'm not going to lie to you, this isn't a simple situation, and all three of us know it. Because of what you just told me, I'll go see Randy myself. We do know each other. If he tells me anything I think will help the investigation, I will pick up the phone immediately. My goal is not the overall investigation at this moment. I want who did it. Whoever put a knife to her throat won't be safe in my presence, I promise you that. I doubt he'd make it to his fair day in court."

Jason wasn't sure if this was a good time or not, but there probably wasn't one anyway. "Maybe they should take Janet's dog for company. They being your family. She gave it to Randy as a gift . . . the dog is staying with me, but I'm not there much. He was worried about her so I picked her up. Louise isn't going to offer much in the way of protection, but she's cute enough."

The breeze was soft and warm and incongruous to the conversation, which appeared to be over. Locke hesitated but nodded. "I'll ask my wife. That might offer her some form of comfort . . . I admit I'm hard pressed how to deal with her grief, much less mine. I do think she'd like that. I'd appreciate it if you'd keep me informed about the investigation, and if I'm not immediately available, contact Assistant District Attorney Michael Lambert. We work closely together."

"It goes without saying that if Randy offers anything to you he didn't tell Detective Santiago, we'd like to hear it. You know how to find us." Ellie nodded and headed for the driveway.

"Good night, Detectives."

When they left, Jason couldn't help but say as he started the vehicle, "You know how sometimes you dread something and it isn't that bad? Not so. This was worse than expected on my scale of one to ten. I think I just heard a district attorney threaten to kill someone."

Ellie didn't argue. "You did. Who can blame him?"

"You look pale."

"I feel pale."

She was telling the truth. The first trimester had been on the rough side when it came to nausea. Jason said, "Take a deep breath. Do I need to pull over?"

She closed her eyes. "No. At least I don't think so. You'll be the first to know. I wish Locke hadn't said the last thing, but I agree with him, so how can I argue?"

"Great idea about your house." Jason wanted to distract her and she knew he meant it. "We wouldn't be able to use it until the case is settled anyway."

"Yeah, thanks for offering up my house for a dog that isn't reliably housebroken, by the way."

"I've been thinking over the buying-à-house thing." Maybe something good would come of this day. "Three bedrooms. Three baths. Hell, I can't remember other specifics, but I think it said updated kitchen, which for me means a decent microwave that wasn't bought on clearance. It's going to be hard to disappoint me in the kitchen department."

Ellie shook her head. "Why do I believe that?" She paused, but did say on an encouraging note, "I'm still on the fence about a living arrangement, but I'll go look with you."

They spent the night together frequently now, but hardly always. He understood she needed space and options. He wasn't used to sharing it either. "You could have your own bedroom. And closet. I own, like, three shirts. You could have my closet too. Think about it, two closets. If that doesn't win you over, I'm not sure what would. I've been watching TV and women really like that."

"Don't try to bribe me."

"I've never bought a house before. You have. I'm asking for an opinion."

"I'm not you, but not shy about that sort of thing either. You'll get an opinion." She switched back to the topic at hand. "If it wasn't Randy, who killed Janet Locke? We're going to have to start with the Lane family."

He flipped on a turn signal. "I'll take Grasso with me. Those high-end types admire his style."

"How about *I* take Grasso with *me*?"

"I'll wear a tie. I want you under their radar. Even if the Lane family had nothing to do with Janet Locke's murder, they are letting their son just sit in jail without even paying a single visit."

Her voice was crisp. "Jason, you can't have this both ways. Are they uncaring? It seems so, but that isn't really our problem. Are they dangerous? If they are, I'm sure they already know we've been assigned to this investigation."

She rarely called him by his first name when they were on the job. And he didn't agree. "I can minimalize the likelihood of someone wanting to do you physical harm if you don't appear to be involved."

"I *am* involved. What do you want me to do? Just sit at my desk?"

"Yep. Maybe knit me a sweater or something. Answer my calls. Do your nails."

"Why do I think Metzger would take exception to that?"

"Knit him a sweater too."

There was a stifled but exasperated laugh. "Um, I've seen your wardrobe, and you might wear it if I did, but most people would not. I'd forget a sleeve probably, and then there is the single major problem that I can't knit. My sister swears to me that you're the one man who wouldn't mind what I did for a living. I'm going to love telling her she's evidently wrong."

"Right now it's a love/hate thing. I love that you're good at it, and I hate that you're good at it. Make Metzger's sweater slime green, okay?"

"We're all vulnerable in some way. Do you think I want *you* out there?"

He might have commented it was just nice to have someone care at all, but refrained because it sounded like self-pity when for the first time in his life he was cautiously happy. She was well aware of his past. "That is the single nicest thing you've ever said to me. By the way, is there a class you can take for changing diapers? I've never done that."

"I'll teach you, don't worry. Aunt Ellie has changed her share. Here's your first lesson. Boys might give a special shower you never wanted. You see, you learn something new every single day. There's an art to swift coverage while yet getting the job done."

"What else does Aunt Ellie know?"

"How to catch a killer. Let's move forward on that."

Chapter 5

"Lane."

"Yeah?" Randy sat up groggily. There wasn't much to do except sleep, and he knew full well depression had that effect on a person anyway. Janet had been getting a minor in psychology and they'd talked about it often enough. He specifically remembered one dazzlingly beautiful afternoon when they'd had lunch by the lake and chose to be seated on an outside balcony—she'd looked so beautiful he'd decided then and there he wanted to sit across from her the rest of his life.

Depression was an understatement and he had uneasy dreams, so sleep wasn't the best therapy, but it was about all he had.

The deputy unlocked the door. "Get up. You have a visitor. Follow me."

Randy rolled off his cot and knew he probably looked like he'd been asleep, but he was really starting not to care. He ran his fingers through his hair, just on the off chance it was his mother. Old habits die hard, he thought ironically. The impeccably groomed, expensively dressed Mrs. Lane would never set foot in a county jail, though, so that was a ridiculous hope. He would bet money had exchanged hands to keep his arrest on the back page of the paper.

Maybe it was the blond cop with the eyes that looked right through you. He kind of hoped so, because he wasn't going to get Janet back, so just getting a reasonable existence was about all he could hope for right now. He'd wanted to live, not rot in jail. He seemed like someone who might help him out.

His heart sank. It was not the tall detective. Janet's father sat there in an interview room and motioned him to the opposite chair. Randy wished he was still asleep on that hard bunk. He said stiffly, "Sir."

"Sit down and let's have a conversation."

There were some things you could argue and some you just plain couldn't. When a person was in jail because they had been arraigned on murder charges, you did not argue with a prominent district attorney.

Especially if you supposedly killed that attorney's daughter.

Randy sat. He had no idea what the appropriate greeting would be in a situation like this so he said nothing. In dealing with his own father he'd always found that silence until you learned what the agenda might be was the best option. He eventually said, "I didn't kill her."

Nathan Locke looked emotionless. "I don't think you raped her. I'm going to have those charges taken off the table. Even if I wasn't her father, I wouldn't find the evidence enough for a conviction on that count because the medical examiner is one of the best and she can't say conclusively one way or other. There were some bruises indicating a struggle and we have your DNA, so we could probably make it stick, but I've decided to not push for it. I'm not a fool. I knew you sometimes spent the night."

Well, that was something, but it certainly didn't solve all his problems.

"I would never do that. Not to Janet and not to any woman." Randy's voice broke like he was just hitting puberty. "Oh God. That anyone would think I could—"

"I believe that she trusted you, maybe even loved you, and if you did kill her that makes it more of a crime." The man's eyes held an unrelenting look. "But she seemed happy, so I accept that you had an intimate relationship with my daughter."

Randy found his throat was so dry he could barely speak. "We've been together for months. I was in love with her. I still am. Imagine that hell for me."

It was said bitterly and he meant it.

"Oh, I can. I'm living it." Locke said it with lethal softness. "This is your chance. I'm willing to listen, though it costs me. Here's your situation." Locke leaned forward and Randy noted he looked about a decade older and there were lines around his mouth he'd never noticed before. "It isn't complicated. If it was you, you will never see the light of day again. If it wasn't you, I want their balls in a sack. Hand them to me. No one has a more vested interest in finding out the truth than you. If we go the route of a hypothesis, we have three choices. The first is it was you. Lovers' quarrel. She wanted to break up and you wouldn't have it. You erupted in a rage, and killed her because if you couldn't have her, no one could. That's happened before. I'm sorry to say, too many times."

He was on trial at this very minute. Randy knew that. No jury, but certainly a judge right in front of him in the sterile room with drab walls and no doubt every word recorded. He took a breath and said carefully, "That is absolutely *not* what happened."

"Explain what did happen."

This was a pivotal moment in his life, he knew it. Randy was surprised he even cared, but he did because, ironically enough, he knew Jan would want him to care. "Yes, it was a nice afternoon, the windows were open, a breeze blowing, we were talking . . . and I asked her to marry me. Maybe I should have asked you first for permission, but the words just came out. She said yes."

"Did she?" Locke was unreadable.

"We did go into the bedroom." That was fairly diplomatic for an awkward as hell confession considering who he was talking to, but he might as well tell the truth. "Afterward she wanted to take a nap, and I said I would pick up some food. I came back about thirty minutes later and the front door was slightly ajar, but it was sometimes sticky to latch, and if the air-conditioning came on, it would open an inch or so. So I didn't think too much about it except I really needed to fix it. I found her in the living room with blood everywhere. I thought I would die. I wanted to. I tried for a pulse, tried to see if I could do something for her, but she was just . . . gone."

Locke didn't act like he believed him, but not like he didn't either. "Is this your family? That's the second guess. It doesn't seem like a clean, hired kill, but maybe you were as much of a target as my dead daughter. Would they frame you for her murder so it was made deliberately to look like there had been an argument? A bum on the street corner would even realize you had both opportunity and motive if that was the case."

It wasn't like he didn't sit and think about it all day. He wanted to say a vehement no. But he couldn't.

Instead he said, "I'm not like my two older brothers. Well, I'm not like Rob. John is mostly okay. I came to the conclusion a few years ago that their vision of me and who I truly am doesn't fit. I grew up in an illusion. I don't know. When I realized something wasn't quite right, I rebelled."

"Is that an admission to possible family ties to organized crime?"

They had cut him out without mercy, but he had no proof they would go this far. He hadn't been a model child, but that was rebellion against the wrong people. Randy waited a definitive moment that could save his life or waste it before he responded. "I *really* don't know. I was truant. I dropped out of high school. I was arrested for the first time at sixteen for giving—not selling—weed to a minor, even though I still was a minor as well. I think my parents didn't want the bad attention. I embarrassed them, but even after I got my diploma, enrolled in college, and had my act together, I was no longer really part of the family. They wouldn't forgive me for not having any interest in the family business either."

This wasn't news to Locke. Not any of it. Randy could see it in his expression. He wasn't really ashamed of anything he'd done, but in retrospect he wasn't proud of a lot either. He'd been the example of a rich kid who took his lifestyle for granted until it was yanked out from under him, but when it came down to it, he'd straightened up, gotten school loans on his own, enrolled in college, and in general learned a lot about life. Jan had pointed that out more than once.

"So they had reason to frame you and get at me at the same time. I'm not leading you, I'm just stating what I see as the truth and asking your opinion if that could be a fair assessment of the situation."

"I would like to think they wouldn't do any of those things." It was the raw truth. "They taught me how to ride a bike and bought me my first car. My brothers and I played hoops in the court out back when we were kids . . . I don't think . . ." He trailed off miserably.

He did think.

Randy asked hoarsely, "What's the third possibility?"

Locke was an attorney and used to questions. "I suppose it is possible that some random deviant saw the door wasn't secure and decided to take a look and Janet heard him and got up and startled him."

Randy said in a subdued tone, "I sincerely, since I can't change things, hope number three is the case."

Locke leaned forward, elbows on table. "But you don't think so, do you?"

Randy had to be honest. This was Janet's father. He just shook his head. Locke was hurting, but so was he, and as far as he was concerned, his grief was compounded by betrayal as well as loss. His answer was a whisper. "No."

There was obvious wealth and there was understated wealth that was even more ostentatious.

Ellie had the feeling maybe she was experiencing the latter.

The Lanes lived outside of the limits of Milwaukee in a neighborhood that had houses with actual acreage that wasn't found in the city. Trees and the occasional pasture with horses, and long, low-lying houses that were deceptively modest from the façade, but if you were paying attention and knew the area—like Jason did because he *really* knew this area of Wisconsin—were at least in the million-dollar range and maybe a lot more.

He informed her, "There's a lot of money floating around out here. If every house we just passed doesn't have a home theater and an indoor pool, I'd be surprised. A gym or an art studio is also a possible/probable. These are rich people who don't really care if you know they are rich at first glance. Their kids go to private schools and get a muscle car on their sixteenth birthday."

"Is that what happened with Randy Lane?" she asked.

"I'm guessing. The problem is, he and I were in the same boat in some ways. No muscle car; let's not get nuts here, sometimes he didn't even pay the mortgage, but my old man didn't care enough about me to worry about what was going to happen to me when he kicked me out. In his mind I was old enough to take of myself. Maybe Randy has it worse. Though my stepfather was abusive when he drank, I don't think he would have ever deliberately set me up to take a fall. If he'd have conformed, the gravy train would have continued. Randy didn't and now he's sitting in a cell."

"We can't assume anything just because we know the family is part of a widespread investigation." Ellie had to point that out because assuming anything was like catching a virus. You could treat the symptoms but not the evidence. It was proven that detectives wanted to successfully solve a case. She had an uneasy premonition this one wasn't so easy. "You can be a criminal and not involved in murder. You can be a heartless parent and not be guilty of implicating your son in a brutal crime."

He shook his head as they pulled into a long, winding driveway. He really had worn a decent tie for a change, and a nice dress shirt. "Considering the identity of the victim, you do have to wonder. If they have even a whiff of the investigation—and I'm betting they do because they have friends in high places—this is a definitive warning off for Locke."

She thought about raising a child—all of the late nights, the investment of time and emotion, the worry, and the vulnerability. The love. She had been attached to the baby from the first moment she'd even suspected she might have been reckless enough to get pregnant. "I really can't imagine, but in our job I think one of the casualties is that you can't imagine a lot of things. Luckily, I think that perspective makes for a better law enforcement officer. It forces us to look at the evidence for what it is, not what our personal reaction to the crime might be."

"Jesus, you've been hanging out with Dr. Georgia Lukens too much."

Georgia was a personal friend as well as a psychologist. Ellie had to laugh and it was welcome at the moment. "I think you hang out with her, too."

"I need more help than you do, let's face it. You're practically normal." He parked the truck. "Drop the analytical bullshit. My personal reaction is there is a dead girl and my job is to find who killed her. If I try and open your door for you are you going to shoot me?"

Her very own Prince Charming, but in his own way. "Shooting you is always tempting. I can get out all on my own, thank you."

He held up his hands. "Whatever point you're trying to prove, I'm starting to get it."

The door went unanswered once they navigated paving stones bordered by a small waterfall and went up the steps. Yet they could hear music pounding in the background, which seemed awfully festive for people who had a son in jail for murder.

They walked around back, where they found three

teenage boys playing volleyball over a net in the pool, the source of the music a boom box on the patio. Most of the time, Ellie did the interviews, but with boys this age, she automatically let Santiago handle it. He started by walking over and pushing a button on a device attached to a set of speakers. The music immediately stopped.

"Hey." One of them shouted the word as all three of them turned around. He was about fifteen, cocky, and dark haired. "What the hell? We were listening to that."

Santiago pulled out his badge. "Milwaukee Police Department detectives. And you are?"

"Cameron Lane. This is my house."

"Nice place. We knocked and guess what, no answer. Where are your parents?"

"Inside. They don't answer the door very often."

Ellie's partner said succinctly with pure male authority, "Get out and go tell them we want to talk to them."

"They aren't going to do it." He was sullen, but grudgingly honest.

"Do what? Talk to us? Let's give it a try. Get out."

There might have been a small grumble, but the teen climbed out and grabbed a towel. He went into the house through a sliding door and emerged a few minutes later alone. "They said to tell you they called their lawyer. They don't want to talk to you without him around, and he's a fat guy lying on some beach somewhere having a drink with an umbrella in it. So basically, they told you to fuck off. Hot blonde, by the way, you guys in a sitcom or something?"

Oh yes, very cocky.

Ellie had heard it all before, but not necessarily from someone his age.

"We're homicide detectives trying to help your brother." Santiago fished a card out of his pocket and flicked it onto the pavement. "Have them call us if they are interested at all in his welfare." Then he added as he took Ellie's elbow, "I'd watch my back, kid, or they might throw you to the wolves too."

As they walked away back toward his vehicle, she said acerbically, "Was that last comment necessary?"

"Absolutely. It was good advice. I'll bet money they don't call. But now maybe he will."

"Him?" She was incredulous.

"Want to make a bet?" "

How she'd ever become involved with the single most irreverent man on the planet she wasn't sure. "No, he won't call."

"He might. Self-preservation is a powerful thing, and if he has a brain at all, he's already thought over how his parents cut off his older brother. I know I would have. Kids process in a lateral unique way. I think as adults we forget they are always learning. They are used to it. I learned to duck out if my old man was drinking. No one told me to do that. I paid the school of hard knocks a classroom visit and took a few notes. Booze equals a bad mood. I'm sure that kid's aware that they aren't big on loyalty, but he might like his older brother enough to do something."

She thought that over. He'd nailed it once before. They had gotten a valuable clue on their last big case from a bunch of teenage boys because he'd recognized the animal. "What could Cameron possibly tell us?"

"I bet he pays attention to his parents' friends. He's met them, and for sure knows what kind of cars they drive because boys his age notice that kind of crap. My father's best, and probably only, friend drove this vintage Chevy pickup. Orange. It had been done over top to bottom. If I saw it on the street right now, I'd know it, make and model. We need to develop a sight line. If someone else orchestrated the murder, who would it be? He might not know, but maybe he'd have an idea."

"We could never use that. It might put him in danger." She was absolutely sincere.

Jason pulled away from the drive. "He knows that. Trust him. He won't tell us anything that could be traced back to him."

"You're so sure."

"I've met his kind before. Hell, minus the pool, I *was* his kind. Teenage smartass is a beloved brotherhood that transcends all economic levels."

It was an impossible invitation to resist. "You seem to still be in it."

"That could be." He wasn't fazed. "I definitely also think you are a hot blonde."

Chapter 6

The public defender did say earnestly, like he'd accomplished something, that the rape charges were dismissed. "The arraignment went as I thought it would. It was over a weekend, so it took a little longer than it normally would have, but that couldn't be helped."

It had been a nightmare. To have the words "rape" and "murder" directed at you was a surreal experience. Randy was beyond shaken at sitting in a chair and listening to the charges.

Bail set at a million dollars. It was probably Locke's influence that he even got bail.

"I didn't force her into anything. We were sleeping together." Randy wasn't ungrateful, he was overwhelmed, angry, and about a dozen other things, including being inwardly frozen with a sorrow so profound he wondered if he'd ever find joy in anything again. "How long are they going to keep me here?"

"They aren't going to drop any of the other charges. Second-degree murder and aggravated assault. It stands. Be grateful that they didn't add premeditated. I've seen the evidence. They might have gone for it and they might have won."

In other words, he wasn't walking out that door anytime soon. He steadied himself with a long breath. He'd known it was wrong to hope for a miracle, but of course he had anyway.

"Her father told me there was evidence exonerating me."

"It doesn't exonerate you." The young man adjusted his glasses. He was about six inches shorter than Randy and had the build of a gymnast, and this morning looked like he'd just come off the tennis court, white shorts and all. His first name was apparently DJ, which fit. "It puts an interesting light on the evidence. There's still every possibility a prosecutor could come in with a reason that could convince a jury you had a reason to wipe off that table. For instance, all counsel needs to do is suggest you started to clean up the crime scene and realized it wasn't possible."

"Why then wouldn't I just wait until it was dark and drive away, quietly dispose of my bloody clothes, and let someone else find her? I called the police!" His voice went a notch too high and he fought for a sense of calm.

"Our main problem, besides a preponderance of evidence like your fingerprints on the knife, your bloody clothes, your DNA, is that there is no other viable suspect. I think if we go to court and enter a plea we could maybe get it down to manslaughter, but I can't be sure of that because it was such a graphic crime. I'm going to always be straight with you, and here's the situation. It looks like the two of you got into an argument and you impulsively lashed out and started assaulting her, slit her throat, and then realized what you'd done. If I were trying this case on the other side, that's what I would present in a courtroom. You have a fairly long juvenile record of minor offenses, one of them being a fistfight at school that got you suspended, which of itself shouldn't mean much, but to a jury it might look like a predisposition to violence. It isn't sealed, because you were never charged. That can be trotted out at any time. At least we have a plea."

His lawyer might look about twelve, but tennis boy did seem to know his stuff.

That was not good news. It meant what he just said was entirely possible. "I can't take a plea for something I didn't do."

"I can't say I understand what you are feeling right now because I haven't been on the other side of this table. I just want you to be aware that even with a district attorney on the fence over whether or not you killed his daughter, I do think there is enough compelling evidence you might have done just that. It isn't beyond a doubt. It is beyond a *reasonable* doubt to convict. There are hung juries now and then because that comes down to what one person thinks is reasonable another one might not. I'm not promising anything, or even advising you one way or the other, but I need to prepare you for what might be in the future." He closed his briefcase and rose.

Randy rubbed his forehead, thinking furiously. "Can you do me a favor? I need you to call a detective at the Milwaukee Police Department. He and his partner are involved in Jan's investigation. His name is Santiago."

DJ gave a short laugh. "Santiago and MacIntosh? I know them. Those two have a habit of making the news. They didn't arrest you. I would have noticed it on the report."

"He came to talk to me."

"That's actually very interesting. It's a high-profile

case because of who the victim is and who you are, but—"

"Who I am?" Randy interrupted bitterly. "I'm a poor college student with a murdered girlfriend and a family that doesn't give a shit about me."

"The Lane family name goes a long way. They are making this worse by refusing to comment and handing you over to the system for representation. It makes you look guilty in their eyes."

This wasn't new information. "Just ask both Mac-Intosh and Santiago to please come and talk to me. All I have is time to think. I might be able to help them find who really did it."

"Okay. I'll relay the message if you are sure. Please remember, anything you say can and will be used in court."

"I'm sure."

He left, and Randy was led back to his cell and heard that fatalistic slam of the door.

There was no way he was just going to let this happen without fighting back. Not only for himself, but for Jan.

This wasn't the easiest phone call of her life. Ellie had really played in her head what she might say. *Hey, Mom, I have some interesting news . . .*

Interesting? It wasn't interesting, it was life-changing news, and there had to be a better way to express it.

I'm so excited to tell you . . .

She wasn't excited to tell her. Her mother wasn't going to like she wasn't married. She wasn't going to like she wasn't considering getting married. Who could blame her? Jason wasn't exactly easy to read, and she needed to know he hadn't just offered because of the situation. Not to mention her own conflicted feelings. He might be the best husband, or the worst. Good father . . . yes, she thought that was not really a question, which was a point in his favor, but that didn't necessarily translate to a good life partner.

This was a very untraditional Macintosh out-of-wedlock-baby situation. Her mother didn't like Ellie's job, and she sure wasn't going to be happy that Jason had the same profession. Ellie also questioned now and then if two homicide detectives should have a baby.

It all came down to that they *were* going to have one, and that was the end of the story.

Time to bite the bullet.

Her mother answered right away. "I've been hoping you'd call soon. I always hesitate to ring you up because I never know where you are or what hours you're keeping."

"I'm sorry. New case for me now that is interesting to say the least. How are you feeling?"

"I feel good. Stop worrying about me. I hope this new case is better than the last case. That one scared me because the real threat was to you."

That one had scared Ellie too. She said reasonably, "All murder cases are frightening. I think we should talk about something more cheerful. What about babies? You know, chubby cheeks and diapers."

Her mother might have a cancer battle on her hands, but it certainly hadn't affected her sharp intellect. "Okay." There was a pause. "There's only one reason I can think of we would talk about babies. I'm guessing we are having this conversation for that reason. When are you due? I've drawn the right conclusion, haven't I? I thought when I talked to Jody this morning she was edging around something. To her credit, your sister didn't tell me."

Surprising. Even when Jody was trying to be secretive, she rarely pulled it off. "You have drawn the right conclusion. December."

"Well, it's better to be pregnant in cooler weather, so you planned that right anyway."

"It wasn't exactly planned."

"How does Bryce feel about this?"

Here came the difficult part. "I haven't told him, since it is none of his business. This isn't his child."

"Oh . . . what? Then I sense there's quite a bit I don't know about what is going on in your life, Eleanor."

"Eleanor" usually meant she was in trouble. She'd expected an Eleanor from this conversation anyway. "Bryce is in New York and I'm involved with someone else. The pregnancy wasn't planned necessarily, but it has happened and I'm happy about it and so is the father."

"Who would be . . . who?" It was delicately asked.

"Jason Santiago."

Another pause. This was going about as well as she thought it would, Ellie decided. Her mother finally said, "Isn't he your partner on the police force? Was that wise?"

"No." She was able to say that honestly. Then she sighed. "But I don't know it was the worst decision of my life either. I suppose time will tell. I know you are going to ask, so I'll just say he's suggested marriage, but I'm the one who is unsure."

To her surprise her mother started laughing. "Of course you are. You'd love a black-and-white world, and, honey, it doesn't exist. You've always been that way. It makes you very good at your job, but if I can offer some motherly advice, relationships don't work on a straight, hard line. He isn't going to be perfect, and I think you recognize that. Maybe he is just your type.

Tell me about him. Bryce was essentially everything a woman could want, and you didn't want it."

Well, it was a valid point. It had been more complicated than that, but that was probably a fair assessment in the long run. "Without the tailored suits and the accent, Jason Santiago is best described as a profane James Bond with cheap beer instead of a martini. I've seen him do some truly stupid dangerous things that have miraculously worked out. All we need is for him to jump out of a helicopter without a parachute and land on a great white shark in the middle of the ocean as he saves the world. The man has been shot three times in the line of duty just since I've known him."

At the very least her mother had a sense of humor. "Goodness! I believe I want to meet him, and, honey, you've been shot in the line of duty yourself."

Ellie chose to ignore that observation. "He's a unique experience."

"Are you happy?"

It was odd, but maybe she was. "I think so," she answered cautiously. "If you had asked me when I first met him if this would ever happen, the answer would have been a firm no along with an incredulous laugh."

"Did you know I despised your father at our first encounter? Absolutely did not care for him. I wanted nothing to do with him. Oh, he was handsome enough, but there was nothing else I liked at all."

Ellie had not heard this particular story and was astonished. "Are you serious? Why?"

"He was an arrogant ass. I so miss him, but not that swaggering athlete who thought he hung the moon. He was a star baseball player, so he thought he was a young god of some sort. Wrong."

"Mom. He was *not* an ass." Ellie was truly stunned. "He was the nicest man I've ever known."

"You remember the mellowed version. He sure was an ass, at first. When he asked me to go out on a date, initially I said no. He clearly couldn't believe I turned him down. So I explained very frankly why. I was very lucky in that your grandmother was a wonderful woman. When he complained to her bitterly about what I'd said, she agreed with me and told him he should think it over and humility was a virtue, and she'd told him that more than once, but maybe now he'd believe her. He must have very much wanted that date, because he certainly behaved a lot better. I know his circle of friends increased dramatically."

"So you went on that date."

"Honey, you and Jody are here, aren't you? As soon as he was no longer constantly trying to impress me with how wonderful he was, he grew on me. The point of telling you this is that if you had told me when I first met him I'd agree to marry him, *I* would have laughed."

Could Jason be trained to the point of complete tolerability? Ellie really wasn't sure. "Jason is someone who has his self-preservation skills honed. He's extraordinarily self-sufficient."

"Would you even consider a man who wasn't? But he's pleased about becoming a father?"

At least that was easy to answer. "Very."

"Then I definitely want to meet him."

"He wants me to help him look for a house. He wants to get a dog, and for all I know, he's already picked out the swing set. However, the man is no sitcom father who reads the paper while he drinks his coffee and wears cardigan sweaters. He's more ESPN with holes in his jeans and a T-shirt with a motorcycle logo. I bet he still wears the shirts with bullet holes in them, because as far I can tell, if he considers them functional, he wouldn't bother to buy new ones."

"Jody told me he was attractive, but in a bad-boy sort of way, whatever that means. How are you feeling physically?"

He wasn't good-boy attractive, that was for certain. And the second question made Ellie unexpectedly tear up. "More emotional than usual. The fatigue is better, but I could still take a nap every day, and don't mention the word 'smoked' in my presence. No smoked pork chops, no smoked sausage . . . nothing smoked. I made myself nauseous just saying it out loud right now. Strong flavors aren't working out for me."

"With Jody it was cinnamon. Just the thought of it sent me right to the bathroom."

The conversation was a relief in some ways. No advice, either way. She said, "I needed to tell you."

Her mother's voice was calm. "Well, of course you did. I might notice a baby on the way on my next visit to Wisconsin."

Jason was walking toward her desk like a man with a purpose. Ellie said swiftly, "Have a good evening, Mom." So far it had been a good conversation, but not the time to push her luck. "Love you, but I have to go. I'm still at work."

"I love you too, and, honey, as far as I can tell, you are always at work."

With his usual lack of any cordiality, Jason planted a hand on her desk and said, "Randy Lane wants a face to face with us. His lawyer just called me. He doesn't sound in favor of it, but his client insists anyway."

"What about?"

"About finding who really did it. Maybe he's thought of something, because I promise you I'd be sitting there brooding about it. It's my impression that for the first time in his life he's realized he needs to be afraid of his family. Damn, he's in the county lockup now that he's been arraigned. I hate that place even more than the jail at the police department. All those guys waiting for their day in court? Talk about the smell of fear."

"Men in general smell. Sweat, socks that should have been washed three days ago but looked clean enough to wear again . . . the list goes on."

For that comment she got a glare from narrowed blue eyes, and maybe she deserved it.

"Look, Detective MacIntosh, I wash my socks."

She switched off her computer and got up. "Good, because don't ever expect me to wash them for you. Who's driving?"

"You. There might be a bunch of socks in my truck, and now you have me all nervous I'm nose-blind to them. Like I needed something else in my life to worry about. Thanks."

She highly doubted he was nervous about anything, and he really was a sarcastic smartass. "Let's go. I don't know about you, but I'm dying to hear what he has to say."

Chapter 7

He'd been in jail for three long days.

They called him "Prep Boy."

Randy had gotten into a fistfight late that afternoon when he went to shower, and quite frankly, he'd been surprised he gave as good as he got. Though he'd only thrown a couple of punches before it was broken up and had some battle scars in the form of a cut lip and a black eye, his opponent didn't escape unscathed either. He was amazed at the culture of incarceration and how gossip was traded more freely than at a church function for little old ladies.

He suspected it worked in his favor that he was waiting for trial for the brutal murder of his girlfriend. There was a certain respect offered to someone who would do what he was accused of, and the fight had only been a draw because he was so angry that being taunted about anything sent him right over the edge.

Still not one gesture from his family. Not his parents, not his uncle, neither of his older brothers, and he didn't want his younger brother anywhere close to the jail, so that was fine. He considered it pure good luck he'd gotten someone he thought was probably a competent lawyer not making nearly as much as he could in the private sector, but the idea of a plea bargain was just out of the question.

His options were limited.

The female detective didn't look very formidable in comparison to her partner until you looked into her eyes. First impression was sorority girl. Second was tough as nails. At once, from the moment he was told they'd arrived and they all sat down, he noticed MacIntosh—how she introduced herself, did the talking. All of it.

"You asked us to come. Why are we here?"

"Because I didn't kill Jan, and I'm counting on you to find out who did. I want the hell out of here. I don't even get to go to her funeral."

Of course not. He was supposed to have killed her.

"Please tell me that there's some information included in this visit, because so far you are the only suspect and a judge agrees."

His lawyer's words exactly. Randy drew a breath. "My father has a business associate. His name is Hank Darnel. I accidentally walked in on them when they were having a very specific conversation a few months ago at the pergola by my parents' pool. I wasn't eavesdropping, I swear, but I froze because of what I accidentally overheard." His throat tightened. "I think that moment, me standing there, killed her. They knew I heard it. They tried to brush it off by just offering me a drink, but I knew, and they knew I knew. We all pretended it didn't happen, but it did."

Detective MacIntosh asked, "All right, don't keep us on the edge of our seat, what did you overhear?"

"Darnel said: '*We need to send a serious message that*

won't be ignored or we might go down. Locke is all over us.'"

Was there some reason they didn't have this information before?

Randy Lane was young and he was obviously not enjoying his jail stay from the bruises on his face. She didn't discount he had a certain loyalty to his family that they didn't have to him, but at least he was letting them know now.

Ellie wasn't positive about how to respond. She finally decided on saying, "You maybe face life in prison unless we can prove something else happened. Unless we can find that something else, then it is your word against theirs. I think the district attorney would back you up if he heard this. He's backed you up already by pressing for some of the charges to be dropped, but in a court of law, we need evidence. A jury will try you. We didn't know Janet Locke, but we want justice for her. We want justice for you. Give us more. You could just be making this up. It's been known to happen. Suspects lie to us all the time."

"Then I wouldn't want your job. I'm not joking, because this is my *life*. I did hear him say it. Investigate Darnel. He owns a company called LOD. He has all the regular things like a big house and a trophy wife who I get the impression hates his guts but screws him with his wallet in plain sight, and I know for a fact my mother doesn't like him because I've heard her mention it to my father. I don't like him either. Talk about a shark; but if money really is everything, he has a lot of it."

At least they now had a name, but Ellie had the sinking feeling this might leach into the federal investigation. "He would never have committed the crime himself, I would guess, so any thoughts on who might have done it?"

"No, but I bet one of my brothers might know. Start there."

Randy looked stoic, but Ellie thought he fought for that reserved expression. She asked quietly, "What makes you think—"

"They play by my father's rules. I never did."

She sat there for a moment, wondering what they could even do with this. "Your parents wouldn't talk to us. Why would your brothers?"

"Try John. He and I are closest in age. He's also more influenced by authority but doesn't like it, and at least has a sentimental side. He might care. I can't promise it, but he'd be a place to start."

"Would he condone murder?"

"I don't think so, but he has an inside view. He might know who did it, and yet he might not say. But he's worth a try. Robert won't help you. We never did really like each other."

Since she adored Jody, that was hard to fathom, but Ellie tried. "Would he have been a part of this? I'm talking Robert."

Randy considered it. "I wouldn't toss it off the table. He has no loyalty to me, and I doubt he likes Darnel either. If he could send us both to hell, he would. John would do whatever he said. If he could also get to Locke, he would sit back and sip a nice whiskey and call it a good day."

Jason shook his head. "He sounds great, and to think I regret not having siblings, not that it was really my decision. So John is a minor douche and Robert is a major douche? We straight?"

"Sounds about right. I doubt Robert would help me,

like . . . ever. If I was drowning, and it kinda feels like I am, I doubt if he'd bother to get up if he was sitting on a life preserver and toss it to me."

Maybe a suspect? If his own brother disliked him so much, that seemed possible. But it had been made clear this was a touchy investigation. "Any good friends of his you can think of who might stomach the kind of crime that was committed?"

Randy nodded. "Porter. Elias Porter. I'm going to guess he has a juvenile record a lot longer than mine. Ely has been banned from strip clubs and brags about it. I've never asked why because I don't want to know. They went to college together. He's a sleazebag in an expensive sweater and alligator shoes. I hate guys like him, but my brother is exactly a guy like him. Robert is an Ivy League asshole."

To her absolute amazement, Santiago pointed at her. "Hey, there's a lady present. Keep it clean."

If this wasn't a murder investigation, she really might have fallen off her chair laughing. It was chair abandonment mirth-worthy to hear Jason Santiago advising someone to keep their language clean, but the situation certainly was not. She said, "If he is one, he is one, I'm not offended. I can handle a swearword or two. Just tell us the truth. Do you think this Ely might murder someone?"

"I think he might get off on it." Randy turned his head, eyes glistening. "Like that? I saw her . . . I don't know . . . It was so bad. I get the impression he's rough with women."

Ellie had seen the gory pictures. "Your younger brother, could he help us?"

"Cameron? I hope not. At his age I didn't have a clue."

Her opinion was his brother really, really had a clue.

"I dislike Ely. Intensely. Maybe that's it, but if he did it, Robert might have suggested it. I don't know anything more, but I know that much. Ely doesn't have the brains to breeze in, do the crime, and leave no evidence. He's a thug with an ascot and a fancy car. His father paid for his exalted law degree. He sat around and drank beer at frat parties. He's a waste of carbon. His office is about a block south of our corporate office downtown."

"We'll look into it." She got up. Not a bad interview, because they at least needed a place to start. She couldn't help but ask, and maybe it was newfound motherly instinct because she knew he was of age, but his mother hadn't bothered. "You look a little worse for wear. You okay?"

He shrugged, but there was a grim expression on his bruised face. "I'll live. Or I hope so. This place isn't exactly a friendly resort. They took my phone when they arrested me, but I know John's number by heart. Want to write it down?"

"Absolutely."

As Ellie and Santiago left the county facility, she breathed out. "Okay, that smell of fear thing, I get it. I can tell you Randy is sincerely afraid. The Lane family seems lovely and close knit. I'm glad my last name is MacIntosh."

"Yeah. It could be Santiago. Maybe then we could make that sitcom."

She didn't want to talk about marriage, but it would have to happen eventually. The discussion, but not the marriage necessarily. "Is that another halfhearted proposal? I've never had a desire for television fame, so you're safe. Should we go talk to John Lane?"

"Halfhearted? You're so sidestepping."

"Then get the message. I'm not ready to think about it yet. Let's see if he cooperates."

"You are the one that needs to cooperate."

"Jason, we aren't having this conversation right now."

He didn't give an inch. "When *are* we having it?"

She relented. A little. He deserved that. "Soon."

"It's important to me the baby has my name. I've never had a family."

It really hadn't occurred to her—at least in that light. It seemed right to give a little. "He or she will. I agree to that right now. If you want me to put it in writing in case you really tick me off in the meantime, I will. Baby's last name will be Santiago."

He clicked his seat belt. "I'm fairly sure the ticking off might happen. In the next six months I won't tick you off? Really?"

"You will," she muttered as they pulled away. "In the next six minutes."

"Oh yeah." He didn't even sound sorry. "Let's figure out exactly how to question John. He sounds like a pendulum. Might help and might not. He could swing either way. Funny to think I always wished I had a brother. It hasn't seemed to do Randy much good and he has three, though I do think we should have more than one kid, for sure. I was kind of thinking four or so."

"I'm going to strangle you."

"There, you see? Less than two minutes. Do we ask him directly about Darnel and Porter, or do we sashay around it and start with how someone beat up his brother in the lockup?"

"Sashay. My grandmother taught me that guilt works. If he cares at all, he'll feel remorse, and if he knows anything, maybe offer to help us in order to get his brother out of there. Our biggest problem is that he'd be stupid not to fear these people. Randy isn't stupid, so maybe

John isn't either. I wonder if he'll even talk to us. Maybe we should ask him to meet with us somewhere neutral, like the coffee place we like on KK Avenue. If we show up at the corporate office, I feel confident he won't say a word."

"I agree." Her partner was already on his phone, all straightforward cop again. "Let's see what he says."

He said yes to midmorning the next day.

John Lane looked a lot like his younger brother, minus the facial damage. Thick dark hair, solid build, and there was a wary look in his eyes. He wore a suit but no tie, and there was a heavy watch on his wrist.

But he'd said yes, and he'd shown up. The shop was perfumed with the scent of roasting beans, since they did that on site, and it was busy as always. Jason stood briefly and John spotted him and walked over. By way of greeting he said, "Cameron described you both pretty well. Let me go get a cup of coffee. It's already been a long day. Couldn't you have suggested a three-martini lunch or something?"

"We actually aren't supposed to do that." Jason said it pleasantly. "There's a law against driving intoxicated and possible high-speed chases and all that. Ours is an exciting profession. We'll wait."

He went to the counter and came back with a frothy concoction, which did not raise Jason's opinion of him as he pulled out a chair and sat down, but his first words did. "How's Randy?"

Ellie said succinctly, "You mean other than his split lip, black eye because he's getting harassed in jail, and not to mention his dead girlfriend, he's about as well as could be expected. He thinks, of your entire family, you're the only one who might help us figure out who really killed Janet Locke. Detective Santiago and I hope that isn't misplaced faith."

"I don't know who killed her." He took a sip from his cup and used his napkin. "I would love to help Randy if he didn't do it, but I don't know anything."

"Do you think he *did* do it?" Jason had to ask it. "We have a lot of evidence that suggests he did, and some that suggests maybe his version of the story is plausible. He says he came in and found her murdered. Quite frankly, considering who her father is, that's quite possible. It wasn't all that brilliant to kneel in her blood or touch the knife, but they had what sounds like a pretty serious relationship. Both shock and grief don't make for cool-headed decisions. He's the one who called 911."

"Our goal," Ellie explained in her most reasonable tone, "is to determine who killed Janet Locke, whether it was Randy or not. I'm sure you agree she didn't deserve to die, and if you could help us in any way, we'd greatly appreciate it. I understand Randy is estranged from your parents, but it seems harsh to me they won't lift a finger to help him."

John Lane said defensively, "He was one pain-in-the-ass kid. Getting kicked out of school, smoking weed, dating the wrong girls—he wouldn't even take the job my father offered him. I can't speak for them, but I think they got fed up. He's in trouble and it is his problem in their minds."

Ellie wouldn't let him get away with that. "There's trouble and there's real trouble. He borrowed the money and went responsibly to college and got good grades, and unless it is determined in a court of law when he goes to trial for murder, he's never been convicted—or even accused—of a serious crime. No assault, no battery, no restraining orders . . . nothing significant. Smoking pot, one DUI, and skipping high school doesn't make you a violent criminal. What do you think?"

She was so good at this. Rational and restrained described her. Jason would probably have said, "*Look, dickweed, your family might have just set your little brother up for life in prison. Talk to us now.*"

He still wanted to say it, but didn't.

Cars rolled by outside the windows on the busy street. Put on the spot, John wasn't quite ready to talk, but at least he seemed torn. "I don't imagine him doing anything remotely like what I heard happened, but I also don't *want* to imagine it's possible."

Good point.

"Let's pretend he didn't do it. Who would you first point your finger at and what would be the motive? We have a few names and a couple of ideas, but input would be nice. We aren't going to reveal you as the source, and don't expect you to do anything but tell us what you think. All we want is a rudder to point us in the right direction. It is up to us to gather enough evidence for a different arrest."

"You really think he's innocent, don't you?" John Lane sounded shaken.

Ellie answered him evenly. "If it wasn't for the contradictory crime scene, we'd just let it all stand. But, you know, despite that we often don't get a lot of credit for it, law enforcement really is interested in justice for the victim and their families. If Randy goes down and he didn't do it, that's really a shame. Two victims and not one. Let's not talk about how someone who would do something so vicious might walk around free and perhaps do it again. We are also here to prevent and protect."

"I don't disagree, but I'm not sure I can help." John hedged, but Ellie didn't let him.

"Could it have been Ely Porter?"

"That killed her? He's a lawyer, for Christ's sake. And a family friend."

"He's a person. She was clearly killed by a person, unless wolves have learned how to use a knife instead of their teeth. Randy has a low opinion of him. What's yours?"

"He . . . isn't nice all the time. Has a macabre sense of humor that borders on lewd. But let's face it, that's a lot different from being capable of murder."

"Let me put it another way. Would you believe it more of your brother, or of Porter?"

He did, in the end, answer. "Porter. Randy might have been a kid that strayed across the line, but just once or twice. He isn't violent in any way. Here or there offenses. He went to jail for that DUI. He got his license suspended because he wrecked his car when he wasn't supposed to be driving. He was uninterested in authority really until he grew up. Porter is another animal. But why would Ely do something so terrible? He'd not likely risk his own neck."

"To scare off Locke? Maybe he represents an influential client who is in the crosshairs of an investigation by Locke's office."

"I can't see him doing it." He took a gulp of coffee. "Oh God, tell me Robert isn't involved."

"How about if *you* tell *us*," Ellie said with pointed emphasis. "What about Hank Darnel? Would *he* be involved in something like this?"

"Not directly. Never. He's very into self-preservation. I deal with his company all the time. Hank is very into Hank. He wouldn't get his hands dirty with something like what happened to Jan. Too much risk."

Jason had to ask, "So if you don't think Porter and you don't think Darnel, any other ideas? Another suspect might help your brother's case."

"Which brother?" His smile was humorless. "The only one I can think of who really has it in for Randy is Robert."

"Why?" Jason was truly interested in the answer.

"I think because before Cameron, Randy was the baby for a long time. Definitely my mother's favorite. No question he was spoiled, but I never felt the same way about him as Robert did. Look, I need to get back to the office. Please excuse me."

He left and both of them watched him go out the door. Jason murmured, "Man, I thought my family was fucked up. I'm feeling kind of slighted on the it-could-be-worse scale."

Chapter 8

Randy had no choice but to be evaluated by a court-appointed psychologist. The judge had ordered it and he had to sit down and take it. Two deputies took him to an interview room, and at least they stayed outside rather than insisting on hearing about whether or not he wet the bed or sucked his thumb far later than most children.

He resented having to do this, but at least he'd gotten out of the cell.

The woman had all the personality of a beer-stained 1950s tabletop in a cheap diner, and it was apparent to him she had obviously already made up her mind about him before she walked through the door and sat down across from him.

"I'm Dr. Gregg. Can we talk about what happened and how you were feeling at the time?" She wore a ruffled shirt and dark striped pants, had hair a shade too dark for her brows when it was usually the other way around.

Randy took a moment. "At the time of what? The murder? I didn't commit it so that's difficult for me.

I think I was looking forward to egg rolls when it happened."

She didn't appreciate the levity and he wasn't trying to be funny by any stretch of the imagination, but it was the truth. Jan had wanted Chinese food and she was alive and well when he left to go get it. It had sounded good to him too. He might never eat it again, but then again, he had no desire to do so, and he suspected that feeling wouldn't go away. The smell of the spilled food mingled with the sickening odor of blood was a vivid memory. Maybe it was true that olfactory senses were more powerful than visual images.

"Do you feel you have issues with anger?"

"No. I mean everyone gets mad now and then over something, but 'issues' is a strong word and it doesn't fit."

"What does fit Randy Lane? Describe him to me." She wrote something down, and when she looked up there was no sympathy or even empathy in her expression.

In her defense, he guessed morosely, she probably talked to a lot of disturbed people.

That was a difficult question to answer. He shrugged helplessly. "I'm ordinary, I guess. I study, I follow sports, I read some books, mostly sci-fi novels. I'm not political really in any way, and I love my dog. Jan gave her to me."

He did. And since he didn't know where Louise was, it was unexpected, but he felt the burn of tears in his eyes.

"Tell me how you felt when you found her."

Tell me how felt after you killed her. It was implied and he thoroughly resented it.

"There aren't words. I don't want there to be words. I made some stupid mistakes like kneeling in her blood and moving her body, but I have come to the conclusion I *don't* regret them. If there was one single chance I could save her, then I don't regret it. I really wasn't thinking of myself for once. Maybe I should have done that earlier in my life."

"So you *do* have regrets."

He so wanted this interview to be over. Hell, he was past caring. "Don't we all?"

Was it too much to hope Dr. Gregg wasn't going to testify at his trial?

Probably.

Carl thought Dr. Georgia Lukens looked more than gorgeous in a brilliantly patterned sundress, the fading sunlight shining off her hair. He very much appreciated the view. Not just of her either, because they were having an after-dinner cocktail by the pool and the sunset was a spectacular splash of red and indigo that reflected in the water, the leaves on the maple tree his mother had planted in the corner rustling in the warm breeze.

The tree was a monster now, and probably would come down one day soon and cause damage, but he did faithfully have it trimmed, and he still remembered the day vividly when his father had brought it home from the nursery as an impromptu gift for his mother and her delighted smile when he gave it to her. A few days later they were both killed in a tragic accident.

That tree wasn't going anywhere. He wondered what a psychologist would have to say about that. They'd been seeing each other for a while now and maybe one day he'd ask her.

"What a beautiful night." Georgia had slipped off her shoes and her feet were propped on the small glass table. She wiggled her manicured toes. "I love summer."

The toes were nice, but he really admired her bared shoulders and the hint of cleavage. "I'm a fan myself. You're beautiful all the time, but covered up in boots and a long coat it isn't quite the same view."

Her smile was playful. "I like it when you lose the tie. You look more like the man Carl Grasso than the lieutenant with MPD."

"I'm doing my Jason Santiago impression."

"Hmm, you haven't said a swearword all evening. Keep working on it. You also need some torn jeans, and I haven't seen one, but I'd bet he has a tattoo somewhere."

She had a point. He chuckled. "I'll try to ease profanity into the conversation, but no to the last two things. Maybe I can undo another button on my shirt."

"That might help."

"I really hope he and MacIntosh are making some progress on this new case. I haven't heard any drums beating in the background, so they haven't stepped on any toes that I'm aware of . . . yet." He'd given her a very generic sketch of the situation by saying multiple agencies were involved.

"Your problem is that Jason is all action and intuition, and Ellie seems like the calm one, but she's not the type to avoid her gut instincts either. If there is a fox in the henhouse, as my grandmother used to say, they will sense it."

"I'm hoping they don't. The foxes have been working this case for a long time."

"And I'm going to predict they figure out who they are, but all that should really mean is that they steer clear of involving them."

Carl wasn't quite sure how to bring up the subject. They walked a tightrope sometimes on what he could tell her, and what she could tell him. "I'm not asking for confidential information, but I'd like to think I'm observant since I've been a detective for quite some time."

She gazed at him inquiringly.

He might as well just ask bluntly. "Is it possible MacIntosh is pregnant? I'm not, by the way, the only one wondering. Rays said something to me the other day. She's dressing differently and not staying as late as usual. I remain at my desk longer than anyone, but she's a close second."

Georgia lifted her brows and didn't give an inch. "Ask her."

"It isn't Bryce Grantham, is it?"

"Ask him. Please remember he lives in New York. It's a long way for a nosy question."

"Damn, Georgia, you are like a tight-lipped lawyer. By the way, I'm not being nosy. I'm curious."

"Doesn't it make you feel better you can trust me to be tight-lipped, and that was a good way to work in that token swear word."

"Metzger is going to be mighty unhappy if it is true. If it is Grantham, Santiago is going to be even unhappier, but he seems to be in a pretty good mood, and you can't tell me he doesn't know."

She poured herself another glass of wine. "From a psychological standpoint, they function on a high level as a team. They have had to rely on and trust each other often. Neither of them have an emotional attachment to anyone else. They are both adults. Why would anyone be surprised?"

"I'm going to guess no one will be. Did you just confirm Santiago?"

"I actually don't know, and that is the truth. Ellie and I haven't discussed it."

"I thought she came to you and divulged her deepest and darkest secrets."

"No, we only talk about things she has on her mind."

"Being pregnant wouldn't be on her mind?"

"I haven't asked her and she hasn't said. She's very concerned over her mother's illness and well-being, partially because she lost her father so abruptly. She would freely tell you that, so I'm not violating confidentiality. It makes sense, and surely makes sense to you, who lost both parents at the same time. I understand that young men don't like to discuss their feelings, but I do wish you'd seen a competent therapist just so you had talked to someone when your parents died."

At the time he hadn't wanted to talk about it. At all. He still didn't. "Because I'm so ill-adjusted?"

"I didn't say that. I didn't even imply it. It just probably would have been nice for you to not internalize."

"I was still in college, and suddenly having to manage that loss and the house, the vacation house, and other financial things such as investments, the cars, the yacht, I admit I was overwhelmed. If ever there was detective work to be done," he admitted, though he still didn't like to think about it, "it was trying to figure out how to handle my father's business affairs. I was barely out of high school. My grandmother did her best to help me, but quite frankly, though she was a very nice woman, she'd never even driven a car. My father had balanced her checkbook for her. When she passed away just a year later, I had to go through the nightmare again."

That was the most he'd ever said to anyone on the subject, and he had the feeling she knew it. "Growing up should be a more gradual process, I agree. But, look at it this way, Ellie was over thirty when she experienced her loss, and she still is coping with it and feels the pain and the panic of no longer having that shoulder to lean on. I have always wondered after having read many highbrow academic articles on the subject, if any of us really have the coping skills, including myself, to deal with a sudden void in our life. Trust me, I have patients who lose a pet and go into a tailspin."

"I thought if they weren't in a tailspin they didn't come see you in the first place."

"No, not necessarily, but we are talking cause and effect." She tilted her glass and studied the liquid in it. "I admit if Ellie is pregnant, it will change everything."

That was an understatement. "I would bet I'll become her new partner eventually."

"You think so? How do you feel about that?"

It was interesting to have a personal relationship with someone like Georgia Lukens. He gave her an amused look. "In case you haven't noticed, talking about how I feel isn't exactly at the top of my list of favorite activities."

"It's a perfectly normal question anyone might ask. Give it a shot."

Obligingly, he thought it over. "She's a very good detective. Bright, intuitive, and she is probably more sensitive to victims and their families than I am. I'd work with her. I *have* worked with her. I've been assigned cases on an individual basis for the most part since I moved back to homicide, but she tends to get the high-profile ones. I wouldn't mind that, because my assignments seem to involve more unsolved cold files than anything else."

"More action, less desk work is what you'd prefer? I suppose I can see that in you. Are you going to talk to Chief Metzger about it?"

"No." That wasn't an option. Carl wanted another scotch, but he'd had two and that was most certainly his limit. "Metzger will decide whatever he thinks is best, and my input won't push him an inch one way or the other. Beside that point, I don't know if it is true. If it is, he'll reassign them both, and I agree, because that is a very significant conflict of interest."

"How so?"

That was an easy question to answer. "You are supposed to have your partner's back, yes, but you are also supposed to do your job, which is the investigation. Worrying about one part of it more than the other doesn't work. This will shift their balance, which was precarious already. Santiago was too protective from the beginning. Day one he disliked getting a partner who was a rookie in homicide, and by day two it was pretty clear he was all on board with it once they met. Knowing the department, I was surprised no one started a pool on whether or not he could ever get her into bed."

It was Georgia's turn to look amused. "Since they're mostly men, I'm surprised they didn't. Has it occurred to you that maybe they did, and as a lieutenant you weren't asked to participate?"

"I wouldn't have if I'd been asked, if that improves your view of my character. They all know that."

She responded comfortably, "So do I. I have a high view of your moral character, for your information. If I didn't you wouldn't have gotten a second glance."

"I have second-glance status? Good to know."

"Maybe a third glance applies."

That was even more promising.

It wasn't Jason's phone that rang, it was hers.

"A juvenile asked to be patched in to you," the male dispatcher said in a dry tone. "I assumed it was you, but don't get all full of yourself. He had Santiago's number. He said he wanted to talk to the hot blonde instead."

"Go ahead."

Cameron Lane. Ellie answered, "This is Detective MacIntosh."

"What are you wearing?" A young voice, slightly cheeky with male bravado.

Definitely him.

"A purple muumuu and dark-rimmed glasses. I've gained fifty pounds since we last saw each other."

"Aw, don't do that to me."

"Cameron, do you have something to tell me that will help your brother, or are you wasting my time?"

"Okay, I've been thinking about it. There's this guy named Reid. If I had a dog, I wouldn't let him walk it. He lives down the street. I would swear he's spying on us. He's always hanging around. Randy stopped by the house one time to get something he'd left in the garage, and I saw this guy go over to the car where Jan was waiting and talk to her through the open window, like maybe he was sort of hitting on her."

"Do you happen to know the house number?"

"I walked over and looked: 918. He's not young, but he isn't as old as my dad or anything. Maybe thirty."

So nice to hear that wasn't perceived as young, but that the man had come over to talk to Janet Locke was interesting. "We appreciate the lead."

He hesitated, but then said in a rush, "I'm feeling pretty sorry for Randy right now. I think I was trying to avoid imagining how he feels in jail. It has to suck. I agree with that Santiago guy. My parents are being way harsh on him by not believing him. So he partied too much and got kicked out of a couple of schools and wrecked his car. He didn't hurt anyone."

Which was pure luck if Randy had driven while

intoxicated, and he admitted to the DUI, but it had been quite a few years ago now. "He's broken some laws, but it seems like he's straightened up. I don't want to lecture you, but maybe you should consider that his mistakes are catching up with him now whether he committed this crime or not."

"We used to text sometimes after my parents stopped talking to him. He told me once he graduated from college and actually had a job that made some money, he might ask Jan to marry him. You don't think he really killed her, do you?"

At least, with that question, he sounded fifteen instead of fifty-one. A little vulnerable and more like an uncertain young—almost, he wasn't there yet—man.

She wasn't going to tell him about his brother's bruised face. "I've talked to him and I don't yet know the answer to that question, but I'm inclined to believe his story. Certainly I think if you found someone you love murdered, you might react the way he did and panic without thinking that you might become a suspect. Unfortunately, though, a lovers' quarrel that becomes violent happens far too often. Why do you think when a wife or husband is murdered, the spouse is always the first person we consider? He shouldn't have touched her, and he certainly shouldn't have touched the murder weapon."

"But he was, like, freaking out. I keep pointing that out to my dad, but he says he believes Randy did it."

Where was the eminent Dr. Lukens when you needed her? Ellie wasn't qualified to counsel a confused fifteen-year-old torn between his parents and his brother. "Detective Santiago and I are usually pretty good at figuring out the truth and we will do our best. I suggest you talk to your brother John. Go out for a pizza or something, because I think he's with you on this one. In the meantime, we'll check out Mr. Reid. If you come up with anything else, please let us know."

"Okay."

The call ended and she went out to the balcony of the apartment, where Jason was sitting with his beer, and as far as she could tell just looking out at the stars. It was a noteworthy stellar display this night, diamond sparkles against velvet black, and a crescent moon. She took a chair and informed him about the call. "Maybe a lead or maybe not. Cameron Lane seems to think this guy is sketchy."

Her partner argued, of course, because he frequently did, and she was guilty of that now and then too. If she didn't agree with someone, it didn't mean it would change her mind, though sometimes it did make her think about the issue all over again. Jason said, "Or maybe he's starting to realize just how much trouble Randy is in, though I have to admit this Reid going over to talk to the victim makes him worth a close look. If you are thinking what I'm thinking, he could effing be one of the feds. Spying on them? That sets off bells ringing for me."

It had occurred to her too. "I know. Sharp kid notices him hanging around a little too much and might have made him? Not as an agent necessarily, but as someone who doesn't seamlessly fit into his world. Kids are way more observant than we realize. The agent could just be worrying about the Lane family with the adults in the forefront, and has dismissed Cameron. Big mistake. He's got a mouth on him, but he isn't stupid."

"I agree. So tomorrow we pay a visit."

"Right. We have, if we count Randy, now three suspects in the murder of a district attorney's daughter. It's a start. Let's talk to Reid and see what we think. I, personally, believe they should just tell us who is who.

Don't waste your time here, because he's FBI, don't touch this one because he's DEA. It would really help us out."

Jason just stared out over the starlit parking lot. "What if they're worried it was one of us?"

"Meaning law enforcement?"

"Deep undercover is a culture of its own. They want you to play with really bad people on a daily basis. Maybe they are concerned an agent either turned or was forced to do it because otherwise there went years of work."

Ellie was horrified to hear it put that way, but it had occurred to her too. "Neither of those agencies would ask you to murder anyone."

He turned his head. "You and I don't know what they expect. That's why I want you off this case. Come on, Ellie, you and I have both killed people in the line of duty."

"Because we had no choice. No one asked us. Lives were in danger. I'm not undercover and never have been, but those people really put it on the line."

"Locke's daughter's murder was not self-defense."

"I agree. We have guns to defend ourselves, but mostly to defend other people. She was a target, straight and clear."

Jason looked away for a moment, his expression tense. "That's how I see it, and how you see it, but the day of black hats and white hats has gone, and I think everyone wears gray now."

He had a point there. Ellie took a moment and regrouped over her cup of decaf tea. "So you're postulating that if it was for the greater good, if an agent had put in the time and effort to infiltrate an organization that was full of bad people who need to be wiped off the face of this earth, Janet was a sacrificial lamb?"

"Postulating? What the hell kind of word is that? Around you I frequently need a dictionary. Let me get out my phone and ask that app what it means."

He was so deliberately irreverent at times she somehow found it forgivable because she knew he was avoiding the answer. Really? She'd have to ask Lukens what that said about her taste in men. Ellie said, "Oh shut up. You know exactly what it means. My point is I don't believe it. I thought we were having an adult conversation here."

"Oh hell yes, we are." He looked at her then. "Ellie, we might find out who really did it. What we need to do is bury Randy Lane and see him sentenced to life in prison. Have a press conference and all to announce that Metzger put two top detectives on it, and unfortunately, facts are facts, and Randy is the one. We've done our part and life goes on. I think it is what the good guys want, and for sure what the bad guys want."

"I can't do that. She was beaten and her throat was slit." Ellie couldn't let it go, hands down. She looked at him speculatively. "Jason, you don't mean it."

He didn't and she knew it.

"I don't," he conceded. "I said 'need' to do. Like you, I care about the truth, but this is a work in progress, and the other players aren't going to tell us anything." He rubbed his hand over his face. "Look, I've been really thinking this over. We were asked to investigate the murder because of Locke. It's a show of good faith on the part of the MPD. I'm just worried about the ramifications if we find the truth."

"What ramifications?"

"That's the hell of it, I don't know."

Chapter 9

His current cellmate was a pedophile, which was good and bad. Randy figured he wasn't the guy's type because he was way too old in his twenties, so that was the good part. And the bad part was that he found the man's crime so disgusting he really couldn't even look at him. Of course, *he* was being held for a brutal murder, so maybe it was a draw.

He'd written to his grandmother, not to ask for anything, but she'd had the letter returned. He could swear the deputy that handed it to him even felt bad. "Wrong address, son."

"Oh yeah, since she's just lived there my entire life." Randy was both hurt and disillusioned. She lived right there in Milwaukee. "It isn't the wrong address. I guess it doesn't matter."

The deputy hitched his belt and produced keys. "I doubt this is going to improve your mood, but those two detectives are back to talk to you. At least it will get you out of that cell for a while again."

How ironic was it that the staff where he was incarcerated ended up being nicer to him than his family.

"I'm starting to think they are the only friends I have." Randy tossed the letter onto his bed and reflected it had at least given him something to do when he wrote it.

"If you are innocent yes, but if not, I doubt it. Follow me."

The blond female detective was a nice visual; attractive but professional, and Randy wasn't put off by her no-nonsense attitude. He wanted her to be good at her job. She said first thing, "Your face looks better. Things going okay?"

She cared more than his grandmother.

No one in his family had asked about his welfare.

"Yeah. I sleep in the same space with a child molester right now, but hey, I'm not a kid. He isn't the type for a fair fight anyway. I'm getting by."

The tall officer with her who looked like maybe he could handle a close encounter involving fists just fine, cut to the chase. "Good point. It could be worse. Tell us about Reid. You know him? Cameron said he came over and talked to Jan one afternoon when you stopped by your parents' house. Did she say anything about it?"

He remembered it. Randy frowned, thinking it over. "I wanted a box of books I'd left at my parents' house, so I called Cameron to ask if he'd let me in. There *was* a guy out there talking to her when I carried it out. I didn't think too much about it. She didn't seem upset in any way. I asked who he was, she said a neighbor of ours, and we left it there. Keep in mind I haven't lived with my parents for quite some time. It's an established neighborhood, but people do come and go."

"Did she say what they talked about?"

"No. He was middle-aged, looked fit, and was well dressed, so I thought he was just out walking and saw her sitting there and said hello. Nothing to it to my knowledge."

The blonde said, "Maybe."

"Fed."

Jason said it succinctly.

Ellie nodded, walking next to him. "I think we've made one of them anyway. I'll feel better if he just says who he is when we interview him, but I doubt he will. It's like swimming in black water without a moon on a cloudy night."

"It's like skinny-dipping in black water," he corrected. "Everyone knows who we are and knows why we're here. We're naked and exposed, and other than Cameron, and possibly John, we're not getting any help."

"Randy would, but he doesn't have a lot of choices."

"I think he knows something he doesn't realize he knows."

Ellie didn't disagree. "I think it is possible."

"Reid, friend or foe, probably isn't going to be honest with us. It feels like a dead end to me too, but I've been wrong before. Like maybe when I took your word for it we shouldn't worry about birth control."

A low blow if there ever was one, but he was pissed at her on a certain level. She didn't even want to talk about it.

Ellie swung around, her stance defensive. "That's not so nice. I thought you were happy about this baby."

"Oh, I am." He really was. "Except you won't marry me or live with me, but that's another issue." He gazed at her across the top of the car. "My point is that misplaced trust is the basic theme in this entire case."

"I never said 'trust me I can't get pregnant.' I said don't worry about it."

"Did you plan it?" He wasn't doing himself any favors by asking that, but he'd wondered.

Luckily, she didn't get mad; instead she sighed. "Of course not. Unconsciously, maybe I said to myself that if it happened, then it happened, and I could handle it."

She was 100 percent right, but he had a few issues of his own, and all of this affected his life too. "That's true enough," he admitted. "But we are going to have to have a discussion and I don't think *now* works."

"I'll pen it into my schedule."

"Ellie, we have to talk sometime, right?"

She let it go by saying, "Our victim let someone through her door she trusted and it wasn't a man she'd casually met because she was waiting in a car for her boyfriend to retrieve a box of books. I don't know about you, but if he showed up on my doorstep after a causal hello, I would find that unusual and disturbing. Reid isn't the answer. She wouldn't let him through the door. Killer or cop, he'd probably know better than to try it. If your father is a district attorney, you've probably had so many lectures on personal safety that every creak in the night makes you hide in the closet."

"That doesn't work, by the way. Bad guys look in closets. It's a go-to. Don't head for the basement either. Don't you watch horror movies?" He was also relieved at the change in subject back to the case.

"It's always worth a try. And I don't need to watch horror movies, since I live in horror reality quite a bit. So why did she open the door? Someone she trusted?"

"I mean this sincerely: I wish we could ask her."

She got into the car and started it as he slid into his seat. "I do too."

Mr. Reid's house proved to be modest for the neighborhood, staid brick with white trim, and a row of neatly clipped bushes under the front window. He promptly answered the knock and they produced their badges. "Can we have a few minutes of your time?"

"Maybe. May I ask why?"

"We just have some questions."

He hesitated, but then caved, "Of course, Officers. Please come in."

Nicely groomed brown hair, tidy nondescript clothes, and he looked calm. But his eyes were intensely observant, and immediately Jason noticed it too. No personal pictures on the walls, and no pet. Maybe just an average bachelor, but he somehow doubted it. Ellie took out her phone and brought up a picture. "We are homicide detectives. This young woman was murdered, and we know you had a conversation with her recently. Do you mind telling us what was said?"

He peered at the image. "I recall her certainly. I think I mentioned it was a nice day. She was . . . murdered?"

Jason wasn't into games. "The Lane kid called us and said he'd seen you talking to her. All we want is to solve this case and call it a day. Can you tell us anything?"

Ellie might have kicked him, but he had some good instincts and he was on guard. It had served him well as a cop all along, so he just waited for the answer. He hadn't really said anything overtly suspicious and there would most likely be some reason to kick him later, so she could wait.

Reid at first tried to look bewildered but then gave up. He pointed to the doorway. "I'm not sure just what you're saying, but let's go out back. It's such a nice day. I don't think I have much to contribute, but I'll try."

Once they followed him onto a boring cement porch with a dying plant on a table, he said tersely as they all sat down on faded cushions on old chairs, "I sweep the house but don't quite trust it. Are you trying to get me killed? I was promised you would stay out of my hair."

"We didn't make you." Jason said it in a matter-of-fact tone. "The kid did. If he bothered to call us, and he did, and we didn't come talk to you, now *that* would be suspicious."

Reid, or whatever his name was, didn't look all that happier. "They may have to replace me. I knew this murder was going to cause a ripple effect, but I was hoping it wouldn't wipe out months of work."

"It hasn't yet," Ellie pointed out. "We are just following a lead. I'm not even going to ask if you are DEA or FBI. All we want to know is if you have information on who killed Janet Locke. Look at it this way: We just did you a favor. My first thought after that phone call was that talking to you might be bad for everyone, but after some consideration, I think not talking to you would be a big mistake. If people are watching, Detective Santiago here is correct, that would be suspicious. Why did you take the chance and stop to talk to her?"

"To keep up the appearance of being the weird nosy guy down the street going. How would I know she was going to be murdered? I don't think I can help you."

"Robert Lane?"

Reid took a moment. "Okay, interesting theory. He's a shark in a suit. I don't think he has the guts for it in the long run, but maybe he'd hire it out if he was motivated enough."

"Would Locke be part of that motivation?"

"Not just Locke, you already know that."

"But you aren't going to say more."

"No, I'm not. I've said too much already."

Jason informed him bluntly, "You've just spoken to two of the most reliable people on this planet to keep their mouths shut. If your cover goes south, that's your fault, not ours."

Reid didn't exactly back down, but he sure took

notice. "Robert isn't the muscle. I'll let you out the back gate. We're done."

"It's like driving off a cliff into a canyon," Jason muttered as they walked out into the sunshine. "It isn't going to end well. With my luck I'd probably land on a cactus just to make it worse, not that I'd be alive to realize it. At least Cameron helped us out. Let's go try Randy's parents again. Maybe their lawyer has his tan in place and is back here in the land of muskies and river otter. Why does that sound less appealing than a nude beach?"

"Your obsession with nude beaches worries me."

He got into the car. "I'm a Renaissance man. I appreciate the female form in all shapes and sizes."

"No comment. This is from the man who wants to wear a Speedo on a desert island?"

"I thought you weren't going to comment."

Ellie said evenly, "So, try the Lanes and see if their high-powered attorney can deign to talk to us? That's the entire plan?"

"Locke deserves and expects whatever we can do."

She didn't disagree. "Reid doesn't know anything, whoever he is and whoever he works for. I think he would have steered us the right way if he did."

"He isn't FBI. Not polished enough."

"I don't argue that. What about U.S. Marshals Service?"

He considered it. "Possible. They hunt down fugitives, and if the organization tied to the Lanes has links to some people with questionable backgrounds, I'm sure not going to topple over in surprise. Who are they looking for if he is? Could this be important to our case?"

"It could be."

"Multiple agencies . . . Jesus Christ. How many?"

"I don't really think they are all talking to Metzger either."

"I'm not feeling warm and fuzzy about the cooperation."

"What cooperation?" Ellie asked, sounding bitter. "That really hasn't happened yet. Our best information so far has come from a smart-aleck fifteen-year-old."

"Who was absolutely right."

True. "We can't mention to his parents he called us."

Jason gave her a scathing look. "Like I would. Give me some credit and remember, I've been doing this longer than you have."

His phone rang then. And he took it from his pocket. "Santiago."

Chapter 10

"You made bail, Lane. Let's go."

Randy glanced up, incredulous as the door slid open. "What?"

His lawyer was waiting for him after he changed into street clothes, not his own, but he wasn't going to complain. "Your bother John gave up the pants and shirt."

Randy already knew his bloodstained clothes were evidence, but was glad to relinquish the jail-issue attire.

"He also put up the bail money. You can thank District Attorney Locke for getting your bail reduced to one million dollars, which means your sibling is in for a hundred grand, but you do not currently have a valid pilot license. That has been suspended. I figured you'd agree to that concession to get out of jail. Your brother doesn't want you to contact him, by the way. You can thank him at some other time, and I quote."

Randy understood full well why John didn't want any acknowledgment in the effort to help him. "I'll not say a word. Trust me."

"I'd ask where he came up with that kind of money when he isn't much older than you are, but I have a fair idea of your family's net worth. Wasn't your first car a Porsche? I've checked your record very carefully. It was registered to you."

"I wrecked it." Randy owned that one. "But yes it was. Too fast for conditions was the ticket. I did a downward spiral from there. Trust me I don't drive a Porsche now. I didn't know what I wanted to do with my life, but I did not want to work for my father, or maybe I would be driving one again. I knew for a fact he'll never forgive me for that decision, and I don't care."

"Well, I don't drive a Porsche, but at least you have a lift."

His attorney certainly didn't drive an expensive car, but then again, he worked for the state. Randy got into the compact vehicle gladly, and while he'd been ambiguous lately about whether he wanted to live or die, he buckled up. "This is just fine, thank you."

"I'm not taking you home."

All he wanted was a cold beer, his ramshackle couch, and some privacy. The single worst thing about jail was no privacy. It eclipsed the boredom. "What? Why not?"

"The order came down through my office. There will be two officers guarding you. I don't know exactly why, but I think it has something to do with those homicide detectives following up on your case, and perhaps other law enforcement. While I'm supposed to be apprised of new evidence, no one has said anything. I'm supposed to drop you off at a certain location and they will take it from there. My only responsibility is to represent you in court when we go to trial."

Randy was not at all happy. "If I knew anything, I would have said so. There's no need for this."

"Someone thinks there is."

"Who?"

"Excellent question."

"Fergusson." Metzger looked about as distraught as Carl had ever seen him. He wore his bristly hair short, but it still managed to look messy, like he'd been raking his fingers through it. "His daughter called me this morning. A massive heart attack while floating down the river somewhere between Budapest and Amsterdam or something. I'm pretty sure I have that wrong, but what I don't have wrong is that his wife wants him to retire. I think the relaxation probably did him in. We aren't programmed for it. He'd told me multiple times Marie was pushing for it anyway, but I never thought he'd do it." Carl was taken off guard at his visceral reaction to that news. He would miss him. It was difficult to speak. "He was a good detective and leader." Hard nosed like Metzger, but essentially fair. No wonder they'd worked well together.

The chief looked at him. "You'll replace him?"

Carl wasn't surprised necessarily at the question, but it was an unexpected complication and he was still off balance from the revelation. Georgia would probably point out sudden change was not easy for anyone, but especially not for him if it involved possible mortality issues. "I was more expecting to be assigned with MacIntosh."

"I'd thought about it." Metzger took a drink of coffee and set the cup aside. "This absolutely is not the bump in my road I wanted, but it isn't like Fergusson wanted it either. He likes to fish, and now he'll have the opportunity to do it whenever he wants. Tell me what *you* want. Lead is more a desk job. You'd be my first choice, but you are a good investigator. I need an administrator. I think you'd be good at that too."

"MacIntosh."

"No hesitation?"

"None." He meant it without even having to think it over.

"You might have to work with Santiago for a while. He's not exactly a walk in the park."

"So she *is* pregnant."

Metzger just shook his head. "Those two are a giant pain in my ass. All I wanted was a well-ordered life. Today I'm just glad to be alive . . . Fergusson . . . I'm sick about it, but at least he survived."

"Me too." Metzger wasn't talking. Not a yes, not a no, but Carl felt he had his answer. "We've been kind of speculating among ourselves about MacIntosh."

"I thought they might have good chemistry, but didn't count on it being that good." Metzger grumbled the words in evident frustration. "Is there a plan between the two of them to make my existence on this planet a living hell? Beside the fact I have to reassign them, I'm not interested on a purely selfish level having MacIntosh out on maternity leave."

"You might want to take up matchmaking as a second career."

"If I wanted input like that I'd have waited for a Santiago moment, but it's a thought right now. There is a detective who wants to transfer here from the Twin Cities and she holds rank. I talked to her chief this morning. I warn you, she plays hardball according to him. I just wanted to offer it to you first. You're sure?"

Georgia had asked him once if he would ever consider being chief one day. It was clear in his mind the answer was a resounding no at the moment.

"I appreciate it." Oddly enough it wasn't a hard

decision. "I don't mind responsibility, but that's not why I'm here. I want to work homicides. It's the challenge and not the glory with the weary details."

"And you have a choice most people don't because you don't have to work at all."

"Being promoted isn't all that important to me, true." He wasn't going to apologize for it. Wealth came with a hefty price tag all its own.

"We'll see how this all goes." Metzger took in a deep breath. "Since you're right here and Fergusson isn't available to ask, which hurts my heart—and here all the time you didn't think I had one—if you want the truth because things are set to change if he really is going to do this, what do you think about me promoting Santiago to lieutenant?"

Losing Fergusson was not good news, even though he could be a proper bastard. Carl was surprised—and it showed—about Santiago. "I'm not even sure how to respond to that suggestion. He's earned it, but then again he's off the wall sometimes. I confess I'm on the fence."

"Me too." Metzger leaned back, rubbing his chin. "One day I want to fire his ass, and the next I really do think he's one of our finest. I honestly think he gives everything he has, but sometimes it is just too much. He's been suspended how many times now? Sure, he walked away clean from every single investigation, but he's like an outlaw who successfully robs banks. Good at it, so you have to give him credit for that, but either he gets hurt or someone else does. I can't decide and I need a second opinion. You win the prize. Talk to me."

"Just don't assign him desk duty."

"That's not an opinion, Grasso, that's plain common sense."

Carl thought it over and shrugged. In his mind Santiago fell into the "nothing ventured nothing gained" category. It all came down to if he wanted someone at his back, that's who he'd choose right next to MacIntosh. "I think you should do it. Give him lieutenant. In none of the investigations did he act in any interest except that of the people of this city. He tends to risk his life maybe more than he should, but that's not at the risk to anyone else. This last investigation he saved the life of a young mother whose husband was trying to strangle her. Cops come in all shapes and sizes like everyone else, but he *is* one of the good guys."

"Well, that's what I was thinking, but he is just not a predictable law enforcement officer. Sometimes I feel he's like letting a tiger out of its cage."

"No, he is not completely manageable, but then again, that might be just what we need."

"I'm still thinking it over."

Carl left him to his dilemma and of course met MacIntosh on the way back to his desk. He felt like maybe he should—and could—handle this for Metzger. "You have a minute?"

She said hesitantly, "I suppose . . . sure."

"Have a seat."

She sat down, holding a file, looking apprehensive. "What, Lieutenant? Or am I talking to Carl Grasso?"

"Fergusson had a heart attack on vacation."

She looked stricken. "What? Is he okay?"

"Yes, but he's decided to retire. You have to admit this is not a stress-free occupation and his wife put her foot down. It looks like you and I will become partners."

Well, that was good news and bad news. Ellie liked Grasso and he was a top-notch investigator, no doubt about that, but she would miss working with Jason. God help her, she knew exactly what her former partner was thinking most of the time. Grasso was more of an enigma.

The horrible news was Fergusson. He was a devoted police officer, and certainly by all accounts a good husband and father and she knew he loved the job, but his wife hated it.

She chose her next words to Grasso carefully. Her father's similar death came immediately to mind. "I'm more than sorry in many ways, but I don't blame his wife for being concerned. I would think you'd be slated as next in line for lead."

"Metzger and I just had a meeting. I stated my preference for working active cases, not managing how they'd be worked. It looks like we're going to get a transfer detective from Minnesota. How is the Lane case going anyway?"

She really did not want to go to another cop funeral, so maybe Fergusson's wife was exactly right.

Grasso wasn't exactly handling it smoothly either, she could tell.

Ellie steadied herself. It seemed like they did need to get down to business. "Randy Lane is out on bail thanks to Locke in part, and he's in a safe house being guarded by U.S. marshals. This is by far the most complicated case I've ever worked because it seems to me like the law enforcement side thinks he knows something important, and the opposition thinks he does too, and he has no idea what it might be. Orders from above, as you know, are to just investigate the homicide and stay out of the rest of the mix."

It wasn't possible. Already they'd crossed a boundary with Reid, but they hadn't known it. Now they didn't have the slightest idea where Randy might be.

"You'll finish the case with Santiago. Hopefully soon. When is the baby due?"

She hesitated. Metzger would not have told him. Grasso must have figured it out all on his own, but she wasn't about to lie to him either. There was no point in it. "I'm not four months along."

"So roughly five months."

"That's how it is supposed to work. This is definitely my first attempt to navigate this experience. Who told you?"

"No one. From one detective to another, there are subtle things, like the way you are dressing, but it's all Santiago. He's . . . downright cordial, and he is not a cordial man. I think he's glowing *for* you."

Ellie had to admit to a dry laugh even with the news about Fergusson weighing on her. Jason . . . glowing? "This was obviously not an anticipated curveball."

"Some of the best things in life are not." Grasso straightened his tie, which as far as Ellie could tell he did unconsciously about fifty times a day. "I didn't plan on meeting an attractive psychologist who probably has me slated as a research project, but so life goes. No doubt I could use the help."

"You've always seemed decently sane to me, and that's all I ask for in a partner."

"Decently? Does Santiago qualify?"

"No comment. Take it as a compliment. I was trying to be kind."

"Ellie?"

She had no idea what she might have said next, but the familiar voice sent a shock through her. She turned and saw Bryce Grantham standing there, well dressed, his dark hair stylishly disheveled. A faint apologetic smile was on his mouth. "Hello, Lieutenant. Am I interrupting?"

Of course, to add to the dubious ambience of her day, her ex would show up out of the blue.

Grasso was obviously just as surprised. "No, we we're done. Nice to see you again."

He really beat it and Ellie understood why. She wanted to outdistance him down the corridor. Instead she said as calmly as possible, "Hi, I guess I didn't know you were in town. Everything is okay with your parents?"

"Everything is fine." He had a slow, attractive smile. "I just thought I'd let you know I'm moving back to Milwaukee. I loved New York, but this is home and I still have the house."

The one she'd lived in. Where they'd lived together. "I'm sorry I just moved out."

"No, don't be. I really moved out too."

He was right, she hadn't abandoned him, they had, in short, abandoned each other. At least it had been amicable.

That was illustrated by what he said next. "My parents have been handling it with the house. Would you like to have dinner one night?"

That wasn't expected. She would but . . . this was awkward.

"Yes." She meant it. "I'd love that." She paused, but she owed him this much. "I'd like for us to talk and catch up."

After the conversation with Grasso, she was really tired of the pregnancy reveal, and this was a complication she didn't need. "I am seeing someone, just so you know, but dinner would be nice."

Bryce actually didn't look all that surprised; he just crossed his arms over his chest and said quietly, "Santiago?"

Males had a culture all their own. It was like learning a foreign language. "How could you know that?"

Bryce didn't hesitate. "Not how he looked at you, but how he looked at me. We sized each other up. I knew there was competition from day one when you moved here and were assigned him as a partner."

"Men are difficult. I work with a lot of them, and just when I think you are all hopeless, you surprise me."

"The question is will he mind if we go to dinner? He carries a gun. Why do I get the impression he uses it now and again?"

Ellie knew Bryce was kidding. "He doesn't own me and he knows that."

"You'd be hard to own." Bryce smiled, but then sobered. "Santiago, huh?"

"It is an interesting development in my life, but then, so were you."

"I suppose I was. I haven't gotten over you, by the way."

That was not necessarily a welcome revelation.

Ellie chose to walk around it. "I . . ." She trailed off as Jason came around the corner, stopped dead in his tracks when he saw Bryce, and then visibly squared his shoulders and came toward them.

Bad timing.

They would both be civil—she wasn't worried about that—and Bryce had to be aware he might run into her partner if he just showed up, but Jason was at a disadvantage over the surprise and she could tell he wasn't happy about it. He said with no real inflection, "Grantham."

"Detective Santiago."

Why on earth couldn't she just have a normal day? Was there even such a thing? She thought probably not.

She wasn't going to get into this mix. "Do you have information on Lane? Your text indicated you did."

"I know where he is and he wants to talk to us again. Grantham, are you visiting your parents or what?"

Luckily, Bryce handled it well. "I'm in town and wanted to say hello."

Also luckily, Jason accepted that. With a caveat. "I know you and Ellie are still friends."

"I certainly hope so. There's no reason we shouldn't be."

It was clearly a warning off on both sides, and Ellie was relieved it was going as well as it was, but she wanted it to stay neutral. "Bryce, give me a call and please tell your parents I said hello. It appears we have to go talk to a murder suspect."

He took the hint and left. Jason said predictably as he watched him go down the hallway, "Give me a call? What the hell?"

"Can we go?"

"No." Jason wouldn't budge. "I so don't like he's ever touched you."

She didn't need that information because she could tell. "You lived with Kate and I doubt beds in separate rooms were involved. Somehow I don't think she was the first woman you were involved with either."

"You haven't found Kate at my desk, chatting me up."

"Chatting me up? I somehow never expected you to use that phrase. This isn't London." She was unwillingly amused because jealousy annoyed her. "Here's some news, he's a nice man."

"Part of my problem right there."

Maybe it was the baby, maybe it was that she knew everyone would figure it out soon, but she went around her desk and looked him in the eye. "So are you, just in a different way. This kind of thing is exactly why we are being reassigned, but for now, we still work together. Ready to go? I want to catch this killer. You're driving, by the way."

Chapter 11

Early evening, but at least he could see the sunset. He'd never thought it over before and just took it for granted. Tomorrow, he vowed, he'd watch it rise.

They honestly thought someone was going to try to kill him, or he was going to run.

Randy couldn't believe it.

It wasn't like he didn't understand the legacy of his existence, especially now, but this was, to his mind, just as much of incarceration as jail. Nicer digs, but the same amount of freedom. At least there was a television, but they'd removed the phone and he still didn't have his cell back.

If the police knew what they were doing, they'd realize he didn't have the money to run.

Only he didn't think it was the police particularly. The landscape was bigger and he was scared, for both Cameron and John, who had stood by him. He had the ominous feeling their world might come crashing down.

He wasn't worried about Robert. Like an alley cat, his oldest brother would always land on his feet.

The room was nice. Plain but clean, and he had a

window with a wide view—of the rooftop, but that was better than nothing

He was going to fail his classes. Maybe the university gave you immunity for certain excessive absent totals, but he doubted being arrested for murder counted. Randy rested his head in his hands and tried to not think about it. At least it was just summer classes, and if they found out who killed Jan, he might get amnesty from the university for the two failures.

He missed her.

There was no one he wanted to talk to as much as her, to hear her warm laugh . . .

The knock on the door was such an ordinary sound it startled him. It hadn't taken long to forget the privilege of having the option to answer or not answer it.

He chose to answer it. He'd watched three movies already, and the news was a mix of violence and politics, not to mention the weather report of a bright sunny week ahead, which to him was even more depressing since he wouldn't get to enjoy it. There was a music channel, but he found then he sat and brooded if he just listened, and so that wasn't a good alternative.

The blond female detective—MacIntosh—wore red today, a long tunic that was a welcome splash of color in his otherwise lackluster surroundings. Her male sidekick came in behind her when Randy stepped back, and Santiago said with his usual abruptness, "You wanted to talk to us. Here we are. Talk."

Randy sat down on the bed and Detective MacIntosh took the chair at the desk he couldn't use because he didn't have his computer. She told him, "It's nice to not see you in jail. You can thank Janet's father for removing some of the charges so you could make bail. Why are we here?"

He could also thank John, and someday hopefully he

could, but he was worried maybe John had disappeared for good. Randy said, "I have a vested interest in helping you with this and it really is all I think about. Let me give you another suspect. I have a cousin who is so sadistic that I could actually see him doing this. As a kid I was afraid of him, and he enjoyed that I was afraid of him. I hate to think this is tied to my family, but if it is, I vote for him as the main suspect. I wrote down his name for you but don't know his current address. He works for the company, though, so you could probably find out."

Maybe at last a viable suspect that wouldn't turn out to be law enforcement?

Jason would normally be elated over having a tip on a possible suspect, but to be honest, seeing Grantham at Ellie's desk didn't help his day. They'd been comfortably talking and he'd felt it like a blow to the gut seeing them together.

He couldn't lose what he didn't have in the first place, if that made any sense at all, since they were going to share a child. He'd been very reluctant to commit, but hadn't expected Ellie's complete resistance once he made up his mind.

Maybe complete was exaggerating. She just hadn't agreed to anything.

Then she'd told him Fergusson was going to retire. It wasn't like he loved that crusty, ornery bastard, but to his surprise he'd miss him. Fergusson had one thing he admired, just like with Metzger. He was fair. Not necessarily nice, but Jason could deal with that if fair was included in the bargain. He definitely told you flat out when you messed up, no question about it, but they weren't on the police force to have their hands held and hear bedtime stories. Fergusson threw his weight around, yes, yet he did his job.

"So Grasso is stepping in," he said. "That won't be bad. I'd rather have him than anyone else."

"No, he's not. He told Metzger apparently that the answer was he'd rather work cases."

Jason was getting a feel for it now. "With you?"

"Who knows what Metzger will decide."

If she had to work with someone else, he'd prefer it to be Grasso anyway, so this shift in his career was not welcome, but this shift in his life was, so he was just going to have to balance it. The entirety of his existence he'd had to deal with the practicality of his current situation, whatever it might be, and Grasso was competent and a tough, canny cop, even if he wore expensive clothes and lived in a mansion. Grasso would take care of her, and for that matter, Ellie would also have his back. They would both win.

It took a few phone calls, but they found Frederick Forsythe's address without too much trouble. He was an accountant for the company called Fund Enterprises, which was a blanket title for a group of small businesses that all sounded legitimate and were owned by the Lane family, but considering all the interest from other law enforcement, probably were not legitimate at all.

It was after six and he was home. He answered the door in an old Packers T-shirt and sweatpants. He must resemble his father's side of the family, because he was squarely built and had reddish hair and a neatly trimmed beard, but ice-cold blue eyes. They both showed him their badges.

They were not invited in.

"Homicide detectives? What? Is this about my loser cousin Randy killing his girlfriend? I don't know what I can tell you."

Ellie wasn't fazed by his caustic tone. "How about where you were that afternoon."

"Me? I'm a suspect? You already arrested *him*, lady."

Jason on the other hand didn't like his aggressive stance. "Ellie, step back, and that's Detective MacIntosh, by the way," he told Forsythe as he angled himself between them. "We could take you in for questioning if you'd prefer."

"On what grounds?"

"Your refusal to talk to us will work just fine."

"I haven't refused, I just have nothing to say. I was here, at home." But he did back down.

"Can it be confirmed?"

"Yes. It was all over the news."

He knew the date, but it was possible he knew it because his cousin had been arrested for murder that day. Though Jason had to agree, he didn't seem like a caring enough sort of guy to remember the actual day. "Confirmed? How?"

"I was working from home. I made a couple of calls."

"Good. From here? We'll pull your phone records."

"Do it. I think I also posted on Facebook that afternoon. Check my page."

It was so easy. All he needed to do was to leave his phone behind and have someone else punch a number. Jason was siding at the moment with Randy, the man was so unpleasant. "We will. Nothing else to add?"

"No, except I'm surprised Randy had the guts. He was such a wuss as a kid."

Normally, they would have thanked him for his time and left a card. Neither of them did.

"What an asshole," Jason remarked as they went down the steps to leave, his hands thrust carelessly into his pockets. "That didn't accomplish much."

"Oh yes it did."

He shot her a look. "Like?"

"He doesn't like women. Or maybe he just likes to dominate them. You sensed it too. Like a guard dog, you stepped right in. It doesn't mean he likes men in a sexual way, but I don't think he is a stranger to threatening the small and weaker."

Like Jan Locke.

He *had* felt it.

"Suspect number one now?" He felt the urge to buckle Ellie's seat belt like a protective mother or something.

She did it herself before he made a complete fool of himself. "I think Randy might have led us in the right direction. Not a crime of passion, but maybe a hate crime. He doesn't like Randy and he doesn't like women. I might talk to Lukens about it. She's not a profiler in that she doesn't handle that work on a professional level, but she's helped us out more than once."

"He's an accountant and a college grad, plus he sat successfully for the CPA exam, so he isn't an idiot." He started the truck, thinking it over. "If we trace his calls, why do I think they will be to be someone in the company willing to swear he's the one who actually called them when he was off handling the murder?"

"We have quite a conspiracy theory going if we are speculating three people at least were involved in such a brutal crime. Forsythe killing her, the person using his phone to give him an alibi and posting on his page, and the person taking the calls willing to say it was him."

"If the hit was ordered to strike at Locke, that person would be on board with helping out. I have fifty bucks—which for the record buys a lot of beer, so I don't throw money around like that lightly—that those calls went to someone high up in businesses owned or run by the Lane family."

"I wouldn't be surprised either. Hey, we are heading the wrong direction. Where are we going?"

He glanced over at her. "To look at the house. We have an appointment, remember?"

The house.

Ellie wasn't aware this was zero hour. "Right now?"

"Yeah, right now. We'll be a few minutes late as it is."

She'd known he seemed serious anyway, but already it had been an eventful day with finding out about Fergusson, Bryce showing up all of a sudden, and the interview with Forsythe had been interesting. It wasn't that she'd ever felt invincible just because she was a law enforcement officer and carried a weapon, but there was definitely a newfound awareness of vulnerability in her life.

Fine, she'd help him with the house.

Jason took them out of the fashionable downtown neighborhood where Forsythe lived and headed south. In four blocks it became more suburban, and in two more he pulled up to a midcentury ranch on a corner lot. It looked nicely redone on the outside, with tidy plantings along a porch, and sure enough the realty sales agent was waiting.

He was middle-aged, overweight, and had a nice smile. He handed over a flyer. "Mr. and Mrs. Santiago. So nice to meet you."

"I'm Detective MacIntosh from Milwaukee PD Homicide Division." Ellie kept the correction pleasant. "I'm just along to give my opinion."

"Oh."

"She really is," Jason backed her up. "I'm not sure I'd marry someone who carries a Glock at all times and has such good aim. What if we had a lovers' spat? She's not all that sweet-tempered either."

Jason could be kind of funny. The humor just needed to grow on you.

The agent looked unsure of how to respond to that. "I . . . er . . . let me give you my card. I have unlocked the front door so you can go in and look around. The sellers have moved, so everything you see stays with the house."

The porch had been freshly painted a soft gray that contrasted nicely with white brick of the house, and there was a pot of bright red geraniums by the wooden front door. So far so good, though Ellie tried to picture Jason watering flowers and couldn't quite summon that particular image. He reinforced that by saying, "If I buy this place, that plant would be toast. If I even look at one it starts to wither. You are in charge of all gardening aspects. I'll mow the grass. The street seems quiet." Jason unlatched the door. "That part is good for us."

"This assumption you have that I will ever agree to live with you is hopefully *not* why you are buying a house."

Jason ignored it, but it wasn't a surprise. He went his own way. He looked around the living room. "Wow, love the exposed beams in the ceiling. Let's go check out the most important part."

"Kitchen?"

"Nope. Backyard for the kid and the big dog."

"You don't even have a dog, or so you claim. You could have kept little Louise, but chose to have Locke take her to his wife."

"If you remember, Louise wasn't my number-one fan. I'm hoping thanks to us Lane can have his little dog back." He opened the French doors to a small deck.

"Wow, this is pretty much like what I was talking about. A couple of comfortable chairs and a little table where you could set your beer and you could sit here and watch them run around."

It was nice, with smooth grass and two mature trees at the back. And it was fenced so there was security and privacy.

Maybe Jody's advice was wise after all. A child could run around here safely. "It's a good feature."

It was amusing that he didn't even glance at the stainless appliances or expensive countertops in the remodeled kitchen, but just cared about this. "I might make an offer on this one."

"Just because of the backyard? Let's look at the bathrooms and bedrooms first."

"I guess we should. I knew I'd brought you for a reason."

In all she also gave it a thumbs-up. There wasn't a ton of charm without any furniture, but a great deal of function, and when a bevy of kids raced by on their bikes on the street as they walked back outside, she knew he'd feel at home. The agent sensed Jason's enthusiasm and informed them, "It is priced to sell, so if you are interested, I wouldn't wait too long."

"It seems like a contender." Jason opened the car door for her and she gave him an exasperated look but got in.

Her phone rang as if on cue and it was Grasso. Before Ellie could even acknowledge the call, he said curtly, "You and Santiago have stepped in it. There are two federal agents right now in Metzger's office, and he had to come from home in the middle of his dinner, so he isn't a happy man, and he isn't happy even when he gets to finish his mashed potatoes. I think maybe you should get back here right away."

"Federal agents?"

Jason clambered in and was now staring at her, his shoulders lifted in question. She said, "We are on our way, but what did we do?"

"We'll talk here."

She looked helplessly at her partner when the call ended. "I don't have a clue as to what's going on, but be prepared for another session with Metzger that will give you bad dreams apparently."

He looked predictably unfazed. "I've served in war-torn countries. I don't have bad dreams. I just rely on bad memories. Okay, let's go find out what's up."

When they walked into the station, Grasso just pointed at Metzger's closed door and went back to his computer. Ellie didn't even want to knock, but there were times in life you did things you knew were going to result in an unpleasant experience.

So she knocked.

The visitors wore nice suits, were clean cut, and one older and one maybe her age. Metzger, as predicted, didn't look too enthusiastic to be there. "Good of you to join us, Detectives. Please meet Special Agent Gregory and Special Agent Campbell. They very much wish to talk to you, and so do I. The two of you seem to wreak havoc wherever you go, so let's hash it out, shall we?"

"What havoc?" Jason jerked out a chair for her, but stayed on his feet. "We are investigating a murder. Last I checked, that's our job. Yes, we got a tip that led us to an undercover agent, but how could we know that?"

"The man you know as Reid is dead, and about an hour after you talked to *him*, John Lane took quite a lot of money out of the bank, paid his brother's bail, and then boarded a flight for Nashville, Tennessee. He didn't rent a car, so either he's wandering through the streets or someone met him there." It was the older agent, speaking in a matter-of-fact voice. "He really was the witness we were counting on. And we are now short a very reliable agent. Both of them were recently questioned by you."

Reid was dead? Ellie felt remorse, but not like they were actually responsible. "We were following a lead. We have no idea even now what agency he worked for, or that he was an agent before we knocked on his door. Reid was seen talking to our victim by Cameron Lane, who might be young, but is evidently pretty observant. He noticed Reid seemed to be paying attention to their household. That's a lead."

Santiago said evenly but with acid in his tone, "It would help if we had the slightest idea who the players are in this game. All we are doing is handling our investigation, and that is to find out who killed Janet Locke. As for John Lane, I'm going to guess the murder shook him up, but even more so his family's determination to let Randy hang for it. I assume he realized a long time ago that he isn't related to the most kind and caring bunch, and maybe he decided to get out before he was put on the chopping block himself. I know I would."

Gregory and Campbell exchanged glances. Grasso had quietly come in and leaned against the wall, just listening so far until he said, "They have a point. It's difficult to solve a case when no one will talk to you."

"What makes you so sure Randy Lane didn't kill his girlfriend?" the younger agent asked with what seemed to be genuine curiosity. "He was immediately arrested, and there seems, from the brief I read anyway, to be overwhelming evidence of his guilt, even his prints on the knife and her blood on his clothes."

"There's also some inconsistencies in the evidence that suggest it really was someone else. Why would he stop and wipe off a table when his prints were going to be everywhere anyway? A blood spatter specialist also thought the blood on his clothes was inconsistent with her injuries and definitely postmortem. We aren't saying he didn't do it, but his story is quite possibly true because it would have taken some real planning for the other scenario. That means two things: We could send an innocent man to jail and then there would be a really dangerous individual walking around out there free and unaccountable." Ellie was emphatic. "We can certainly say Randy didn't kill Reid. He's been in jail or under guard since the murder. Someone else is following our case."

"We wouldn't, and didn't, for a moment think your case was related to what happened to our agent. We are just wondering if your investigation is hampering an effort that has been ongoing for years now by drawing attention to it. These are some very bad people, Detective MacIntosh. We don't want them to wake up and take notice any more than they already have."

Jason had an incredulous look on his face. "What the hell do you want us to do? Just like you, we're doing our jobs. I don't give a rat's—"

Ellie interrupted before he used a word she was sure he was about to use. "Detective Santiago has a point. A little communication would be great, but it has to be from both sides. We are doing the job the people of Wisconsin expect us to do. If you have a solution to this problem, I'd love to hear it."

Agent Campbell stood. "I understand your position. Let's see what we can work out."

After they left, Metzger didn't look any happier.

"Now, the two of you tell me you have at least a viable suspect."

Ellie said firmly, "We do, and if you think this case isn't related to theirs, I strongly disagree."

Chapter 12

Just when he was getting used to his lackluster view of the roof, they moved him. Randy was watching a cartoon that must have been made before he was born when his gatekeepers—he'd started to call them that—came in through the door without knocking and told him to pack up, and make sure he didn't leave anything behind.

His personal opinion on the situation was when two burly men with no sense of humor carrying guns told you to do something, you did it. Besides, he had about three pairs of boxers and a couple of shirts and two pairs of jeans stuffed into a duffel bag. It didn't take long. They even came in to watch him shave and took away the razor immediately. Like right out of his hand.

"I'm not going to slit my throat or anything," he complained, but it wasn't like suicide hadn't occurred to him. He was feeling pretty alone for someone who had absolutely no alone time at all.

"Nope," one of the officers agreed. "Not while I'm on duty. I have an assignment, son, and that is keeping you alive and knowing where you are at all times."

"Then maybe an electric razor would have been a good idea."

"And have you drop it in the bathtub to take care of it that way, or use the cord to hang yourself? Give us some credit."

They had actually been pretty decent, but it was infuriating to be out on bail and have absolutely no freedom. On the other hand, it was better than jail.

Anything was better than that.

The second place was a ground-floor apartment that smelled vaguely like stale cigarette smoke, but at least it had a kitchen and room to move around. There were cans of soup in the cupboard, some bagged lettuce, lunch meat and bread, and two bottles of dressing in the refrigerator. There was even a six-pack of beer and a bottle of wine, screw top of course.

He'd left picky behind quite some time ago so there was no protest. He'd had to borrow the money for college and his apartment was pretty Spartan. The best part was there was a small stack of books, and a pen and a notebook. Still no phone, but who was he going to call?

No options there.

Late afternoon, misty warm rain, and it was almost impossible to keep the windshield clear without the air at full blast, so he was starting to wish he'd kept his jacket in the truck.

Jason was driving down Lincoln when his cell beeped and he pulled off into a parking lot to answer it. The few people who had his number usually had something important to tell him, but after having done a commercial at the request of the governor against driving and talking on cell phones, he made it a point never to do it on the road. "What?"

"Has MacIntosh ever mentioned to you your phone skills could use some work?"

Grasso. Jason admitted, "Maybe once or twice."

Or a hundred times.

"I'll remind her to do it again. She and I are going to see Georgia. I was going to go over later anyway because we have dinner plans, so I thought I'd just take her and listen in on what our favorite psychologist has to say."

"I can't join you right now. I'll meet up with you later after I run an errand."

After Jason saw his mother at the hospital. He hadn't mentioned specifically what "errand" it was he had to run. His very tenuous connection with his family was always an emotional trail ride down the side of a deep canyon on a windy day on a grumpy burro.

No one knew if they would make it to the top again.

All Jason knew was that his mother had been in a car accident and was in fair condition, and his father had specifically requested he visit her, included the room number and the name of the hospital, and the man sounded all shaken up.

Giving comfort wasn't part of Jason's skill set.

This was going to be interesting, but while his appearance was maybe not necessary, he'd found he anticipated guilt if he didn't do it.

So he'd agreed.

He reluctantly asked for her room and said he was family. A nurse pointed the right way and he followed the directions. The door was open and a man in a white coat who was no doubt a doctor was scribbling on a clipboard. There were, Jason saw with a twinge of alarm that actually surprised him because he hadn't even seen his mother in decades before until recently, quite a few tubes attached to the woman lying in the bed and she appeared to be asleep. He saw stitches on her forehead, one of her hands was bandaged, and any other damage concealed by a blanket.

His father rose immediately from a chair by her bedside and came over to hug him, which wasn't all that welcome, but under the circumstances what choice did Jason have but to allow it? The man looked about as strained as he'd sounded on the phone. He told the doctor, "This is our son."

Our son? It was true, but then again, given he hadn't met the man until he was over thirty, not all that true either.

The doctor nodded and said in a no-nonsense tone, "I'll tell you both that I think the internal bleeding is minimal, which had been our biggest concern. She seems to be stabilizing nicely, and in a day or two she should be upgraded to good condition as long as all goes well."

"That's positive news." God, he was bad at this. It sounded lame, and Jason felt inadequate, but he wasn't sure what else he should say.

"I'll be back to check on her later, but the nurses will keep me informed if anything changes." The doctor hung up a clipboard and walked out the door.

And left Jason essentially alone with his father.

A first.

Their interaction so far had been mediated by his mother, so the one-on-one was not very familiar. Jason asked quietly, "What happened?"

"The other driver ran a red light. Broadsided the car. It was a Jaws of Life kind of event. They flew her here by helicopter because they have such a specialized trauma center."

In other words, very bad.

"Intoxicated driver?" He had to ask. It was a police officer question, but then again he was one.

"Speeding."

Jason wasn't surprised. "Intoxicated drivers are being irresponsible, but there is a reason we have speed limits. Speed is almost worse. My apartment isn't that far away if you want to use it. I can stay with Ellie."

"I kind of wondered if the wind blew that direction."

That was unsettling. He'd never thought of his father as perceptive, but then again, he hadn't thought about him much at all. "We work together. She's a friend."

"More than a friend. You look at her like I look at your mother. I noticed it when you came to dinner a few months ago and brought her along. Partner perhaps, but maybe more than that, eh? Pretty young woman."

Just because his father had done time in prison didn't mean the man was stupid. Not perfect certainly, but stupid, no. Their wary relationship was evolving.

His father rubbed the back of his neck, his expression somber. "Let me tell you something about our family: We don't do things halfway. It's in our genes. All in or all out. I haven't told them about you because they'd want to meet you, and I have a feeling you aren't interested."

That was certainly correct. Jason thought about Randy Lane. He said bluntly, "I'm not. Ties to organized crime are toxic. I think that's why you didn't know I existed. No, thanks."

"Don't sell my sources of information short, even when I was inside. I knew you existed, I just didn't realize you were mine. If you don't think I kept track of your mother, you'd be wrong. I only agreed to the divorce because I wanted her to be happy."

Jason didn't even know how to respond to that.

"You're going to be a grandfather."

He hadn't really meant to say that outright to a man he barely knew, but maybe it was just the situation, and maybe it was an olive branch of sorts. The woman lying there attached to all those machines had wronged them both in a way, but then again, her intention had been for the best of everyone. His father took a second, but he smiled wearily. "Thank you for a good moment. I needed one. You didn't have to share with me but you did. Your mother will be thrilled. I know you are working through this distance between us because we haven't had the chance to know each other, but please take a second to realize I am too."

That was at least positive. It had certainly occurred to him that he might not have even known about the accident if Ellie hadn't put him in touch with his mother in the first place.

Jason handed over the vase of flowers that he'd bought at the last moment. "Tell her these are from me."

"I can help with your latest case. The Lane family thing. That murder of the lawyer's daughter." His father held the flowers, which looked incongruous next to his rumpled work shirt. He'd obviously not been home to change since the accident happened. "Heard your name mentioned. I can ask some quiet questions of the right people."

"Hell no!" Jason wasn't sure where the vehemence came from, but it was there. He pointed at the still form of his mother in the bed. "She needs you alive. I realize you understand they aren't playing around probably more than I do, and I appreciate the offer, but all three of the people in this room have suffered from your ties to the right people, and that includes you. You got yourself out of that life, so stay out of it. Don't ask as a

favor to me, please, but more for her. I'll solve this problem myself."

He walked out and headed for the elevators.

"Maybe Jason has a point. Bow out of this case."

Ellie glanced over at Georgia from where she was
chopping scallions to put on top of the garlic chicken,
which was simmering away nicely and filling the small
kitchen with the perfume of ginger and the richness of
soy sauce. "He's talked to you about it, or is this Grasso?"

"I'm Jason's therapist. He's supposed to talk to me.
Let's just say I'm aware he's extremely concerned. He
loves you, but he now has other things on his mind as
well."

Ellie was resigned. "I'm glad he's so enthusiastic
about the baby. Without making the claim that I planned
it, let's just say looking back I knew if it did happen, he
would be right on board with it. I think I rationalized
that planning a pregnancy without discussing it with
him first would be wrong, but if it happened, it happened. I *didn't* plan it. He actually asked me if I did."

"Did you?"

"No. I wouldn't lie to him, or to you, I just said I
didn't."

"You *are* a woman in her thirties, so if you did want
a child, the opportunity isn't exactly now or never, but
this would be an ideal time. It's a logical question."
Georgia took a sip of wine and said delicately, "Just so
you know, Carl did ask me if you might be pregnant.
No confirmation one way or the other."

Ellie picked up a wooden spoon and stirred the
chicken. "We've had the conversation. I told Metzger,
so it isn't a mystery anyway. That wasn't easy. I've told

my sister, but the hard one was my mother. The first one didn't go well, meaning Metzger, but the last one was better than anticipated. She wants to meet Jason, which I suppose makes sense, but the meet-the-parents deal is a commitment I'm not ready to make. I'm happy, but only cautiously. He'll be a good father. The rest of it is up in the air."

"Jason is an interesting man. He deals with life in an extremely straightforward way. There is no ambiguity."

"I've noticed."

"Look at it this way: I doubt he'd ever lie to you. He doesn't flow that direction."

That was the absolute truth. "A positive. He isn't shy about putting it out there, I agree." Ellie took the spring rolls out of the oven. "Have I mentioned Bryce is moving back to Milwaukee?"

"Is he?"

"Oh yes. He stopped by my desk to let me know."

"Is that significant to you?"

She weighed her answer. Ellie eventually said, "I don't think so. It was nice to see him and he asked me if we could have dinner together. I said yes. Jason is going to have to learn to handle it. He wasn't happy about it."

"I don't think he has a problem with your independence. In my opinion, part of why he is so attracted to you is that you don't need him. He associates with it, and finds it comfortable. If something happens to him you won't be helpless, you'll cope. I have a lot of patients who suffer from the opposite syndrome. They require dependence to feel important. Jason will never be like that. However, security is different. There has been some serious fallout in that department in his life."

Ellie got out a wide cobalt blue bowl for the rice. "He will always be the father of our child." Her smile held wry humor. "Even if I wanted to run and hide I bet he could find me. That's the downside of having a relationship with a detective."

"But you wouldn't run and hide. If you choose someone else over him, he'd just have to take it on the chin. That, I'm guessing here, he knows full well. He'd survive it, but he wouldn't like it."

"If you are talking Bryce, it's just a dinner. It will be nice to catch up face to face. Did you know Jason went and looked at a house? He's seriously talking swing sets already. I guess I don't need to lose sleep over being a single mother."

Georgia started laughing. "He seems very clear cut but is actually complex like most of us. It's easy to know *how* he feels about something, but *why* he feels that way is more difficult. In your case, I would say that maybe you're still trying to figure out why, aside from the physical attraction, you have an emotional attraction."

"Are you grappling with the same personal problem, Dr. Lukens?"

Grasso had run out to buy a bottle of scotch, since Ellie didn't have any on hand. The invitation to dinner at her place had been impulsive, but both of them had accepted with alacrity. She had the feeling they ate out too frequently and she was cooking anyway.

Her friend didn't dodge the question. "Oh yes. Carl and I are both navigating the harrowing waters of figuring out if you want the same things in life, and there are always white-water rapids along the way. In my experience dependent people commit too easily and the independent spirit uses caution like a shield. We are used to our own lives."

"What is Carl Grasso?" The chicken was done and Ellie switched off the burner and picked up her glass of sparkling water. "An independent spirit?"

"Oh, most definitely." Georgia poured more wine into her glass. "There's a high wall to scale there. The idea of loss terrifies the man. He would walk into open gunfire and not blink an eye and keep a cool head, but certain things he never wants to endure again. I understand it, but I can't decide how to deal with it."

"You are supposed to have all the answers."

"Dream on, sister. Feel free to think I do, but I don't."

It was Ellie's turn to laugh. "I'm not exactly sure how to deal with Jason either, and I can't even drink a glass of wine right now." She paused. "I'm going to have to tell Bryce I'm pregnant. He might not be surprised, which makes me wonder if he knows me better than I know myself."

"Perhaps he left for New York because he understood the writing on the wall. Jason is an attractive man and you two spend a lot of time together. You both have a passion for your job that creates a bond that is not necessarily easily understood by the rest of us because, for instance, in my profession I relate to most of my colleagues, but do not have to trust them with my life. The very nature of what you do gives you a special relationship."

"Yeah, well when I met Jason I wasn't particularly fond of him." Ellie said it dryly and meant it. "I don't think he liked me much either."

"It seems to me you both got over that." Georgia's smile was genuine. "Bryce might have seen it coming. Men can also be intuitive. Not necessarily sensitive about expressing it, but they get what's going on. By that I mean they understand more quickly. Our gender tends to stand back and reflect out loud."

"In other words we talk too much."

"We tend to process differently. That chicken smells wonderful."

"Thank my mother. It's her recipe." Ellie heaped rice into the bowl and then poured over the chicken and sauce. "Jody and I used to ask for this on our birthdays." Then she got back to business. "So you do think Forsythe displays overt signs of hostility and maybe a predisposition to violence?"

"I think, from your description, he's like a three-year-old who takes his sibling's toy and breaks it because he's jealous. Randy Lane told you his cousin never liked him. Your interview with him seems to confirm that. A trigger could be anything. All it would take is one remark by a shared grandparent to prompt resentment, or a comparison by anyone, even Janet Locke. That was a particularly violent attack. There was anger involved. It could have been against her, against women in general, or against Randy. I would vote for the latter."

Ellie agreed. Rarely had she had such a negative reaction to a person. "He was hostile enough toward me that Jason stepped between us."

"Instinct. People discount it and think we are far too civilized for it, but I don't agree. Dogs raise their hackles when they sense danger. If we ever think we can't learn from that, I believe firmly we need to take a second look at our visceral reactions. I wish I didn't have to say this, but I have several female patients with a tendency to put themselves in dangerous situations with males they don't know well enough to trust. I'm not their mother or father. I'm just there to help them try to understand why they do it. The frustrating part of it is most of them realize it isn't healthy behavior at least on some level, but they do it anyway."

"In my experience, the really dangerous ones seem like nice people on the surface. How can you know? I don't step in until a crime has been committed. Would

Janet have opened her door for Forsythe? From what I saw today, I'd say no. That question really bothers me more than whether or not he was capable of killing her."

It really did. Unlike her last investigation, where she and Jason had a lot of information about the killer and even a physical description but no suspect, in this case there were suspects, but no information.

She had to add, "I almost think it rules him out. If she'd met Randy's cousin, she wouldn't trust his motives in coming to her house. On one meeting, if he showed up here, *I* wouldn't open my door, and I carry a weapon. From what I know about her, she was smarter than that."

The front door opened and it had been locked, so that meant whoever just arrived had a key.

It was Jason and he looked strained as he walked into the kitchen and dumped a sack on the counter. He said, "It smells great in here. My mother was in an accident and I don't want to talk about it with either one of you, so don't ask. I need a beer."

Chapter 13

Randy used a chair to break the window.

He wasn't an expert, but he could recognize the sound of gunfire. When it happened he'd been reading a murder mystery set in Minnesota, which wasn't a very cheerful pastime with dead bodies turning up everywhere, but at least it was entertaining and he'd devoured the other books so it was about all he had left.

Two loud pops. He froze in the act of turning a page. No return fire.

He just knew. *Get out.*

The gatekeepers usually sat on the front porch and drank coffee in the evening, talking to each other. Sometimes they played cards; they were two older officers and they argued amicably. He was aware they'd come to the conclusion he wasn't really a flight risk, so they mostly left him alone, which was well . . . lonely, but better than jail.

As he brushed aside the broken glass, cutting the hell out of his hand, he wondered if jail wasn't a lot safer even if he lived with the dregs of society sleeping on the next bunk.

The drop landed him in a rosebush and he'd heard the sound of tearing fabric as he'd struggled to get out. Scratched and bleeding he staggered up and tried to decide which way to run. He literally had no idea where he was exactly because it wasn't like anyone had handed over the address.

But he ran. There was a wooded area behind the house, not big by any means, but at least cover. He would have run through it to one of the houses in the next subdivision, but he was bleeding, and what if he was already being followed and the people had kids. He couldn't live with putting anyone else in danger, especially children.

If he managed to live at all, which might be a legitimate question. Safe house was . . . not so safe.

He hid behind a thicket of young trees, unarmed and helpless. They would know which way he'd gone, he couldn't stay there. He heard the back door open and took off.

Ellie's phone rang, and at least she'd finished eating and was cleaning up when she saw the number with a small frisson of foreboding. She handed over the sponge. "The ID says Locke. This can't be good news."

Jason said grimly, "Why is it I think I'd rather wash dishes than take that call."

"No one wants to wash dishes." She slid her finger across screen to accept and put the phone to her ear. "This is MacIntosh."

"Hello, Detective, this isn't a call I wanted to make, but Chief Metzger told me to go ahead and handle it because of the intricate nature of the case. We have a double homicide that happened this evening, and unfortunately, now Randy Lane is missing. Two U.S. marshals are dead. Single shot for each of them at close range."

Ellie was literally speechless. She sat down. "What? No. How could he even have gotten a weapon? It wasn't Randy."

"Neither of the federal officers were missing their weapon, and the forensic team said the guns were fully loaded. The back window to a bedroom was broken out, but from the inside from the glass pattern. I think someone tried to get to him. What's your opinion?"

She really thought it over. "I agree. No way he could get a weapon on his own with those officers right there with him. He heard it happening and ran."

"Or he's dead. There's evidently some blood on the ground outside that window. There are investigators already on this scene, but since my daughter's murder is your case, I thought you might like to know about this development."

Ellie said slowly, processing out loud, "He doesn't have a lot of choices . . . he might come to you if he escaped. I assume he's been to your house often enough so he'll know where it is. He's a smart young man and wouldn't want anyone to think he'd jumped bail, and you've been willing to at least listen to his side of the story. If I were him I'd do that or else head for the nearest police station."

"I have to let all of you handle the different aspects and do your job before I can do mine. However, this is personal to me as you know. By the way, my wife says your house is lovely and very comfortable. She's catching up on her backlist of books she didn't ever have time to read. I think it takes her mind off the terrible reality we are experiencing as a family. I get the impression the change in surroundings is therapy for her overwhelming grief, as is that little dog. That Janet held it and selected the animal in the first place gave them an instant bond." He added formally, "Thank you."

Milwaukee certainly didn't seem the safest place at the moment for the Locke family, or anyone else at the moment.

"Can we have the address where the murders took place?"

"No. I asked. I don't have it. This is a decision made higher up than my office and I'm not happy about it."

She wasn't either. It was hard enough to get a feel for this case without all the roadblocks, and they were about three stories high. Whatever happened to the cooperation they'd discussed with Campbell and Gregory?

Jason had heard enough that he didn't need a full report. He'd also cleaned that extremely messy pan and ferreted out a towel to dry it. "It takes balls as big as canned hams to kill two U.S. marshals. Who are these people? How did they manage that?"

"Single shots," Ellie informed him, picking up her cup of tea. Grasso and Georgia had departed fairly quickly after dinner, but Ellie didn't mind that at all . . . they were an odd couple, but she liked them both. A healthy romantic relationship would do them, in her inexpert opinion, a lot of good. "It's out of our hands apparently since we aren't allowed to even find out where it happened. Balls as big as canned hams? Really?" The expression Jason had just used made her exasperated, but she knew he did things like that on purpose, plus she didn't in principle disagree.

"My old man used to say that when watching pro football. It kind of stuck with me." He was predictably unapologetic.

She let it slide. "How did they find Randy? *We* had no idea where he was. I actually still don't, and apparently someone else is in charge of the crime scene. Randy Lane is gone."

She had a small bistro table in the kitchen where she had her coffee in the mornings and he came over and sat opposite. "We might as well resign ourselves to the fact this case has a lot of angles and we have been directed down a straight hallway. If we don't know where it happened or who is investigating it, those two downed officers are a mystery to me. I think I'm pretty good at my job, but my crystal ball is AWOL. Those agents are trained to spot anything suspicious. That is what they do. How the hell did this go down?"

She was wondering the same thing. Her response was measured and thoughtful. "We track down murder cases, but what if we are in the middle of a war between *two* factions of organized crime? Maybe that's why all these agencies are involved and no one will tell us anything."

"It certainly sounds like someone knew what they were doing. Our problem is even if Randy is gone it doesn't mean he murdered Janet Locke." Jason shook his head. "I just don't think he did, and if it wasn't for Locke we could just drop it, but he will never allow that. I don't really blame him either. He wants someone accountable, and to see justice. It is his job and our job."

Ellie agreed. At that very moment, her phone rang again. Not a number she recognized. She answered it anyway.

"Are you Detective Ellie MacIntosh?"

"Yes."

"Okay, well that's true, so here goes . . . I'm an urgent-care physician and a young man came into the clinic and needed stitches to his right arm, left hand, and thigh. No insurance and no ID. I treated him because that is what we do when someone is bleeding everywhere, and he asked me to call you. He had your card in his blood-soaked pocket and seems lucid and coherent. No alcohol or narcotics involved in all this that I could tell. I believed him enough to call. He said he thought you might come pick him up. I can release him, but he says he has no transportation."

"What's his name?" At least Randy was still alive.

"He told me I was better off if I didn't know."

"Dark haired and not tall but with a wrestler build?"

"Yes."

"You *are* better off not knowing. My partner and I will be there as soon as possible. Give me the address."

"Detectives? I truly don't want to know what's going on, do I?"

"No."

"Come get him then, since I gave him a shot of painkillers and it doesn't appear he has a car from what he told me. I said if I gave the medication to him, he shouldn't drive, and he replied I had no worries there. I'll leave him in an exam room until you arrive. But we are unfortunately busy tonight."

She was already waving Jason toward the doorway and he was grabbing his keys. "We are headed your way. Do *not* let him leave."

Metzger was going to be unhappy at her giving out his number, but she did it anyway.

"Call this man and ask him if you should just lock up the clinic and keep everyone there until he can send officers to back up your security. He will sound like a bear that has been in hibernation but he knows more than I do. We are now running out to the car. It is ultimately his decision. If he says yes, he can describe us and we have our badges. Let us in, but no one else."

"It's that bad?" The doctor sounded horrified.

"Oh, yes it is. That is the number of the chief of the Milwaukee Police Department."

He stammered, "I . . . I don't have a clue if I have the authority to lock anything up. I'm just a resident physician on rotation."

"Don't worry, *he* has the authority. That's why it's quicker for you to just call him directly. We really do appreciate your cooperation. We'll be there as soon as possible and then this won't be your problem anymore."

An appropriate night for a full moon.

Two murders and a wounded young man sitting in the backseat wearing bloody clothes half asleep on whatever they'd given him to help with the pain.

Jason got to be the one to call Metzger. "Okay, got him. We have Randy Lane. They called us from a clinic. We'll file a report in the morning."

"Do you think I don't know all about it, Santiago? I believe someone also called me from that same clinic. Here's an address. Two agents who are well aware of what happened will take him off your hands."

"Is that wise?" Jason knew he was out on a shaking limb here, but he was really not in favor of doing that. "Look, how'd they find him? It was inside information. It had to be. I'm not taking Ellie, or for that matter even Randy Lane and myself, to that address. I know it wasn't me, and I know it wasn't Ellie who revealed his location since we had no clue to where he was. But I'm not walking into a firing squad. We will figure something out and be in touch. I don't think we know who we can trust. Someone is in bed with the bad guys while posing to be a good guy."

Silence. Then Metzger said heavily, "Well, hell, you

could be right. We've lost three law enforcement officers already, not to mention the daughter of a district attorney."

"Not everyone can walk up and kill two experienced U.S. marshals. I'd start there. I'm going to bet they knew whoever did it. In the meantime, I'm not going to tell you where we are."

"Santiago, dammit—"

Jason pushed a button.

Ellie was driving since for a good reason she hadn't had a thing to drink. She glanced over in dismay. "Did you just hang up on *Metzger*?"

He really just had. "I have a bad feeling in the pit of my stomach like I ate a burrito from a convenience store, which I don't recommend by the way because I tried it once. Bad decision. I did the man a favor. What if he gets a direct order from whoever is running this circus to reveal our location? This way, he can honestly say he doesn't know."

"It could get you fired."

"That's better than getting me dead, in my opinion."

Hard to argue that point.

"If you haven't noticed, the chief is ticked off at us already, but I'm agreeing with you on this one." She looked extremely unhappy. "I think it is inside too. But why all this focus on Randy? At this point I think if he knew something, he'd tell us."

"I believe that too. Okay, next phone call is Grasso. I don't want to ruin his evening, but maybe we can stay at that mausoleum he calls a house. If whoever killed those officers knows we are with Randy, my place or your place doesn't sound like a good idea. Sure they might know we work with Grasso, but I doubt anyone would think of his house, and it has a top-notch security system. I'm not a character in an action movie, but

I think using a credit card right now would be a mistake, so no hotel. Besides, I'd probably have to help Randy inside the way he's conking out, and if I was a desk attendant and saw a bloodstained man being carted through the lobby, I'd call the police."

"I would too. Grasso it is. Call him. I could sleep anywhere. This fatigue thing doesn't really work right now. Randy also has a reason to be comatose. I'd be grateful if you could figure something out that involves a pillow and a bed."

This was his first experience with a pregnancy, but he'd heard enough about the process to know that growing another human being wasn't exactly without some very real challenges. Ellie looked tired, and usually she could hold her own.

Grasso answered right away. "I've talked to Metzger, so I know what happened. You don't have to tell me your plans, but if you want to, go ahead."

"Be careful what you wish for. How about your house? Big enough, it has a security system, and is close. I'm with a pregnant woman and a guy who is down and out on pain meds. Possible we could crash there?"

"MacIntosh made that chicken for me. I'd walk through coals for her now. Not a bad call. I have a gun, you have a gun, and MacIntosh has one. I can stand guard. You can take a shift as well."

"She'll probably take a shift if I know her. This protecting her stuff doesn't go over."

"Done."

"I think we are not on the game card with these people, but we are starting to understand the score isn't exactly in our favor."

"In a fair war, you know the identity of the enemy." Jason was really starting to get rattled and he'd been in dangerous situations before, but this was different.

"I think this falls into the category of an unfair war." Grasso sounded neutral, but he obviously agreed.

"We'll be there in about ten minutes or so."

"I'll open the garage door so you can park inside. The way this is playing out, for all we know you're under surveillance. Let's not have your car in plain sight in my driveway."

Now that was a cheerful thought, but it wasn't like Jason hadn't considered that possibility.

The house was dark when they arrived, but the garage door was open. Ellie parked the car and Grasso came out a door that led into the house and pushed a button so the door slid silently closed. It took the two of them to rouse Randy enough to get him to walk into the house, and Jason wondered how much was the medication and how much was just sheer exhaustion kicking in. Being charged with murder and having people out there determined to murder you couldn't make for a good night's sleep. He looked the worse for wear too, and he didn't say anything except to ask for a drink of water when they led him to a bedroom. Grasso, it appeared, didn't own old sweatpants, but did offer him some pajamas, since Randy's clothes were stiff with blood. Jason was fairly sure the pajamas were silk, but didn't say anything. He was more a cotton/sweatpants kind of man, but to each his own.

Ellie had settled into a chair and relaxed in the kitchen, her eyes half closed.

Grasso just pointed at the hall. He said to Jason, "Pick a bedroom. I'll take the first shift. In about two hours, it's your turn to be on alert. I don't want anyone coming in, and I don't want anyone going out. The alarm will be set. After being attacked in my garage not all that long ago, I had the company come and replace the system and wire it into the house."

"Yeah, if we lost Randy now, we would all be in deep shit." Jason pulled Ellie to her feet. "Come on. He's not going anywhere. You need some sleep."

She didn't object, which said volumes. He picked a door, opened it, and found it was dark but had a queen bed. She just lay down on the bed after toeing off her shoes. "I'm glad I already brushed my teeth at home."

He could swear she was asleep in less than a minute.

He wasn't so lucky. Jason lay down next to her, but it just wasn't happening.

The ghosts of his restless mind were familiar. If he wasn't going to go to sleep he might as well relieve Grasso. He went back out into the kitchen and found him sipping coffee and answering emails. He said, "I'll handle this if you want to go to bed. Ellie is sacked out. Normally she'd be pissed if we even suggested she couldn't take a shift, but it isn't remotely normal right now."

"I have to agree with that, but normal has always eluded me." Grasso shut off his computer. "What is that anyway?"

"Normal? Do you think *I'd* know?" Jason pulled out a chair and sat down.

Grasso laughed. "No. Good point. I'd give you a lecture about not touching your partner, but I saw that coming a mile away. We all did."

"Hey, it takes two people."

"You certainly have good chemistry as a law enforcement team. How do you feel about Grantham being back?"

"Jesus, is there no such thing as privacy any longer?"

"As far as I can tell, no."

That he would ever be having a heart-to-heart with Lt. Carl Grasso of all people was disconcerting, but it had been a long, interesting day. It was out of character for both of them. "I'm not leaping up and down with joy," he admitted. "Ellie doesn't like to sit around and have deep emotional discussions. I can't tell if it is because she knows I'm not into them, or if she's not into them either. How I feel about Grantham doesn't matter. How she feels about him does."

"A legitimate question."

"Here's another one. What are we going to do with Randy Lane? You do realize we have to turn him over tomorrow."

"I realize I wasn't going to do it in the dark tonight when he's clearly not safe, and not gift him to two agents I don't know. He was pretty canny to go right out that window even if he cut the crap out of himself."

"They want him bad for some reason."

"His brother gave up quite a bit of money to give him a chance and then went off the grid for the same reason, or that is my take on it. John Lane was slated to be a key witness and so he disappeared."

"Something big is going down."

"And no one is talking. I'm thinking we do turn over Randy tomorrow, but at the station. If they want to come pick him up, fine, but if there's someone feeding information, his location probably won't be under wraps for long. I want to talk to the agents that will now be guarding him, but on our turf. We have three solid suspects that Randy has steered us toward in the Locke murder: Hank Darnel, Elias Porter, and Frederick Forsythe, and all of them are tied back to his family."

"The timeline of the murder is very short." Grasso looked as usual not even slightly tired, just contemplative. "Randy left to go get food for dinner, so they had a window to get in, get the job done, and get out. I still wonder why she opened the door."

"So does Ellie. I'm an ex-military guy who carries a

weapon at all times. If someone comes and knocks, I answer it usually. I wouldn't if I was a single young woman who was unarmed."

"I wouldn't either. But maybe not everyone views the big, bad world like we do."

"She knew him. Ellie and I have already been through that. We agree."

"Forsythe then seems logical. He's family. She might have opened the door."

"Except Randy has nothing good to say about him, and I've met his cousin and don't disagree with that negative assessment. I don't know that Janet would have answered his knock. There was a side panel of glass. Surely she glanced out. We all would."

"Maybe you're looking at the wrong people. I'm not saying they aren't involved, just saying they didn't commit the crime *you* are investigating."

"There's the problem. We are being asked to do the impossible, which is to separate out one crime from what appears to be a mass investigation of multiple offenses." Jason could hear his combative tone and moderated it. "I realize I can't bitch at Metzger because he isn't in control of this. But four people are dead now. I suspect they aren't the first casualties by any means. If it wasn't for Locke I'd just tell everyone to go fuck themselves, but I feel for the guy. I know Ellie does too."

"What about Randy?"

"He's young. He can fall in love again, but Janet's father can't replace his child."

That was philosophical for him, but then again Jason was starting to see the situation in a different way than the detached bachelor police officer he used to be.

"True." Grasso also seemed to grasp it. "You're going to view life from a different perspective now as a parent. But he can't fall in love again if he's spending his life in prison. And you can't say he won't end up there the way this is going. I've a few unsolved homicides under my belt. You and MacIntosh are good, but you've also been lucky. The overall feeling he's telling the truth is in his favor, but to a jury it might not fly. The minute they hear DNA, in my experience, it's guilty until proven innocent, not the other way around. They are going to want to pin this crime on someone. That Locke doesn't seem convinced he did it helps him out a lot, but it sure doesn't help *you*. Arrest someone else and the game changes."

The air-conditioning clicked on with a smooth hum. Jason was humming too, but it certainly wasn't smooth. The case, his mother's condition, two dead officers, and a trip to another medical emergency clinic . . . he needed to decompress, but thought it was unlikely. "Before tonight I found Randy's story plausible, but not necessarily true. Even two downed officers doesn't necessarily mean he didn't kill his girlfriend. However it sure convinces me he might be why it happened."

"His family association doesn't help him, but he didn't take their guns and no one fired them. If those officers allowed him to get ahold of a gun somehow . . . no, I can't see *how* it would happen. I'm with Ellie. He wasn't the one. Why? That is different."

Maye it was his mother's accident and his own experiences that made him say it, he wasn't sure, but Jason had to wonder. "Is it possible they are trying to protect him? His family, I mean."

"By letting him go down on a murder charge?" Grasso looked dubious and wasn't buying it.

This case was so off the charts Jason wasn't sure either, but put it out there. "Maybe. I'm wondering now if they didn't think he'd be better off in custody, since the hit was supposed to be on him. He just wasn't there so Janet was killed instead. They can afford a high-powered attorney to get him off when he actually goes to trial. Look at it this way, in the meantime, we're taking care of it."

"It's an interesting theory."

"Someone is really trying to kill him and his brother John has disappeared."

Grasso said with equanimity, "I can't argue that all has happened."

Chapter 14

Randy woke up disoriented and in pain.

The thigh wound was the worst part. He'd watched the doctor take out one piece of glass the size of a half dollar from his leg from crawling out the window, but he was still alive, so a few injuries were nothing.

Not necessarily the outcome if he hadn't been aware. Maybe he could thank jail for that. He'd learned to only half sleep, on some level always on the edge, waiting for the worst. If you pen men—or women for that matter—like beasts they acted like them, but usually they'd done that already or they wouldn't be there.

He vaguely recalled the big house silhouette and being escorted inside, but everything after his stumbling escape into the wooded area between the houses was a blur. He'd run down the nearest street and luckily—yeah that actually *was* luck, and he'd needed some—almost had been hit by an older man driving a pickup truck.

Even though he looked less than appealing with his scratched face and other minor wounds, he was given a ride to the nearest hospital by that kind soul, since he wouldn't bleed all over his backseat if he didn't mind the bed of the truck. Randy couldn't even shake his hand since both of his were bleeding, but he did manage to say thank you before he walked in through the emergency entrance.

The arrival of the two detectives was foggy, because he'd gotten the shot before he'd been stitched up, but he at least recognized them, and he was fairly sure they didn't want to kill him. That was a plus. He was starting to wonder if his bull's-eye wasn't universal.

The image in the mirror of the bathroom off of the bedroom where he'd slept wasn't all that great. It looked like an angry cat had attacked his face on the right side, and they'd put some disinfectant on the scratches at the clinic that left a yellow residue, so he opened a couple of cupboards until he found a stack of washcloths and managed clumsily with his bandaged hands to wash it off. It stung, but at least he hadn't needed stitches there. He also found a new wrapped toothbrush and travel-size toothpaste and felt halfway human after he brushed his teeth.

There was a clean white T-shirt folded at the end of the bed. His torn, bloody clothes were gone, so he put on the shirt, left on the pajama bottoms, and ventured out into what proved to be a very long hallway. The smell of coffee at least gave him a sense of what direction to go, and he found a pretty grand curving staircase his mother would approve of—she was fond of grand—but his stitched leg hurt at every step down. The male detective named Santiago was sitting in a chair at the bottom, drinking coffee and reading something on his phone. He glanced up and lifted his brows. "It's about time. I'd ask if you slept well, but you know, for some reason that question always annoys me. If I didn't, I feel like I have to lie or something and say I did."

"What happened?"

"Two deputies killed."

"Ah, no." Randy muttered the words, heartsick. "Those two guys were really decent to me. I didn't want to be there, but it was okay. I hope no one thinks I—"

"I doubt it. They were experienced officers. If you'd had a weapon, they would have found it. Plus, it isn't like you got away. You went to seek medical care and had them call us. If you cut the hell out of yourself for something that isn't going to change your circumstances, I can't see your motivation. In short, you didn't have opportunity or motive."

Randy was happy to hear that, but also not happy it had been considered. "I've never killed anyone."

"Good to hear. Want a cup of coffee?"

It was close, but he didn't do it. He really and truly almost said, *I'd kill for one*.

It was an interesting morning.

Ellie didn't exactly blame the federal agents for being abrupt and irritated because Randy hadn't been delivered into their hands, but then again, she still thought she and Jason had made the right decision. Randy sat in an interview room, and they all had a discussion in Metzger's office.

Grasso was lead, so she was more than happy to let him do the talking.

"I can't see why for a moment you would disagree that a judgment call was warranted in the best interest of everyone involved. If someone on your side of the fence knows where Randy Lane is all the time, why on earth deliver him there and risk their lives and his?"

One agent—Ellie hadn't seen him before, the other

was Campbell—clenched his jaw. "We are well aware of the problems in this situation."

Jason, of course, couldn't keep his sardonic mouth shut. "Yeah, well, it would be nice if *we* were aware. He's accused of murdering his girlfriend. That's straightforward enough. But then there's a bunch of bullshit about his family's ties to this and that, and how his dead girlfriend's father is a district attorney and that the killing was a clear message." He leaned forward. "We're all alive. He's still alive. You have three dead agents and a fourth murder victim. Tell me again how aware you are."

If there was one thing about Metzger, it was if he didn't agree he let you know, but if he did agree, he didn't shoot you down just to play politics. So he stood stoutly behind that. "Detective Santiago has a point there."

That agreement didn't improve the tension in the room at all. "We know full well what has happened."

"Because *we* called *you*. Do you understand our level of hesitation?" Ellie kept her tone moderate. "We're all sailing along on a leaky ship. That leak did not spring from our end. Randy Lane is a college kid. We weren't just dropping him off to anyone. He might be a killer, but it does seem like either way, someone wants him dead. On the chance he's just another victim, we chose the safe route. He hasn't been convicted. He's out on bail. Why the safe house and marshals guarding him? It seems unfair to him unless he's part of your agenda somehow, in which case, explain why."

Of course her question went unanswered. "Your attitude is very noble, Detective MacIntosh, but not necessarily the best for everyone."

"I'm very concerned about finding justice for Janet

Locke. No one wants us to be concerned about anything else. We have some names and we've turned them over, Porter, Darnel, and Forsythe being at the top of the list. We've backed off because you asked us to, but you don't seem to be doing anything that impresses me. Who killed those marshals? How could someone walk up and shoot them?"

That was clear enough anyway.

"Randy's girlfriend isn't the only casualty." Campbell was less edgy than his counterpart.

"Obviously not," Grasso said clearly. "If MacIntosh and Santiago just talking to your undercover operative got him killed, how do they know what they're walking into?"

"Reid wasn't ours technically. I think it has been explained to you there is more than one ongoing investigation by multiple agencies."

"It has, just not what these investigations are. Are you investigating Hank Darnel and Elias Porter as well as the Lane family? Randy gave us those names as potentially being behind the murder."

"Let's just say none of those men are going to get a merit award as citizen of the year. Don't interview them." Campbell was pleasant enough but firm. "For one thing, they wouldn't tell you a thing, and we aren't interested in any of them deciding it's time to hop on a plane and fly to a country that doesn't have extradition. Since you seem determined to help out Randy Lane, if any of those men knew he'd mentioned them, his circumstances could get even worse, and he's already charged with murder, not to mention someone wants to kill him. What's more, you're likely to put more of our people in danger. If you were seen talking to any of them, even if you were just asking directions to the nearest bathroom, they'd go under a microscope."

"I guess that 'and justice for all' thing is just rhetoric, huh?" Jason sounded frustrated, and Ellie felt the same way.

Campbell said just as clearly, "Give us due credit. You name the crime and it is probably on our list. We are operating a small secret war against people who have a lot of money and a lot of resources. They are smart and they are ruthless. John Lane disappeared for a reason, and we want to know if there's some internal unraveling going on. Powerful people make powerful enemies. Randy Lane is better off in protective custody. This is going down."

That statement said so convincingly sent a chill right through her. Ellie couldn't help but think of Cameron. "He has a young brother."

Campbell looked weary all of a sudden. "Detective, I thought those two U.S. marshals were keeping Randy safe. How did that work out? I can't answer that implied question. You and I both know there's no legal way to take a minor out of a situation unless you can prove he's in danger, and that would definitely tip our hand, wouldn't it? We might as well put up a billboard on the freeway that says Someone Is Watching."

He was right, but the situation was wrong. "If Locke was targeted through his child and Randy is in danger, surely we can do something to protect Cameron Lane."

"If you think of something ingenious please let us know. Otherwise, interfere as little as possible, please."

They both got up in their well-cut suits and left. Randy would be taken away in a few minutes, and Ellie, Grasso, and Jason were left to Metzger's not-so-often tender mercies. He said, looking at each of them in turn, "If this was a game of chess, we're the pawns and maybe they are a couple of bishops. I don't know what would have happened last night if you'd have handled it differently, but the three of you handled it. Here's what I like and what I don't like."

Jason didn't say anything, which was a miracle. So was his use of the word "rhetoric."

"I don't like the situation, so don't think for a minute I've bought into it. I think our only role is to be a smoke screen, because if we didn't look into this someone out there might wonder why, but then again we have Locke breathing down our necks. The rock-and-a-hard-place scenario isn't good, but we have to make do with it. Unless you can come up with a solid lead for another arrest, Randy Lane will go to trial. Until last night I thought he probably did it anyway, but if you three are in doubt, and Locke isn't convinced, now I have to think maybe otherwise."

The chief leaned back in his chair and blew out a breath before he went on. "I don't like the overall lack of cooperation, but I'm not running those operations, and I downright hate the idea there might be someone who was bought that's supposed to be on our side."

It was Ellie who finally said, "And what was it you do like?"

"Nothing. Nothing at all." Chief Metzger growled out the words with fierce sincerity.

She agreed.

It was midafternoon before she told him.

"The baby just moved."

Jason had brought her a cup of tea, which was nice of him and certainly not his style. She suspected he had to go to the shop down the street that was usually filled with people taking a short break from government jobs. He almost dropped the paper cup, but she reached up and grabbed it in the nick of time. She wanted that tea.

"What?"

"Don't look so surprised. Babies do that." The cup was fragrant with ginger and lemon, and she really could use it. She wished he'd brought one of those white chocolate cookies, but the tea was thoughtful. Ellie peeled off the lid. "Thanks for this."

"Has it happened before?" He almost seemed speechless, but he was Jason Santiago, so of course he managed the words.

"Yes, but not like just now."

"Ellie."

"Ellie, what?" She lifted her brows. "This will be an experience neither one of us is familiar with, but at least I have Jody and my mother to fall back on. Jody said the timing is about right to start feeling movement and warned me that down the line, the nugget—you know how funny she is—will delight in kicking me in the bladder. Maybe I should only talk to my mother and leave her out of the mix. Jody is having entirely too much fun with it not being *her* that's pregnant. What did you find out about Forsythe's alibi?"

He centered back on the job, and that was probably good for them both, but still looked off balance, leaning against her desk. "Well, it checks out for all that is worth. Two business calls from his home according to the tower that was used, and he posted on social media that he was watching a certain show that was on during the time frame we have for the murder. It sounds like a planned alibi to me, but we would have to prove it somehow that he wasn't the one using his phone or doing the post from his phone."

"Easier said than done." She didn't like Forsythe, but she didn't think he was stupid. Not nice, but stupid wasn't her impression at all. "I think we're clear on how he feels about Randy, and he's tightly knit into the Lane business ventures, but the real question is if it was him, would he do it himself or hire it out? My impression is he might do it himself, but I still don't think Janet would answer her door if he came knocking."

"Then Randy moves back into first place as the perp. Why would she open her door for a stranger?"

"Maybe more for a stranger than she would for Forsythe. That would be *my* attitude."

He gazed at her keenly. "You feel that strongly?"

"I do. If it wasn't that I think from what I know about her, Janet was intelligent enough to distrust him, I'd move heaven and earth to prove Forsythe did it. Georgia says there was rage involved, so he fits there, but once again, how did he get her to answer the door?"

"It could be as simple as when Randy left, she'd either forgotten to lock the door or just assumed it would be okay for such a short while. He said he was only gone long enough to pick up the food."

Ellie shook her head. "Do you think, for even a minute that when Locke's daughter became involved with none other than Randy Lane, the man wouldn't have sat her down and talked to her about security?"

"You've never forgotten to lock your door?"

"Of course, we all have, but the killer couldn't count on that. He didn't have time to count on that. I think she knew him or trusted him somehow."

"Maybe Randy forgot to lock it. She was taking a nap."

"Possible, but still, at some point she got up. She wasn't killed in her bed. She'd come out for some reason."

"Maybe to let Randy in or answer a knock."

"I know, but neither of us thinks it is him."

"I agree. I'm just talking what could be argued in court."

Ellie pushed back her hair from her face, looping it

behind her ear. "Locke's assistant DA called me about an hour ago, asking about progress on the case."

"You said what?"

"I told Michael Lambert the truth, which is essentially no progress, and that our charged suspect was now with two new federal officers. Randy was injured and contacted us, but we don't know where he is because he was taken off our hands. That truth won me some stone-cold silence from the DA's office. I'm starting to sense it is impossible to make anyone happy with our investigation. I also suspect Locke might be up north with his family and that's why he didn't call me himself again. I assume Metzger called him and told him we had Randy but that he wouldn't say where."

Jason said darkly, "You can add me to the unhappy list. I'm not thrilled with it either. Every case is different, but I've never been told who I can or can't interview before. Three potential suspects and we've been warned off?"

"The only reason I'm not angrier is I think Campbell was right. Porter and Darnel aren't going to cooperate. He knows what they are. It is in their best interest not to cooperate. We both know Forsythe will tell us to go jump off a cliff."

"I'm not sure what the hell we are supposed to do then."

"The answer is muddy, I agree. I trust Agent Campbell well enough. He seems like a reasonable man, but certainly intent on his own agenda." She paused and then stated the obvious. "Both of us have been in difficult situations before, but this is really out there. Whoever came for Randy last night meant serious business, obviously. I would love to see the forensic reports on how those two deputies were killed that include ballistics. A sniper might have done it from a distance, I suppose. They aren't sharing."

Jason shook his head. "I've known some guys that were that good, most of them military. But there aren't a lot of them out there. From a rooftop you can fire a clean shot, sure, but then to fire the second one as fast as Randy claims seems unlikely to me. You still have to move the gun and focus on the scope, and that takes more than a second or two, especially since once the first shot happened the second officer would react. I think it was point blank. Boom, boom." He demonstrated with pointed fingers, mimicking someone holding a weapon. "That would be fast."

"And that goes back to someone they knew."

"I assume they wouldn't let a stranger walk right up to them. For that matter, Reid wouldn't either because he was so paranoid about us blowing his cover."

Ellie wasn't sure about Reid. "I don't think that was us. I still think that was Cameron. That's why I'm worried about him. He said something to someone and then Reid was targeted as being suspicious."

"He's fifteen, Ellie. Surely they won't—"

"Listen to yourself. I don't think these people get all bound up in sentimentality," she interrupted. "I think we need to go talk to the Lanes, complete with their lawyer if they choose that it has to be that way, and see how the flag is flying, because if your theory is right that they are trying to help Randy by leaving him in custody, they may not even know about Reid. What if they are underwater and losing control? Easy money is rarely easy."

"They can't stonewall us forever. Let's go talk to them."

Chapter 15

Randy declined the pain meds. First of all it was demeaning that they handed them over one dose at a time, and second of all he'd learned the hard way to stay alert was the best course of defense.

"I'm fine." His wounds itched, but he really was fine. Physically, that is. His mental state was something else entirely.

Someone really wanted him dead, and law enforcement really wanted him alive. Not because they valued his life so much, but because they needed him to testify. That was the only reason he could think of why they'd go to so much trouble for him. The problem was he had no clue what it was he could testify about that would help anyone. The two agents with him now were FBI—they'd shown him their identification—and he thought there was at least one more watching the house because they seemed to be in constant communication with someone else, and from the one-sided conversation he could hear, that was the conclusion he drew.

He was definitely living in the twilight zone right now.

Mallory Lane actually decided to talk to them, but whether that was on the advice of their lawyer or not, it was hard to tell. Jason was surprised when they were invited inside.

Nice house—grand foyer, curving staircase, statues on pillars, ornate chandelier, paintings he assumed cost a lot, but he wasn't up on it enough to judge . . . He preferred his simple apartment, but to each his own.

The woman was like her house, elegant but not quite ostentatious. She was wearing a sheath dress in a shimmery fabric on a Saturday afternoon and had the figure for it even though she was at least midfifties. Silver earrings and a silver bracelet that glittered with diamonds, and she had blond hair that was well done but not natural. Usually he wouldn't notice other than to note if a woman looked nice or not; fashion was definitely not his thing, but in this case, because of recent events he planned on noticing everything.

She'd been crying. Her makeup was perfect, but her eyes were red, and no male was immune to the signals of a woman who might cry, who is about to cry, or in this case is trying to cover it up that the event has happened. Not that he really cared whether this woman who had done nothing to help her son was unhappy, but he was curious about the tears.

Maybe she did care about Randy.

The chairs gathered around a marble fireplace had perfectly placed pillows, and Jason decided just to stay on his feet. He was fairly sure they were upholstered in silk and he wasn't dressed for the room, so he'd look

stupid settling down and crossing his ankles in a genteel way.

Ellie spoke quietly but without equivocation as she
sat down. "We are here because we are investigating the
murder of Janet Locke. That is the entire scope of what
we are doing. We'd like justice for her, and for Randy
too. That sounds simple, but sometimes it isn't. Did
he kill her or did someone else do it? Tell us what you
think."

"Of course he didn't kill her. He isn't like that, he was
just rebellious." Mrs. Lane stiffened her spine, knees
primly together, her expression betraying an inner ag-
ony. "My husband and I both struggled with how to
get him to straighten out. He wasn't bad, just irresponsible. Tough love finally seemed to work. We stopped
giving him money and trying to fix his mistakes. If you
ever think that was easy, you'd better think again. Do
either of you have children?"

Jason was glad he had backup. He let Ellie field that
one. She was unfazed. "Neither of us have a child old
enough to test us in that way yet. Of course we've read
over Randy's records and it really doesn't seem like
other than the DUI, which truly *was* irresponsible, he
did anything too out of line."

"When he totaled his car, Cameron was with him. I
haven't yet forgiven him for that. He was going way too
fast. It was a miracle they both weren't killed."

That was a direct hit home to Jason given the last
time he'd seen his mother. Just the night before last.
He'd maybe ask Ellie to go with him to the hospital this
afternoon.

"Evidently you haven't forgiven him, since you won't
help him." Jason was blunt, but neglectful mothers were
on his mind and he resented that he was worried about

his. "Although he wasn't drinking then, speeding is just as bad. Many people don't realize it. Maybe he shouldn't have been given a sports car."

"It's *my* fault?" She took a minute and thought it over. "Maybe you are right, but we thought we were being generous. Helping him doesn't help him." Mrs. Lane didn't even flinch over standing her ground over the not-so-subtle criticism. "In our family, if you made the decision, you answer for it."

"Even if he's charged with a murder you seem convinced he didn't commit?"

"When your child gets older, you will discover how difficult it is, Detective. Children don't come with a handbook you can ruffle through and find what to do on a certain page. My four sons are so different, yet we raised them the same way."

He wanted to point out how lucky Randy was to have Locke in his corner, since this wasn't an accident born out of misjudgment, but Ellie sensed his reaction and gave him a quelling look he heeded. Not that he wanted to. It wasn't like he didn't agree adversity made people stronger, but he also liked to believe that you could count on certain individuals to support you no matter the circumstances.

"Your husband seems to differ with your opinion," Ellie pointed out. "I believe he has stated he thinks Randy is guilty, or so we've been told."

"He's not happy with Randy, I'll admit that. He won't be happy to know I talked to *you* either. I don't have anything to say that will help you with Janet Locke's murder."

"Someone tried very hard to kill your son last night. Would you know why?"

If Jason had to call it, there was enough motherly concern. Mrs. Lane was visibly upset, but she didn't seem shocked. She fingered the bracelet on her wrist and looked at a painting above the mantel of the unlit fireplace. "Is he safe now?"

He didn't mean for the words to come out so caustically, but it happened anyway. "It's polite of you to ask, but we don't know. He isn't in our custody."

That was something he wanted to make crystal clear.

Ellie rose and he was more than happy to conclude the interview himself. She said, "Here's a card. If you think of anything that can help us, please call."

Mrs. Lane was just as glad to see them to the door.

"I have one request. Could I have my mother's engagement ring back? Randy asked me if he could have it for when the time came he felt he could propose to that girl. I gave it to him. I suppose it is in your custody somehow, or else in his apartment. I would like it returned. It is quite valuable."

"We will do our best."

"Polite?" Ellie didn't say it until they pulled out of the driveway. "You told that woman she was *polite* to ask about her son?"

He shrugged, not as indifferent as he wished to be. "Okay, maybe the wrong choice of words, but if you notice, she didn't directly answer one single question. So . . . I stand by polite. 'That girl'? The one her son wanted to marry and she can't even use her first name? I'm not a fan of Mrs. Lane. Look, maybe she knows where John is, she hopefully doesn't know where Randy is, and she won't help us at all except for a small lecture on how difficult it is to parent. I refrained from mentioning how difficult it must be to be her child. I deserve an award or something."

"I think you have an inflated sense of how tactful you are," Ellie observed dryly. "She did talk to us without a

lawyer in sight, and in case you missed it, she was upset before we even got there."

"I didn't miss it." He braked for a stop sign. "It would
be nice if she'd shared with us why. For all we know,
the dog ate her favorite pair of designer shoes or the
pool man didn't show up."

"I didn't see a dog. I'm sure there is a pool, but please
tell me no one cries over that. I got the impression she
only talked to us to find out how Randy was doing."

"Maybe. I suppose that brings her up a little in my
estimation, but not much. She's his mother. She should
be frantically calling us, not waiting for us to stop by."

"Has it occurred to you she is afraid to do so?"

"Occurred? Yes. Am I convinced it is on her top pri-
ority list? No. You should be willing to run into a
burning building to save your child. Hell, last spring
you and I ran into a burning building to save a cat and
it wasn't even our cat. If you ask me, Randy is sur-
rounded by fire and has no way out but us. A talented
prosecutor is going to tie him to a stake and toss in a
match at his feet."

"If you are going to try to be poetic, could you use
different types of images, please? I do agree she wasn't
as cooperative as I hoped, but we did learn a thing or
two."

"Like?"

"I think your theory the Lane family is trying to protect Randy might be right. For one thing, she wasn't
surprised he wasn't still in jail. That means they haven't
entirely written him off because they are paying attention. My impression of what's going on is evolving.
Maybe the message sent wasn't to Locke alone. If Lane
deals with crime lords and really had a falling out with
some not-so-nice business partners Janet's murder might
be a message to Mr. Lane to toe the line. We know the

time window was small, so maybe they thought Randy would be there."

"Double homicide. A two-for-one deal? Could be. One problem, though: There goes your theory she knew the person."

Ellie didn't argue that one. "I know. I was thinking out loud. But either way, mission accomplished. She's dead and Randy is going down for it at this point."

"The killer couldn't count on him being such an idiot to touch the body and the knife."

"But when the killer attacked Janet, he could count on Randy coming back and finding her. No prints on the knife, so he'd know Randy would be under suspicion. Here's another question: How did John Lane get one hundred thousand dollars so easily? I checked. He's twenty-six."

"And neck deep in his father's company. You just saw that house, and I'd bet Mrs. Lane's bracelet cost more than my truck. I'd guess he had access to bank accounts, maybe even from laundered money so no one could really call foul if he appropriated some of it. They trusted him and he didn't trust them. When criminals steal from each other, I don't lose sleep over it."

He didn't really care where John got the money, because Jason suspected John saw what was happening and decided to decamp and figured he'd help his brother out before he took off. It was nice of him, but maybe not the best idea in the world. Randy was safer in jail.

"True enough. How he got the money isn't our problem." Then she said in an offhand way, "Do you care to tell me now what happened to your mother?"

Getting Jason to talk about anything personal was never easy. Ellie wasn't all that great at it either, so the double whammy didn't make for intimate conversations. After her direct question he was quiet, driving more conservatively than usual. She almost thought he'd just not answer, but finally he said, "Car accident. She's in fair condition. I visited."

Short and sweet.

Very Jason Santiago. Maybe it wasn't his conversation with Randy's mother that reminded him he should slow down his driving a little. Ellie sensed a comment wouldn't be welcome, but she also sensed if she didn't make one that wouldn't be welcome either. His conflicted feelings about his parents made them a very touchy subject, so she was careful in her choice of words. "I'm sorry and I hope she's okay. I assume your father will keep you up to date."

"I told him he was going to be a grandfather. I hope that wasn't a big mistake." His tone was pessimistic. "I think in a moment of weakness I felt sorry for him and thought it might cheer him up. It's no secret to me I sometimes open my mouth and later wished I hadn't. I'd feel sorry for anyone lying in a hospital bed attached to a bunch of tubes. Maybe it will cheer her up too."

Ellie had the feeling that even if his mother wasn't awake for it, that her son had bothered to come see her would mean a lot. "Why would it be a mistake?"

"I'm not interested in a warm, fuzzy relationship. A baby would give them a reason."

His parents were trying to foster a relationship. He was just resistant, which she could understand.

She switched the subject back to something they could talk about without complicated emotions involved. "Why hasn't Randy yet suggested his older brother Robert might be involved in the murder? John did."

Well, maybe that question did involve complicated emotions. Randy had said they'd never liked each other very much. In her opinion, while Forsythe was unpleasant, maybe Robert had really resented his younger brother for being a spoiled brat.

"Yeah, interesting. Reid sure wasn't a fan."

"Back when he was alive." It was hard to even say it.

"I'm trying to not think about him or those two marshals. I have to think about Janet Locke, so no choice there since that's our case, but I honestly would rather have my fingernails pulled out, one by one."

Ellie didn't disagree. "Robert is Randy's brother. Janet might open the door for him."

"That negates the argument she wouldn't for Forsythe."

"Except all Randy said was they didn't like each other much. With Forsythe he was up front about his treatment of women in general. Reid didn't like Robert Lane, but he never mentioned a propensity for actual violence. At least not to us."

"Uh, zip, zero on us getting information on what he did know, and of course there are reports. If Forsythe works for the company as an accountant, you can bet he's under scrutiny."

He was right. No one would tell them anything about Reid's notes. She didn't even know who to ask. "I'm going to suggest that since we are getting nowhere, Robert should be next on our list."

"We can pay him a friendly little call. John told us his office is right next to his father's, so I suspect we'll get slapped with the lawyer brick wall again. I wonder if Mrs. Lane plans on even telling her husband about our little chat."

"I'm guessing not." Ellie realized he'd pulled into the lot of a local grocery store chain. She asked innocently,

"Are you all out of boxed macaroni and cheese and hot dogs?"

He parked next to a minivan and gave her a sardonic look. "Very funny. No, all stocked up on both of those. I thought I might pick up a couple of steaks we could grill for dinner."

She'd been avoiding this moment, but then again, as she'd told Georgia, it was just dinner. Bryce had sent her a text earlier that afternoon asking if she was free. "I have plans. We could do that for tomorrow night if you want."

He stopped in the act of getting out of the vehicle, one foot on the pavement, his gaze inscrutable. "Let me guess: Grantham. If you were having dinner with Lukens you would have said so, and if your sister was in town you'd have mentioned that too."

There was a problem with having a relationship with a detective. They tended to process deductive information quickly. "I do have other friends," she said mildly, "but yes. Bryce asked me to have dinner with him. You know there was no bitter split. We just went different directions in a friendly way."

All along they'd talked occasionally, exchanged an email here and there, and he always sent her flowers on her birthday, which was thoughtful, but he was a thoughtful man. Maybe hard to understand, but considerate.

"I don't have to like it," Jason declared curtly, "in a very unfriendly way, but I guess there's nothing I can do about it. I'll be right back."

Talk about hard to understand.

"Jason, I assume you wouldn't like me going to his house for a cup of coffee either."

"You assume right." He slammed the door shut with

a little more force than was necessary, but she wasn't surprised.

He'd become reasonable about it, but it would take him a moment or two. If she had to call it, their professional relationship worked because they recognized each other's strengths and weaknesses, and their emotional relationship was not nearly as solid because they each weighed the other with the perception of someone who didn't trust very easily. In their occupation that came with the territory.

He returned, set the bag between them, and climbed into the car. "I'm fine. Well, mostly. I'll eat mac and cheese and watch beach volleyball. But do me a favor. Come to my apartment afterward and stay the night. Lukens would probably point out a bunch of babble about male insecurity and possessive tendencies, but I can deal with this if you'll say yes to that. At least I'll know you're sleeping with me and not him."

"Do you honestly think I would?" She didn't bother to conceal her exasperation.

"Well . . . no," he at least admitted. "But I'm not finding anything logical about our situation. For a while I thought I might be in love with Kate, but I was dead wrong there. You're different."

For him, that was pretty eloquent.

A concession seemed fair, though he had no choice at this moment but to deal with that she still had her own life, even if it was now intertwined with his. "That's fine. Bring the steaks to my house tomorrow night. At least I will make sure we have a salad."

"You do know you'll make someone a beautiful nagging wife someday. Hey, I eat salad."

"I don't think potato salad from the deli counts."

"It should." He backed out and pulled out in the

direction of her condo. "I don't like the mustard stuff, though, but the bacon kind is pretty good. So, here's a thought. Campbell does seem like he's a reasonable guy. He's obviously in touch with Metzger through some channel, so let's ask if they have a dossier on Robert Lane, and if Campbell would just call us and give his opinion on whether or not he's worth an interview. He wasn't shy about warning us off on Darnel and Porter. I was so pissed it didn't register I should ask about questioning Lane."

She was guilty of that too. The evening before had definitely thrown them both off.

"Last night was clearly not because of us, but if anyone else gets lit up," Jason said grimly, "and we are involved in the equation, I think a lot of people will start to wonder if we are detectives or the Grim Reaper in disguise."

Chapter 16

At last someone had told him what was going on.

"We need to know what you can tell us about a package you signed for in July of last year."

Randy was perplexed and said flatly, "What are you talking about?"

It wasn't just the two agents, but three others had joined them. A bunch of suits, and he was the one in jeans and a shirt he knew he'd worn twice without it being washed again.

The one named Campbell—he liked him well enough—spoke first. "You signed for a package from France."

"Okay." He still wasn't quite following. "Maybe I did . . . I kind of remember that. It just showed up at my apartment."

"Did you open it?"

"No." He hadn't. "It was addressed to my father, but somehow had my address instead. I dropped it off at the house."

"How did they seem?"

Randy knew full well he was missing something, just not what exactly. "My parents? They just took the package. We don't speak often. My mother might have even said thank you. I left and that was the end of it."

"I bet it was a big box. We estimate there was five million dollars in there."

He was . . . stunned. Not because of the number, but because his parents had trusted him not to open it. He groped for words. "I . . . I didn't know that."

Campbell smiled, but it wasn't necessarily warm. "We thought maybe you didn't. They played you, and they used the right decoy. You didn't open it. We figured that out fast enough when you didn't go buy an island under an assumed name and relax in a hammock before you were charged with murder. We've thoroughly checked your financial accounts in the U.S. and tried to find accounts overseas. There are no assets."

"Come on, I drive a used Ford Focus. That has to count." It was a weak joke, because he was thinking furiously. He knew his parents were well to do, rich even, but why would anyone send that much money in a package and not do a wire transfer?

He suddenly didn't want to know the answer to that question.

"You signed for that package. Besides the murder charge, we could technically bring you up for indictment on other charges, because if you did know what was in that package and agreed to have it sent to you, you have committed a serious crime. That's why even though you made bail you are still in federal custody. Now do you want to help us?"

All five of them had intent looks on their faces.

The answer was . . . no, he didn't.

The restaurant was understated and elegant, and Ellie had been there before, with Bryce actually. She was glad that the atmosphere was quiet, the atmosphere subdued, and there was just some classical playing in the background. There was also a spectacular view of the city, just starting to light up.

Long, long day.

Maybe it showed. Bryce, who looked collected and as reserved as usual, asked her, "Wine? I was thinking of ordering a bottle. Preference?"

"No, but thanks. I'll just drink water. I might have half a glass."

He was a very smart man. He thought it over. "You do look a little tired. Are you feeling okay?"

It wasn't like he didn't know her. Maybe it would be easier to just tell him. It was weighing on her anyway. It might ruin the evening, but he deserved forthright disclosure if he'd meant it when he said he wasn't over her, but Jason deserved it too. She had to be honest. "I feel fine, I'm just tired because we are working a complicated case and I'm pregnant."

That was done.

He took it surprisingly well. Dark eyes reflected only a slight shimmer of shock, and then he got it under control. "Pregnant? Oh . . . I see. Congratulations. You love Jody's kids. I'm sure you're happy. I've never been able to decide on kids myself."

"I've noticed that."

He spoke about his ex-wife. "Elaine never wanted them. I wasn't sure if that bothered me or not, which tells me it didn't. I've never not wanted any, but never actively wanted children either."

Jason certainly didn't fall into that category. She thought about the house with the pretty backyard and his enthusiasm about it.

For whatever reason, they both relaxed as the bread was delivered. Ellie was hungry all the time now that the nauseous stage had passed, so she didn't hesitate to take a piece. "I am," she said, "in a certain way, in a complicated relationship."

"Those seem to be the type you choose. Ours certainly was, especially at the beginning."

Well, that was fair enough. He'd been a suspect in a case involving serial killings up in Lincoln County.

"You do as well. I'm not sure anyone wants to live with a homicide detective."

"I'd live with her again. How are you feeling?"

"I'm fine. I get tired easily, though that is letting up a little in the second trimester." She didn't like admitting to the fatigue, but it was true. She also had no idea how to respond to the part of what he'd just said, so she didn't. "But otherwise, yes, I'm good."

He ordered a glass of merlot and ordered her new normal, water with a slice of lemon.

"You look great."

She couldn't decide how to feel about his ambiguity about her pregnancy, but then again, she could to a certain extent understand it. Bryce had always had an approach to life that was both cautious, and if not passive, at least reserved. To her, it was extremely awkward admitting she had an intimate relationship with another man. Considering his earlier remark he wasn't over their involvement, she did ask outright, "It doesn't bother you about the baby?"

He didn't hesitate. "Some. I don't think I have the right to be bothered. I left. It was great for my writing, but not so great for us. I should have asked you to marry me, but I didn't, and so that is entirely my fault. Except you wouldn't have said yes, would you?"

That was very perceptive of him.

No, she wouldn't have. Not at the place they were

when he left for New York. She equivocated. "Neither one of us was ready. So how is the book release doing?"

"Avoidance of the topic?" He lifted his brows. "Okay, we can switch gears. The release is going very well. It's reviewing well also. They have started selling foreign rights, and I have another contract. I still work some at my other job, but more part-time. It's a nice balance. It keeps *me* balanced is how I would put it."

"I suppose that is always something you have to take into consideration."

"That book and I had traveled a lifetime together. The second one was more of a stranger. We got to know each other. My editor now has it in production."

"I find the process interesting. I can't wait to read it."

He smiled. "Ellie, you find almost everything interesting. Your inquisitive mind sets you apart. You should have been a writer."

That he had a way with words wasn't exactly surprising. "I'm not a writer, Bryce. I'm a realist, and that you think one way and I think another doesn't say anything bad or good about either of us, but we don't function on the same plane."

"True enough." He laughed lightly. "I don't disagree. You want facts and I produce fiction."

"I think we both have a very different calling. I can't really see myself doing anything else."

"You and Santiago have that in common anyway. How does he feel about us having dinner?"

It was the question of the hour and absolutely not hard to answer.

"Unhappy." She fingered the stem of her glass, enjoying the soft sound of Mozart in the background. "I said I had plans and he figured out dinner with you in about two seconds."

"I've never thought he wasn't astute. I told you I wasn't over you, but he probably had already guessed it. How badly am I stepping on his toes? If I'd known about your pregnancy I might have hesitated to ask you if you wanted to have dinner."

She'd thought it over. "He might be the most resilient person I know, so he'll deal with it. We are in an extremely committed professional relationship, and I can't quite say the same for the private one. I'm definitely the problem there. I don't know if I can be with any person twenty-four hours a day. We're being assigned different partners anyway once this case is over." She lifted her shoulders slightly. "I got lucky and it looks like Grasso will be mine. I can live with that, but then again, I don't know if this case will ever be over."

"Tough one?" Bryce looked interested, but always had been, at least in the psychological aspects. They'd had an unspoken agreement she could talk about her cases if she didn't go into much detail about the actual killings. That was fine with her; she didn't want to go there again either if she didn't have to.

"Unequivocal yes. We are doing our best to keep someone Jason and I both think is not guilty from going to prison, but there's a lot going on behind the scenes. Unless we come up with something concrete, the accused will go to trial. There's enough evidence the right jury for the prosecution might convict him."

"Pressure on I see."

"Definitely."

The waiter arrived with menus and she was glad the morning sickness—not relegated just to the morning—was a thing of the past, but still cautiously ordered braised chicken. Bryce was predictable and ordered a steak, some things never changed. He caught her up on his family—she did miss them—and she let him know about the adventures of Jody's lively family. The food smelled wonderful when it arrived and she was maybe halfway through her meal before her phone vibrated.

Jason.

She might have been annoyed, but then again, she didn't think he'd actually call her during dinner unless it was important. He got that much credit. She smiled apologetically at Bryce, but he'd been through it before. "I have to get this call."

"Of course you do."

He meant it. That was nice anyway. Ellie pressed a button and said quietly, "What?"

"Anyone ever tell you your phone skills could use some work just as much as mine? Anyway, Forsythe is dead."

That declaration explained the interruption. She set down her fork. "What? How?"

"It looks like suicide. Why do I doubt that? Notice I said 'looks.' The body is in the Underworld with the ME as we speak. Let's see what Hammett has to say. He sure didn't seem like the type to off himself to me."

"With all these agencies involved how are people still dying?" The chicken was delicious and she didn't really mourn the obnoxious Forsythe, but still doubted she'd be able to take another bite because it was so disturbing. "We talked to him and now he's dead? Oh, that's just wonderful."

"I know. If Metzger calls tell him I'm in Vegas or something."

"No. You are talking to George Washington here."

"You cannot tell a lie? Dammit, Ellie. Learn how. It, of course, isn't our case."

"I have an honest soul, so lying isn't option. It doesn't sound like there is a case." She hadn't liked Forsythe, but he was a casualty one way or another. "I guess we'll talk this one over later."

"Someone evidently killed our lead suspect unless it truly was suicide." She said it after she ended the call by way of explanation to Bryce. "I'm sorry. You just recalled why you left for New York in the first place, didn't you?"

"I never left because of your job." Bryce was intuitive almost to a fault. "You don't seem too upset."

"I didn't like the man, but neither did I want him dead. It seems like in the course of our investigation, if we have a suspect, they somehow become a victim. I feel like we are causing more homicides than solving them. We certainly haven't solved the case we've been working on."

The genteel sound of silverware on china, romantic lighting, and the soft music were incongruous to the topic. Luckily, Bryce was used to it. "I assume this won't close said case, but if he committed suicide, it looks to my admittedly amateur eye like perhaps he was guilty and felt you closing in."

"Well, we weren't closing in. He has—or had anyway—an alibi, though it wasn't by any means airtight, and we have absolutely no physical evidence it was him. Let's not forget the suspect is already in custody where there's physical evidence all over the place. But I'm with Jason. This man would not kill himself. If he committed the crime, he'd thumb his nose at us and dare us to prove it."

"It does sound complicated. How is your mother doing?"

It was an effective move. She picked up her fork, maybe able to take a few more bites. "She sounds great. Cheerful and positive as always."

"We email back and forth now and then. I agree, she seems to be in a good place."

They did? Ellie wasn't sure how to take that bit of information, since her mother had never mentioned it. "I wasn't aware of that."

"Ellie, I didn't abandon you, I gave you space."

She replied, "I think we both needed space."

Jason had to admit the balcony view helped somewhat. He liked the lights in the pool glowing, and even if there was a parking lot right behind it, well that was fine.

Ellie pulled in and he uttered a curse not even under his breath because he'd specifically requested she not walk through the parking lot alone. He went out the front door at a dead run, startled some poor lady on the stairs as he flew by, and was lucky he didn't break his neck gaining the main level. He blew out the front entrance like a hurricane.

Ellie didn't appreciate it when he came rushing toward her. "What are you doing?"

"I'm new at this worrying thing," he explained, a little out of breath. "You are going to have to get over it."

As luck would have it—his bad luck—she looked like a knockout in some dark blue flowing dress. He was sure Grantham had noticed as well. She said, "Me? *Me* get over it? You get over it. If you think you have a Prince Charming moment going, maybe you need to think again."

"Let's go inside and I can fill you in on the Forsythe case." It was his best save under the circumstances. Not good, but he wanted her inside behind a locked door.

"Do I have a choice?"

"No."

"I get that impression."

"Let's get safe, and we can talk about it."

She obviously conceded the parking lot wasn't the best place to have a discussion, since she came along willingly enough and he did give an exhale of relief when he got her through the door and locked it, shot the dead bolt, and flicked on an extra light.

Ellie immediately slipped off her shoes and dropped onto the couch. But she was on the same page, since she took out her Glock from her purse and laid it on the table, right within reach. "So talk to me. Tell me what you know about Forsythe."

"Grasso is handling it, since on the surface it looks pretty straightforward. He shot himself."

"We have some pretty valid reasons to think it's a homicide, but Hammett and forensics will figure that out quickly enough." Her expression indicated she was sorting it all out, weighing what they did know against what they didn't know.

Jason was so relieved to have her sitting there, more because she was safe than that she wasn't with Grantham any longer, but it was an issue. He'd never dealt with jealousy before and wasn't enjoying it one bit, but he'd told her the truth, he'd really never had to worry about someone else's safety either. Two people actually, and the list was growing, he thought grimly. Hell, he was worried about his mother, if that wasn't irony for you. He was even afraid his father hadn't listened to him and might do something stupid like talk to all the wrong people anyway as a gesture of goodwill and fatherly affection and managed to get on the watch list.

God help him.

"What would be the purpose in killing Forsythe?" Jason sat down in his favorite chair that even he had to admit was looking pretty bad and needed to be re-placed, but if he was moving, he'd pick some new stuff, so for now that faded plaid was part of the decor. "I get he was an accountant for what appears to be a very questionable operation. He knew something, is my guess, or saw something, or worse, embezzled funds. If he cooked the books and knew they'd caught on that he'd kept some of the cash for himself, maybe he did decide suicide was a better option than what might be in store for him. For all we know someone stood there and forced him to pull that trigger, carefully explaining what would happen to him if he didn't, and dying was the better option."

"Speculation? Drawing conclusions without facts?" Ellie shook her head. "Come on, Detective Santiago, you know better than to spin a yarn without evidence. That's a gruesome picture, by the way."

It was, but maybe a viable theory. "We aren't exactly in the greeting card business, sweetheart." He tipped back the last of the beer he'd been drinking, wondering if he should cut back a little. He wasn't an alcoholic; he'd seen that firsthand growing up. But he did like it; it cut through some of the restless energy.

"No, we aren't," she agreed, her eyes holding a trou-bled look. "We certainly aren't and I'm not your sweet-heart. What are we, in high school?"

"Figure of speech. Maybe we could start a card company with a guy in a long black robe with a hood and a skeleton hand holding a scythe as our advertis-ing. Grim Reaper Greetings. Has a nice ring to it."

"I'm starting to wonder. Someone is following our investigation, but I just don't see what it gains them to eliminate suspects. Reid is certainly a casualty, but I don't cry mea culpa on that one since once Cameron told us, maybe he told someone else too."

"Forsythe was deep in with all kinds of shit if I had to guess. Could just be a coincidence."

"He wasn't going to get my vote for Man of the Year anyway, but you could be right."

"We need to talk to Locke again. If there are charges coming, he would know that much."

"Maybe he isn't interested in risking his life by having a chat with us."

It would be different if she were joking, but she certainly wasn't. Jason argued, "He has more and more reasons to assume he might be in the crosshairs anyway. Whether or not Lane and his partners realize they are subject to a big investigation, killing Locke would accomplish nothing. The DA's office would probably let Lambert handle it with another district attorney or even move him up. He already knows what's going on. It wouldn't stop anything."

"So let's meet with both Lambert and Locke."

"I think they might be as shackled as we are in some ways, but it is worth a try."

"They *have* to know what is coming down the pipeline."

He didn't agree. "Let's see if we can hook up, but I bet they don't know any more than we do."

She actually wanted to hook up, the case aside. She'd noticed that Jason had backed off in a sexual way, but emotionally he was way more available than before. Ellie knew they were both learning as they went along, but . . .

"I'm really in the mood."

Jason looked startled and then wary. "Please tell me this isn't because of Grantham. Jesus, Ellie."

"Yes, because of Bryce, but not how you mean." She was sincere, since an unresolved part of her life had just

been set aside. "I think now I can safely say that's settled."

"In my favor?"

"I'm sitting here with you, right? Let's go to bed."

He didn't need to be asked twice.

Chapter 17

Jan came to him in dreams.

She would lie next to him, warm in his arms, and her breathing was soft in the night. Randy would wake up sweating, wanting to say a thousand things he'd taken for granted he'd have time to tell her, and all he had was damp, cold sheets and a silent room.

This was bad. This was hell.

They wanted him to testify he'd seen certain people over the course of his lifetime actually, as guests in his parents' home. Pictures, names, the works. That package was just the tip of an iceberg that he was about to ram into at full speed in a fiberglass canoe that might shatter on impact.

The worst of it was the realization he'd known maybe his entire existence that this might one day happen. That there was always something going on he didn't quite understand, that all the money wasn't just blood, sweat, and tears, but maybe just blood. Looking back on the things he'd overheard, he could maybe sink a few ships besides his own and that one was going down fast.

But he didn't want to do it. It was hard to decipher

how he felt about it all, but maybe the bad dream was a product of overload. He felt a sense of loyalty that might be displaced, since it wasn't reciprocated, but he still felt it.

He'd guessed who John had gone to for refuge and he was really tempted to do the same thing if he could pull it off.

The meeting went about as well as she expected. Locke was a very tense man under a polished exterior, and Lambert was smoother, more contained, but full of questions. He was maybe thirty, still fresh out of law school, and had landed quite the job and knew it. Ellie had met him before and found him to be pleasant and personable, and he looked like a lawyer: smooth stylish brown hair, nice-looking, good clothes, and a lot of composure. But he did have that same razor focus as Locke, and maybe it was what won him the job. It was there in his eyes.

Locke said briskly, "So what are we going to accomplish here today?"

It was a valid question to Ellie's mind. "We are guppies swimming with piranhas. I get the feeling you are also. I think our main question is when will charges be filed against the major players in your investigation? Maybe then we'll be able to do our job."

"The timing is delicate. Once we start issuing the warrants and law enforcement officers make the arrests, there will be fugitives. As you well know, the burden of proof is on us. The Lane family is outwardly squeaky clean when it comes to their business practices. They pay their taxes like good citizens, adhere to labor laws for their employees for the offices here in Milwaukee, have a 401(k) plan, so everything is legitimate on the surface anyway. But at least two of their companies in other states are front entities used for money laundering, which has been going on for literally three generations. Connecting the dots is the cohesive problem in all of this. We are not the ones to handle that. We are the hammer that comes down when we can make it stick. Evidence is the key word."

Lambert added, "We have discussed asking Chief Metzger to pull you off until our cases are under indictment, but afraid the trail will be too cold, and it looks to us anyway like Randy Lane will go to prison for Janet's murder."

Jason said with remarkable calm for him, "A decent defense attorney could come up with a case for reasonable doubt. Maybe he'd win it, but maybe he wouldn't. I know I have reasonable doubt."

"What defense?" Locke's jaw was like iron.

"We have some, but not much, physical evidence to prove his story might be true."

"As in what? A wiped-off table, a missing antique engagement ring, and a generic knife with no prints on it except for that of the accused?" That was Lambert. "I've read the forensic report. You are going to need more than that to prove it was someone else."

Ellie had to point out her main argument. "We have a little more. She opened the door for whoever killed her. No sign of forced entry, which I know makes Randy Lane look even more guilty, but it makes no sense to us why he wouldn't just kill her and leave, not go get food and come back."

"I'd argue it made a great cover-up for the crime."

"But surely, Counselor," she replied, "it would also seem that maybe that was exactly what happened. He left, and someone killed her while he was gone."

"It depends on the jury. So what you're telling us is

you don't have any leads solid enough to arrest a different suspect." Lambert didn't pull punches." Do I have that right?"

To Ellie's frustration he did have it right. "No. In our opinion, Forsythe was option number one, and he's gone. No solid proof he did it, and no irrefutable proof he didn't. You tell me. The knife that was used is sold by half a dozen retailers in this city alone. According to the forensics report it wasn't new either, because it showed some wear, indicating it had been sharpened before. Tracing the weapon is virtually impossible, since it might have been owned for years. The killer must have used gloves, because only Randy's prints were on it."

It was a very unique experience, and not a pleasant one, to have to discuss the case with the victim's father. He wouldn't handle it in any way since it belonged to the county, but if it was motivated by the federal investigation, then his office would be involved.

"It's always hard to convict a dead man." Locke sounded strained and modulated his tone. "If he did do it and gets off because he committed suicide, we will likely now never know."

It wasn't difficult to read the message. *Work harder. I need closure.*

They were definitely doing their best.

"We've been told there are certain people we can't question or even bring under scrutiny. What we'd like from your office is some support in at least a general overview of how long our hands are going to be tied. Please understand, I'm with Detective Santiago. I don't think it was Randy, especially since law enforcement officers have been killed in someone's attempt to get to him."

"We are well aware." Lambert wrote something

down by hand in a notebook and looked up. "You have a proven track record of success, Detective MacIntosh. If your instincts tell you Lane is not the person responsible for Janet's death, I think this office trusts that, but give us someone else. As for the people you can't interview, that isn't our decision at the moment, but the minute they are charged, you can step in."

"But still no timeline on when that will be?" Jason looked at Locke.

The U.S. district attorney looked right back and said through his teeth, "If you think for a minute I don't want my family back and whoever killed my daughter punished, think again. I am pushing so hard to have this resolved, Detective Santiago, sleep isn't even an option. I haven't made my bed in days because I haven't been in it. But it is a complicated situation and my voice isn't the only one."

"I have a family too. I can't step on the wrong toes either." Jason was unflinching.

Ellie had to admit it was strange to hear him say it to other people so matter-of-factly, knowing he included her and the baby. She clarified. "What he means is we understand. In our last big case the killer threatened my sister and her young children. I did what you did and told her to get out of town until we caught him. I can imagine your resolve to end this is overwhelming, but Santiago is right. We are more handcuffed than the culprit might ever be."

"I'm trying not to lose faith you'll discover the truth. I haven't yet."

"I'm sorry, since I know I'm in the minority when it comes to who is sitting in this room, but I think the right man has already been arrested. That said, I'm not the one investigating this case; the two of you are responsible for that part of the procedure." Lambert looked from Jason to Ellie very deliberately. "Please excuse me, I'm due in court in an hour and need to stop by my office. Good luck, Detectives."

When he left, Locke also rose. "I have a meeting in a few minutes as well, but I appreciate your diligence and fully understand your dissatisfaction with how this has to be handled. No one does more than me."

"Fuck," Jason muttered as they left the building and walked into brilliant sunshine. "That applies to this whole thing. Cluster fuck."

"I think you need some counseling about language before this baby arrives." Ellie wished she wasn't wearing slacks, since it was so hot, but her options were getting seriously limited anyway.

"I get counseling already. Go ahead and mention it to Lukens if you want. Did we accomplish anything? You talk first and then I'll tell you what I think."

"I think at least we proved we are very committed to this case."

"And I think Lambert is up to speed too, but not as convinced we can pull this rabbit out of our hat."

"I'm not convinced either."

His blue eyes looked very brilliant in the afternoon light.

She equivocated, "But don't sell us short just yet."

There were wheels turning. Slowly, but they existed. Jason registered that something had poked him, but he couldn't put his finger on it. Every investigation—or most anyway—was like that. A small phrase, a dangling fact that didn't make sense, and suddenly either he or Ellie caught on. They tended to work off each other, bouncing ideas back and forth, and worked it, and so far, they were doing pretty well with that technique.

"Something was off," she agreed. "I'm trying to figure it out. The conversation was uneven, like we were being led . . . but why would Locke ever do that? He's rabid to find out who killed Janet."

"Lambert has made up his mind." Jason saw it and he'd come across prosecutors like that before. "He thinks we're spinning our wheels. I just don't feel it. My gut says we aren't."

"I don't think so either."

He was so conscious of it he didn't even ask, but took the keys from her hand. "Let me drive. We can talk on our way back to work."

"Jason, we are always at work."

"To our desks then."

"I need pizza tonight."

"I love you. Pizza it is if that is what the baby wants."

He'd never said it that way. Loving someone and being in love with someone was quite different. Not that he was an expert, but settling into the feelings involved a process that meant profound change. Ellie just looked at him as he backed out the car. He shrugged. "I know I could be all crappy about it and claim this is a one-sided relationship since you won't talk about it, but then again you are the one having the baby. I felt like a definitive declaration needed to be out there."

Ellie was very quiet and he let it be that way. She finally said, "We are both working through this. I don't really trust that I'm levelheaded about you right now. I'm being cautious for both of us."

She sure as hell was being cautious. He truly now empathized with his ex-girlfriend Kate, who'd accused him of just not being open to commitment. He wasn't positive Ellie wasn't just as guilty, but he was now on the other side of the equation.

Not fun. It sucked.

Payment for his myriad sins? Maybe. He had them and no doubt would be a repeat offender. His phone vibrated so he didn't have to make a comment one way or the other, which was probably just as well. His diplomacy skills also needed a lot of work.

He pulled over. For once he was grateful to recognize the caller. "Santiago."

"You are promoted to lieutenant. I hope this is the end of this conversation. I don't have time for it. We have a new lead detective coming on board. Don't get all full of yourself. I want you to have the same rank and you will be expected to help her settle in. A lot of cold cases will become your responsibility. Got it?"

He was . . . stunned.

"I believe you never have a problem making yourself clear." He cleared his throat. "Sir."

Metzger hung up. Jason wasn't sure what to say. He just stared at his phone. Ellie asked him, "Is everything okay?"

"Um, I'm not sure."

"The look on your face . . . what?"

"Metzger just promoted me." If Jason had to vote on it, he'd have picked Ellie to be ahead of him, even if he had more experience. After all, he'd been under an IA microscope several times before and she hadn't.

No wonder he loved her. She relaxed. "Thank goodness. I didn't want it to be your mother. Congratulations."

He eyed her suspiciously. "You knew about this?"

"Actually, no. But you seem like a logical choice with Fergusson clearing out his desk. I did know Grasso passed on being lead."

"He said that?"

"He made it clear since we were being reassigned he'd be my partner."

Oh great, now he was jealous of Grasso. Not romantically, but it was almost worse. "Lucky him, since he'll now get all the high-profile stuff thanks to you, whiz kid."

"Jason, *you're* the one that just got promoted to rank. I'd have a glass of champagne with you, but you hate champagne and I can't do more than a few sips, so it would be a waste."

"Lukens would probably tell you I'm struggling a little with the thought of giving up our working relationship."

"I don't like it either, but we will still see each other every single day. Our desks are in the same area."

"And hopefully every single night if they accept my offer on that house."

He would never have blurted that out if Metzger hadn't thrown him off. He wanted to take her out to dinner, break the news in a cavalier way so he didn't give over how much it mattered, but there he was, just putting it out there.

"I wasn't aware you took that step."

Well, what did that mean? "Any enthusiasm, or just 'oh'?"

"I did think it was a very nice house. When did you even find the time?"

That was something encouraging anyway.

"A real estate agent who smells a sale will stop by with the paperwork, so all it really took was a phone call. We could keep your house for a vacation place." He was trying not to push, but failing. *Too many "we" references, you damn idiot.*

"I have thought about moving from the condo."

Score! Not a yes, but not a no. He was careful not to show any elation. "Maybe we've both learned from our initial mistakes when we gave it a try the first time, but then again Kate and Grantham bear some of the responsibility too. I fell down on my bike that initial pedaling attempt as well. It hurt, but I managed to get up, and I was a lot better down the line. I might have wobbled some and hit a curb or two, but I got the hang of it."

"When you try to do an effective analogy, you might want to think it over a little more." She was at least laughing.

"Hey, I thought it was pretty good."

"Not too bad. I've known you for a while now. It could have been worse."

"Ellie, I understand if you want to move from the condo, so really, why not move in with me? I have this feeling I'm going to put beer mirrors on the walls again. It is sort of my go-to decorating thing. Do you want our child seeing a half-dressed woman in a short skirt and a half-open blouse holding a tray full of foamy mugs?"

Now there was an argument.

She sobered, the amusement gone. "I think maybe we could try it."

This really was his lucky day. *Ellie and the coveted promotion in one afternoon?*

Time to appreciate what he'd gained and cut his losses. He said, "What kind of pizza are we talking? If you crave anchovies you've lost me forever."

Chapter 18

"Do you have any idea why your cousin would commit suicide?"

Randy couldn't even summon more than a stony stare. "Freddy? He wouldn't ever be that considerate to the rest of humanity. If you think I'm going to shed a tear, think again. He was one cold, mean bastard his entire life. My father told me when he hired him it took about two days before no one in accounting wanted to work in the same office with him. He only hired him because of my uncle. I honestly don't think my uncle liked his son very much either, but if something shady is going on my cousin wouldn't have any trouble getting his hands dirty for the right amount of money. He certainly seems to have plenty of that."

"Seemed. Definitely past tense. I think all he has now is a pitchfork in his back and hot coals under his feet." That was Detective Santiago, talking to him via a computer screen, because apparently even the cops weren't allowed to know where he was. Campbell had brought it into the sterile living room of the safe house that looked like a throwback to a comedy from the seventies, and was sitting right there, listening to every word. "Know anyone in particular who might want to kill him?"

Why the hell did everyone seem to think he was an oracle or something? "I don't mean to sound like a jerk, but pretty much anyone who'd ever met him, which doesn't narrow it down for you guys. I don't think anyone understands how much when my family wrote me off as a lost cause, they really dumped me. I know very little about his personal life, or his professional life either."

"But you fingered him as someone who might have killed Janet."

"We disliked each other, my family business is apparently under investigation and her father is involved, and Freddy was in my opinion capable of it."

What else could he say? He'd wanted to get his degree, find a decent job, and marry Jan. It was simple enough and now shot to hell, and sorrow had gradually been replaced by anger.

"Had you proposed yet? Cameron said you were going to and your mother gave you an heirloom ring. We are wondering where it is. She wants it back."

Of course she did. It had belonged to her mother. She'd sent it to him by courier out of the blue with a simple note: *I know you can't afford one. I wish you happiness, and your grandmother would agree with me.*

"God, don't do this to me." It felt like a tight knot had tightened around his throat. "Jan should have been wearing it. Just that afternoon I'd asked and she'd said yes. I'd put that ring on her finger. When I found her she was dead. I can tell you right now that ring was the last thing on my mind. I was freaking out."

"In the crime scene photos she isn't wearing it."

Just when he thought things couldn't get worse, it

seemed to happen. Jan had loved the ring, but he'd known she would. She was very into vintage and it suited her. "Someone stole it then."

"That missing ring might hang you. A prosecuting attorney could argue that you asked and she said no, and in a fit of rage, you killed her. It gives you motive."

It wasn't at all what happened. Randy knew he'd lost weight, and it was an effort even to eat, but now he felt absolutely sick again. It had been an olive branch for his mother to offer it, and he was pretty sure his father and Robert would have disapproved and given her grief over the gift. His voice broke. "Whoever killed her took it."

It was more than past dark but with light dawning all the same. Not in a literal sense, but a mental one. There was no way she was going to go back to sleep.

Ellie picked up her phone and hit a button. Jason answered at once. Those years in the military had stuck with him. No one she knew slept as little as he did, except maybe Grasso. She speculated that man might be a vampire. "What?"

Typical Santiago greeting.

"Did you get the impression Locke was aware his daughter was engaged?"

"What? It's three in the morning. I was in bed, finally half asleep at least. I don't know."

"Bed? You were snoring on the couch. That dilapidated thing has to go to the basement or be donated, by the way. Answer my question."

"I think I just did. I don't snore, for your information."

"Dream on. The ring *is* missing in the crime scene pictures, or I sure don't remember it. We have two possibilities. Someone broke in and killed her and stole it like Randy claims, or, for whatever reason, Lambert knew something her own father didn't. He said, 'missing engagement ring.' That's specific. I can't sleep because of it."

"Lucky me." Jason's head was evidently clearing. "He did say that. I remember it. Locke did kind of look surprised."

"I'm just wondering why Jan Locke would tell Lambert and not her dad if she had gotten engaged. We are talking a pretty short time period here."

"Maybe she called the office and got Lambert instead? They have busy schedules I'm sure, and it might be they don't actually see each other all that often except to meet over cases."

"Possible. But why wouldn't Lambert have mentioned it to Locke when she was murdered and Randy was arrested? We are talking the same afternoon here."

Silence. Then he said slowly, "Now I'm wondering the same thing. Dammit, Ellie, I was having a peaceful evening, still basking in the glow of the champagne we didn't drink."

"I'm sitting here thinking the glow was Pabst Blue Ribbon or Old Milwaukee. Anyway, I'm having an issue with the missing ring remark and Lambert knowing she had it. Explain to me if it isn't in the crime scene pictures how he would know that. I don't remember that ring on her hand, which fits with it being missing, but if Randy had just proposed, how would Lambert know she had an engagement ring in the first place?"

"Ellie, Randy could be lying to us. I believe he's innocent, but I wonder now and then as facts don't add up. I told him if we find he hocked that ring, it could make the case against him."

"It still doesn't explain Lambert."

"Maybe he just assumed she had a ring."

"He's an attorney with the U.S. district office. I don't think they operate too often on assumptions. Considering the Lane family wealth, I bet that was one very nice ring. I have two big questions. Where is it if Randy is telling the truth? And how did Lambert know she had it on her finger in the first place? I want to look at the crime scene pictures again, and I want a warrant to search Forsythe's house and office."

"I don't know if it will fly. We have nothing solid to make a case except Randy's dislike of his cousin."

"If we find the ring there, Forsythe is our guy and Randy could be off the hook, or at least it is one less nail in his coffin. There is no reason for Forsythe to have that ring except if he killed her and then couldn't resist and took it. I can't believe I'm saying this, but the whole case could hinge on that ring. Let's try that angle."

"It's better than the nothing we have so far," he admitted. "What if Mrs. Lane hadn't even talked to us and been venal enough to want the ring back?"

"I don't know she was venal. For my part, I think it has sentimental value. I'm glad she mentioned it. I'm also encouraged she gave it to Randy. It means she does care."

"Or had some extra jewelry just sitting in a drawer in that fancy house of hers and thought what the hell."

She was well aware part of the problem was when his mother let him down, Jason lost faith in women in general and was leery of changing his stance, so that he was the one pursuing commitment was more than a little surprising.

Georgia Lukens would reiterate that since they had to rely on each other in dangerous situations now and then, Ellie had gained some hard-earned trust another woman might not be able to accomplish. The physical chemistry probably didn't hurt either.

"Jason, she wants it back. That doesn't signify 'what the hell.' It means it meant something to her and she still gave it to him."

He ignored that observation. "We could, as always, use a breaking point. Let's go for the search warrant so Forsythe's father can't object because he is also under investigation and we don't want that screwed up."

Ellie objected at least a little to that. "We haven't been warned off him at all."

"We both know that, but I don't think there would be loads of agreement from all different sources it's a good idea."

"Oh no, now you sound like a lieutenant. I might strangle Metzger."

"Go ahead. I might place you under investigation though with my new unlimited powers if he turns up dead."

"Unlimited powers? Me and the nugget are proud of you, but please—"

"Can I come over so we can talk about this face to face since you can't sleep?"

"Jason, it's three in the morning."

"If you are awake, and now I've no hope sleep will happen for me, what's the difference? We can 'not sleep' together."

It wasn't like she didn't know they needed time together now and again away from work if their relationship was going to go anywhere. "I don't think I have more to say about the case until we get the warrants and look at the crime scene photos again."

"I'd just like to snore next to you in the dark instead of alone in my apartment. Talk about some boring stuff, okay? Maybe I'll doze off."

"I'm boring?"

"I didn't say that, did I? But if you'd talk about opera, I would think that was boring."

"I want to talk about the case."

"Of course you do, because you're you. Just keep in mind murder isn't dozeworthy."

There wasn't going to be an argument on her end over that. "Agreed."

"I'll be there in a few minutes."

No matter the time, Jason was more than happy to show up on Ellie's doorstep. She didn't seem adverse to it either, and that was progress toward the idea of living together might just work out. She was wearing a light pink camisole and matching cotton shorts, and very definitely the scanty attire did not conceal that she was pregnant, which to his surprise he found pretty sexy. Maybe it was simply the knowledge that it was his baby, or maybe he was just drawn to her no matter what— he wasn't sure.

Her condo was a nice place, forever tidy, and it always smelled good, like someone had just baked a cake or something. He was never sure if he was nose blind about his apartment.

The loan preapproval on the house had been a breeze, since he was paying mostly cash. Ellie's furniture was much nicer than his and would look good in the new place if she hadn't changed her mind about them giving it a try. They'd spent plenty of nights together, especially on their last high-profile case when she'd had a stalker and it was dangerous for her to be alone, but *every* night sounded better to him.

To his disappointment, she didn't suggest her bedroom but settled back down into what appeared to be her favorite chair and put her feet up on the ottoman. "I've really been thinking."

"About me?"

No luck. She shot him right down. "No. You know, this might sound ridiculous, but this Lambert angle . . . I'm wondering, did they know each other out of the office? I'm talking about him and Janet."

He sat down on the couch and took off his tennis shoes so he could also stretch out, arms behind his head. "I don't know. Where is this going?"

Ellie frowned. "Lambert. I like him basically. That's a complication when thinking about all this. He's intelligent, though argumentative, but he's a lawyer. They get paid to argue. I do like Locke also, who weighed in on hiring him I'm sure. They would have been introduced. Lambert and Janet would have known each other if I had to guess. That Lambert knew about the ring is really raising a red flag and waving it in my face."

"I can see that, but I can't see why exactly. I still say maybe it could be easily explained."

"Crime of passion. If it wasn't Randy, who was it?"

He'd just relaxed, but he sat up abruptly. "Are you really suggesting we question *Lambert*?"

She didn't budge. "I just don't think this was a professional hit. I'm looking at it from an emotional viewpoint. I'd at least like to find out how he knew about the ring."

"Evidently." He considered it. "If rage really was involved, Forsythe is obvious to me. He seemed mad at the world."

"Before yesterday I would agree. If Randy is telling the truth, someone took that ring. I don't know if it was personal, or if it was a robbery, but the irrefutable truth is it is missing. I refuse to let Janet lose her life and lose the man she loved as well."

This wasn't the Ellie he knew. She really wasn't sentimental but instead pragmatic and straightforward. He pointed out, "If you think we've started a shitstorm with the people we've questioned so far, imagine what might blow up if we suggested Lambert might be a suspect. He just can't be."

"I didn't say that he was a suspect. I just wouldn't be a decent police officer if I didn't pay attention when something struck me as unusual. You're right, it's probably as simple as she called to tell her father she was engaged and got transferred to Lambert instead and told him and mentioned the ring. But . . ." She trailed off.

He finished it for her. "But if he hadn't mentioned it to Locke, why? Oh crap, that bothers me too now. If he knew about the ring, he knew she was engaged. You would think when Randy was arrested, that would be the first thing he'd mention to Janet's father."

"Maybe he wasn't surprised she was engaged, just maybe surprised Lambert knew before he did that it was official."

"Can I point out Locke only looked, to us, like he was surprised. He's under a great deal of strain. Let's call him in the morning and just ask him if knew already. If I was him, I wouldn't even look at the crime scene photos. I couldn't handle it. Maybe he was just surprised the ring was missing because didn't realize it existed. Ellie, it's late. Let's get some sleep. Can we just go to bed?"

"I'm kind of wired up."

"I know the feeling."

"You do realize you haven't touched me since you found out I'm pregnant unless I suggest it. I don't know how to feel about that. No interest now that the nugget is starting to blossom?"

Subject switched.

He couldn't be more astounded. Jason sat up and stared at her. "You've got to be kidding. I think I'm happy I won't be your partner any longer because you've lost your mind. Lots of interest. Like every minute of the day interest. I understand you've never dealt with this before, but I haven't either."

"Are you always going to detach yourself?"

He didn't need Lukens grilling him because he had Ellie asking him uncomfortable questions. Why was he paying for therapy? The answer was a struggle. "I can't mess this up," he conceded in a halting voice, but it took something to admit it. "Like . . . not at *all* mess it up. I'm worried about our relationship, and I'm worried about the baby. What if I did something wrong?"

"Something wrong? In bed? You have a long list of problems, but so far that isn't one of them."

"Ellie, you're pregnant."

"I've noticed. You do realize pregnant women can have sex?"

He did, and she was dead wrong if she thought he was turned off. "On an intellectual level, yes I do. If I am operating on pure protective mode, no I don't. If you'd let me, I'd just carry you around all the time. You wouldn't need new shoes for quite a while."

At least he'd gotten a smile out of her. "Not effective, and I might gain a few pounds before the nugget emerges waving and already able to recite the alphabet. You might need to work out more."

"I never worry about anything, but I'm finding that's not the case any longer. I'm gaining a whole new perspective on life."

"Keep seeing Lukens. Your insecurity issues are sky

high." To his surprise she got up and came over to touch his cheek and said the most romantic thing possible. "You do know you are an idiot, right?"

"Oh yeah, well aware."

"Let's go to bed. Maybe it is hormones or something, but I'd like to address this. Maybe then we both could sleep. Let's agree next time *you* romance *me*?"

He couldn't resist, because a man could have worse problems. "Sure, yeah. We have a deal."

Clothes off. He must have listened at least a little because he was really into it, which was so much more like him than his recent cautious approach, soft touches, intense pleasure, whispers in the dark, and afterward she murmured, "You did not mess that up." Then Ellie did drift off to sleep literally naked in his arms. It would have been helpful if right after six in the morning the phone hadn't rung, jarring him awake. "Lieutenant?"

"Uh, no." Sleepy and disoriented it took Jason a minute. "Oh, wait. Yeah, I am. If you want Santiago, I'm him."

"Chief Metzger wanted me to call. You have a crime scene. Let me give you the address."

"What? Who? Text it to this number." He was instantly awake. "I don't exactly have a pen and paper on me right now." Or anything else for that matter, he thought wryly.

"Will do. Not a homicide, but they think you'd be interested."

"Thanks."

Though he hated to do it, he nudged Ellie awake. "There's no rest for the wicked. Metzger thinks we should look at a scene."

She sat up sleepily but nodded. "Give me five minutes."

She emerged from the bathroom with her hair in a

sleek ponytail, wearing jeans and a dark blue sleeveless tunic. He wanted nothing more than to just drag her back into the rumpled bed, but he also wanted to find out what was going on.

Chapter 19

Wisteria vines, palm trees, sandy white beaches, and crystalline water had spelled the fond vacation memories of his childhood. He and Robert and John trying to learn how to surf, laughing at each other every time one of them lost the battle, and Cameron protesting he was old enough to try but given a firm refusal by their mother. He'd never been a good swimmer.

John had loved it the most, and the feds were after him, and beyond a doubt Randy knew where he was, but whether or not the gift of bail money had been a bribe not to tell anyone or just a brotherly gesture it was hard to say. Maybe, like his parents trusting his integrity enough not to open that package, John believed Randy would do the right thing.

Whatever that was. There had to be a handbook for betraying your entire family. Some of his relatives evidently had a copy.

He hadn't read it.

So someone had tossed Freddy's house.

There was evidently speculation they were looking

for something pertaining to the business nature of his dealings with some unsavory people. That part didn't surprise Randy too much, but he viewed the pictures of the chaos and had no answers for what the culprits might be looking for or why.

"I can tell you it wasn't me. You know it wasn't me because Agent Campbell can testify I haven't gone anywhere. I would guess financial records would be well hidden. My cousin was mean spirited, but he was smart. A safety deposit box would be where I would put a flash drive like that."

"We found one in your name. Did you open it?"

The noose around his neck got tighter and tighter. "A what? I'm sure you've seen my apartment. I have nothing of value enough for a safety deposit box."

At least he got a nod from an agent he hadn't met before. Holister was young and tough looking and didn't wear a suit-and-tie combo but instead khakis and a brown polo shirt. The man nodded. "We had the signature checked out, and according to our expert it doesn't match yours."

Frustrated, Randy wished for another cup of coffee, had the feeling it wasn't coming at this moment, and asked, "Then why are you asking me?"

"Who do you think has the key?"

"Doesn't the bank have security cameras?"

Agent Holister said succinctly, "It certainly does. Mr. Forsythe emptied the box three days ago. We have it on tape. Our question is who was *looking* for the key? Have you seen this man before?"

The kitchen table was functional but old, and when he pushed over the photograph, it caught on the cracked surface. Randy picked it up. Reluctantly, he said, "Yes."

* * *

"Who called this in?"

The uniformed officer said, "Neighbor saw a light moving around. It didn't seem right to him because he knew Forsythe was dead."

Ellie surveyed the damage. The residence had been torn apart in a way that suggested speed rather than stealth. Rifled drawers, spilled silverware, broken dishes, open closets with garments on the floor with pulled-out pockets, the desk emptied, and the theme followed through the whole place, even into the garage.

"Ransacked," Jason muttered. "They were in a hurry. Why?"

She wasn't sure, but it didn't help their case. At all. If Forsythe murdered Janet, then either someone knew about it and had enlisted him to do it, or this was part of the greater problem. As if there was a greater problem worse than murder, but she had the impression that since the death count had mounted, no one involved was safe.

That included her and her current partner. Jason was taking pictures with his phone, walking around and surveying it all with a look on his face she'd come to know well.

"We were going to request a warrant," she told the officer who was in charge. "It seems like someone beat us to it."

"For my report, do you know what they might have been looking for?"

"We were going to search for a ring that was supposedly taken from our victim and would nail the homeowner as her probable killer."

"Is that so? As you can see, it will be hard to tell what is here and what isn't. I'm afraid the family is going to have to do the inventory for their insurance company." The officer adjusted his hat and wiped his brow. "I've been thinking all along 'those poor folks.' He killed someone?"

"Maybe."

Those poor folks had encouraged Forsythe to enter a life of crime, of that Ellie was fairly certain from the information trickling in reluctantly from various sources. However, it had been his decision, but Randy was proof maybe declining to accept the recruitment wasn't a good idea either. She'd save the information that while Forsythe had residue on his hand from the gunshot wound, the medical examiner thought it was possible he was unconscious when it happened. Very slight, but still there, traces of latex were found on his fingers. He'd been fairly impaired by alcohol at the time of the shooting, well above the legal level. It was the opinion there should have been more residue from the gunshot, so homicide was more likely than suicide. But Freddy's hand pulled that trigger. Did someone wearing gloves help him along with that? It was possible.

Cause of death was gunshot wound to the head. Manner of death was officially listed as undetermined by the ME.

But someone had visited the crime scene, or even perhaps revisited it, looking for something.

"What are you thinking?" Jason walked over, his expression speculative. "I don't actually care if he offed himself or not since it isn't our case. I just care about whether he had Janet's ring at this point. I sent Metzger a text asking for that warrant. I highly doubt whoever did all this was looking for it. I think it was more tied to the federal case. Documents or drugs? Or a key to a separate safety deposit box? All possibilities, but I can't see someone caring one way or the other if Freddy got nailed with Janet's murder."

Ellie eyed the unattractive blood spatter on the leather couch. "Except it would exonerate Randy."

Jason slid his hands into his pockets and followed her gaze. "I somehow doubt that would set him free. The feds are hanging on to him with both hands."

"What the hell?" An older man came charging through the front door and looked around furiously at the damage, his jaw so tight a muscle pulsed. He was dressed in knee-length shorts and a salmon-colored golf shirt, and looked a little short on sleep from the redness of his eyes. "How did this happen? I think it is bad enough my son is dead."

Randy's uncle. He certainly had the family features. Ellie wanted to talk to the man anyway, but she wasn't in charge of the scene. Luckily, the police officer who had greeted them had different ideas. "These are two detectives that I have been informed could be investigating something tied to this, so talk to them. All I'm doing is playing guard dog until any prints have been lifted and the neighbors have been interviewed. Sir, if you'd look around to see if you can tell anything is missing after we are done here, we'd appreciate it."

At least Sherwood Forsythe said grimly, "I will."

He turned to them with an assessing gaze. "Don't fault me for not being pleasant. I'm still trying to process. What could be tied to this subhuman crime? No one with a lick of decency robs a dead man."

"Murder." Ellie said it with definitive emphasis. "We are detectives with the homicide division of the Milwaukee Police Department. You do know the cause of your son's death was ruled undetermined."

She left it alone that they weren't officially assigned the case but more in his son's possible involvement in the death of Janet Locke. He responded testily, "I've been told that. How is it possible the investigators can't tell?"

How is it he didn't seem all that shaken by the fact someone might have staged his son's suicide, Ellie thought darkly. She said, "Forensics is a very exact science, but in the case with your son, just as in the case against your nephew in the Locke murder, small factors that aren't easily explained raise questions. Was he depressed? Did he have money troubles or a recently failed relationship?"

Was he somehow aware there was an investigation under way and unwilling to go to prison but pretty sure that might happen? She didn't say that one out loud.

"Freddy didn't get depressed. His relationships tended to be short anyway, because fidelity wasn't in his vocabulary, and though he had his faults, he was really good with money." Forsythe shook his head, his hair well on its way to being all gray, suddenly looking damaged and weary, the anger fading. "As for my nephew, I found that hard to believe as well. Randy was a wild kid, but not really in a bad way. He wouldn't kick a dog."

"Your brother-in-law thinks he's guilty according to everything we've heard."

"Robert Lane Sr. wants things like he wants them. Randy showed a lot of initial promise. Gifted at school and yet irresponsible by not willing to do more than just get by. My sister's husband couldn't handle it. He's very much into control, but Randy was a free spirit if you will. He certainly won't be free now."

Maybe not, but maybe. Jason gestured at the destroyed room. "That giant television is still here, so is what looks like a pretty high tech video game setup, so this doesn't look like an ordinary robbery to me. Any idea what they might have been looking for?"

Mr. Forsythe took a moment to answer as he surveyed the damage, the bitter look returning to his face. "If he was murdered, it wasn't for a petty amount of money. I've picked up his personal belongings. He had four hundred in cash in his wallet and his credit cards. He liked to drink and he liked to gamble. The kind of 'behind closed doors, special invitation only' games where the stakes got high. Maybe Freddy took a bundle off a high roller. They have a long reach."

It was possible, but Ellie wasn't convinced. She wanted to ask if it perhaps had anything to do with the company, but refrained only with effort. She didn't want Metzger in the hot seat because she'd given anything away.

"If you could convince your brother-in-law to talk to us, we'd appreciate it. He doesn't need his lawyer. We'd just like to talk about Randy. We'd appreciate his take on what possibly happened. I'll give you my card."

He took it, but grudgingly. "Robert always wants his lawyer there. He's very careful in business and other aspects of his life. None of us can tell you anything that would help. If we knew, we would—"

He stopped himself with obvious restraint.

"Carry out the old eye for an eye?" That was true Santiago sarcasm in the tone of the question and his eyes held an unrelenting look. "It seems to me people are keeling over in unpleasant ways all over the place. You've lost a son and essentially a nephew if Randy goes to prison, and we've had casualties on our end already too. Think about it. Any special reason the daughter of a U.S. district attorney would be viciously murdered in her own home and the crime pinned on Randy? That weighs on our minds."

When they were back in the car, Jason said tightly, "I

probably said too much, but I'll be damned if I could keep my mouth shut."

"A frequent problem." Ellie didn't really blame him, though. The song and dance was getting to her too. "We should take up spelunking after this. We've been practicing."

"What the hell is that?"

At least the sun was shining and the heat made a shimmer rise from the pavement. "Spelunking is exploring caves with nothing but dim lights usually. I think you usually don't find pirate treasure, but instead a blind fish that resents your presence and maybe a bat or two."

"Sounds about like where we are." The familiar restlessness had set in and he was driving a little too fast, as if it would help him find the solution. "The collision of our case with all this other shit is really getting to me. It is interesting that Forsythe's house was gone over with a baseball bat, and it might help the feds, but it doesn't really help us. I can see why Metzger wanted us to know, because our lead suspect is dead and then his home was burglarized, but it gave me nothing."

Ellie agreed. "My guess is someone heard about the suicide or murder, and decided he had something that would be better off in their care, either worth money, or incriminating."

"My guess is the latter. Forsythe was an asshole, but a smart one."

It took about two seconds flat for Jason to dislike the new chief detective. Andrea Karsten was auburn haired, tall and buxom, and could have been a knockout, but her attitude was absolutely like Fergusson in that she didn't pull punches and had no sense of humor. If she had testicles, he wouldn't have been surprised.

She now had Fergusson's office, so gone were the pictures of his family put neatly in boxes somewhere, since he was still on official medical leave before his retirement, and replaced by various awards and citations issued by the state of Minnesota. She didn't have the untidy scattered piles of paperwork on the desk, but instead just a laptop, and Jason realized as he took a seat in front of the desk that he really had not allowed himself to grieve in any way for a man he did miss.

Grief was not his specialty. If you ignored it, it went away eventually. Maybe Lukens could explain to him if that worked or not. He'd guess she'd say no, but on the other hand, dwelling on a situation you couldn't change wasn't productive, so maybe she'd agree. Toss-up right there.

Detective Andrea Karsten asked in a steely voice, "I'm looking over the cases assigned to homicide and not noticing any progress on yours. I'm not as convinced as Chief Metzger it is worth wasting the time of what I understand are our top two detectives when we have a suspect who has been arraigned on murder charges, but go ahead and change my mind."

Fergusson would have called them out too, so maybe she was just doing a job he wouldn't want in a million years, which involved a desk and endless reports.

Ellie said, "This is a messy case. I feel confident you know that from the reports."

Karsten wasn't very forgiving. "I'm walking into this late, but your mission seems clear enough to me. Find out who killed Janet Locke. So far we need a suspect that hasn't killed himself unless it means he did the crime, or one that is not in federal custody. I fully understand the victim's father is an important man and he doesn't feel like the case is cut and dried against his daughter's fiancé, but looking at this with an objective eye, Mr. Lane will go to trial and a jury will make that decision."

Ellie's voice was calm, as always. "We think we have a new lead, but like everything in this case, it is tricky, and that is not an exaggeration at all."

Jason contributed in a level tone, "Don't you think all the deaths indicate Randy is a possible target, not a criminal who would murder the woman he just asked to marry him that afternoon and then left to pick up food?"

Andrea Karsten said in the same reasonable voice without a hint of conceding the point, "I think that it is very possible a number of scenarios could have played out, but you deal in facts, Lieutenant. I understand you are playing this from the gut, and I've done it myself and tricked myself into thinking something that was straightforward wasn't, and in fact, it was."

Her opinion apparently. Jason didn't agree necessarily in this case. "Tell me why he would wipe off that table and why someone is trying to kill him. Where is Janet's engagement ring? Did someone trash Forsythe's apartment and take it? You've read the reports."

"You tell me why those events are part of the same equation."

He couldn't, that was the hell of it. He laid his cards on the table. "We can't, but that's a *not yet*. Not a throwing up of our hands. They came for Randy, but they got her."

"Possible. What are you going to do now?"

A legitimate question. Luckily, Ellie was up for it. "We aren't done with Freddy Forsythe. Our hands are so tied by the long list of who we can't question it's ridiculous. We certainly can't question him any longer, but we did just talk to his father. What I think we took away from it was that he gave us every indication Randy's father was unlikely to help us, and when you talk to Metzger, be sure and have him let the federal officers know this case is not off the radar. The Forsythe robbery tells us that someone has something to lose a lot more valuable than four hundred dollars and a big-screen television. His house was looted, but they were looking for something other than what you could sell easily on the street."

"Like?"

"We have no idea."

"My job is to give you input on how you are doing on a scale of one to ten. I think you are nailing a solid two."

Well hell.

"That's . . . unfair." Ellie wasn't about to give. "At every turn we find a wall to climb."

"I didn't say this was an easy case, but there's no pay dirt so far."

"But there's dirt."

At least Karsten showed a hint of humor. "Up to your neck in black soil. I'm new here, but my job is to make sure you aren't wasting talent on a done deal. Make or break this soon, and I'm talking soon. I have other cases that could use your attention. So solve this one and move on."

He was all for it. This one was far too dangerous. "Ellie has an interesting theory."

"I'm listening."

"You don't really want to hear it." Ellie shook her head. "Not one shred of proof."

"Then find the proof." Karsten looked at both of

them one at a time. "I understand you are both being reassigned for a certain reason."

"Not entirely my fault I'm so charming." Jason tried to diffuse the moment and gave her his best contrived boyish smile.

It didn't work one bit. "I don't think the word 'charming' came up in the conversation. Chief Metzger believes witches gathered over a cauldron right before he hired you, and I quote. He did say in your defense that though I'll find you a pain in a certain part of my anatomy, you are a good detective. He would have promoted you a long time ago if you didn't continuously fuck up and use your heart, not your brain. That is also a quote. I try to keep profanity to a minimum."

Jason was going to have to mention that one in his next session with Lukens.

Karsten went on. "Okay, this is where we are. You are, Lieutenant Santiago, responsible for this investigation. I have never walked into a situation like this, but my position is pretty clear in my head. Detective MacIntosh isn't asking me for anything special and you don't speak for her, no matter the circumstances. Go forth, both of you, and solve the case."

It was possible he would have said something he'd regret, so instead he left the room. Ellie was right in front of him and grabbed her keys. "Locke left me a message. He agreed to talk to us and has a window here in about twenty minutes."

"Ellie, he's talked to us. Quite a few times now." Jason just didn't see the point. They had nothing to offer the man. "He'd tell us anything. We've been over every inch of ground."

"I have done nothing but think about this. We need

to talk to him again. I have some questions about Lambert and he's the only one to ask."

She seemed to have made up her mind, so Jason threw up his hands in acquiescence and followed her down the hall.

Chapter 20

Torn loyalty just plain sucked.

Randy signed the deposition anyway. He didn't want to be involved in a trial that involved his father, but he wasn't being given a viable choice. Maybe "turncoat" looked good on a résumé.

He really didn't know how much of a betrayal it was to admit he'd seen his estranged parent with certain people, but that did not constitute witnessing a crime, so he just admitted he knew his father met with them.

His house of cards seemed to be wavering in a breeze. Hurricane force winds actually.

Being seen talking to someone was not breaking the law, unless, of course, the person was a wanted criminal, which might bring you under intense scrutiny.

That wasn't enough to bury him as far as Randy knew, but it was certainly enough to tick off the wrong people.

It had weighed so heavily against him that he'd declined the invitation to the party by not accepting his father's offer of a job. His decision not to climb on board with Robert and John made him unpopular—if, to be fair, he hadn't done that all on his own already.

He couldn't decide if Cameron should just say yes or stand his ground.

The former hadn't worked for John, and the latter not so well for him. Either way his younger brother could be in trouble.

It worried him, and he had enough troubles of his own.

Locke was in his office, showing the strain of recent events in the tautness of his face, as if the skin was too tightly stretched, and Ellie had to wonder if he'd slept at all yet. There was a picture of Janet on his desk, obviously her senior high school picture, and she looked young and radiant in a cream-colored top with ruffles on the sleeves and fashionably torn jeans, one arm propped on her knee as she sat on the steps of the federal building. She had no idea if it would be better for him to put it away or if it helped him to look at it every day.

Ellie took the offered chair in front of the desk and sat down, wondering if maybe she was playing a risky hand. However it went, there would be very little happiness on the horizon. To her surprise, Jason also sat down, when he usually preferred to restlessly walk around the room.

"Thanks for the impromptu meeting." Then she took in a breath and said it. "I want to ask a fairly simple question, but this needed to be face to face."

"I gathered that."

"Did you know your daughter was officially engaged?"

Nathan Locke frowned. "I expected it, certainly."

"With all due respect, sir, that was a yes or no question. I don't need a lawyer answer, just a direct one. Did you know? Had she called you?"

"No. She'd call her mother first."

"I'd do that too . . . Um, it brings up an interesting question. When we last spoke, I got the impression you didn't realize it had happened. I'm curious as to why Lambert knew Janet was engaged and you did not."

Locke looked nonplussed for a moment. Then he got it together. "She might tell him before me. I can see her doing that if I was out of the office."

Ellie leaned forward. "Why would she do that?"

"They were involved at one time. They dated for maybe half a year. She might want him to know before he heard it from me."

The stars—they weren't good ones—started to come into alignment.

She needed to play this so right. What she was thinking was pretty grave. "How involved were they? Serious?"

"It seemed so at the time . . . Detective MacIntosh . . . where is this going?"

"Who broke it off?"

Behind her Jason muttered, "Oh Jesus, Ellie. No way—"

Locke cut him off. "She did."

"Was he upset?"

There was a reason Locke was a U.S. district attorney. He certainly wasn't slow on the uptake. He said carefully, "I actually don't know. I'm her father, and in this office we certainly strive for a certain level of professional behavior. If he was angry about it, I'd be the last person he'd tell. Janet did tell her mother he was far too possessive."

"He'd know about the federal investigation too, wouldn't he?"

"Of course. My entire office knows. Are you suggesting he could be the one who murdered Janet?"

She exhaled and took her time. "I'm extremely curious how he knew about her missing ring. The only two people besides Janet who knew she had a ring on her finger were Randy and apparently Michael Lambert. I realize engaged implies a ring but, he *described* it. It *was* antique. You heard him say it."

"We all did." Jason backed her up, looking grim.

"Think about it," Ellie said, pressing her point. "Would your daughter call him and simply say she was engaged because she wanted him to hear it from her, or would she be mean-spirited enough to tell him all about her beautiful antique ring? I can't see it. It has been bothering me all along. Unless you are a cruel person in general, do you say to your former boyfriend it is an expensive opal with garnets around it? Do you use the word 'antique'? No, you don't. I'd even venture to say you don't call him at all. I don't get the impression she was a cruel person."

Silence. She might have just made the mistake of her career, and there had been several of those lately, but she didn't think so in this case.

Locke looked positively like he'd taken a hit he really hadn't seen coming and was sidelined.

It was Jason who said, "The nature of the attack was vicious and Janet opened the door. No forced entry. We've thought all along she knew the person or she wouldn't have let them in. Crime of passion has come up more than once. It was what hung Randy from the beginning. Lambert might have killed those two marshals as well. I assume he could get access to Randy's location."

"Yes. All law enforcement involved is keeping our

office informed, but not through me, through him."
Locke briefly shut his eyes. "No. You have to be wrong."

"We don't want to be right. A nightmare for you, and
it is also a nightmare for us. I'm speculating that Lambert's rage at Janet would be twofold against Randy
Lane. If he could get access to information on where
Randy was being held, then I assume he could walk up
to two federal marshals, produce his identification, and
say he needed to talk to Randy, and shoot them both
dead at point-blank range. I haven't understood that all
along either. They wouldn't let a stranger just walk up."

"No, I doubt they would." Locke's face was set in
grim lines now as he visibly processed.

"Lucky for Randy, he's learned the hard way to watch
his own back and not count on anyone else to do it for
him." Jason was the voice of experience on that aspect
of life, Ellie knew that.

Locke was actually pale now. "I'm not dismissing this
as impossible. I want to, but I can't now, dammit. How
did he know what the ring looked like? Did he use the
power of this office to gain information with intent to
commit murder for personal revenge? I would find
those significant points in presenting a case."

"I think so." She was right. Ellie was sorry, but it was
falling into place. In every way this was a worst-case
scenario. "He took advantage of his position to get back
at Randy Lane because Janet had chosen him instead.
Can we ask for the phone records to see if Janet ever
called Lambert? Either at his office or on his cell? If she
didn't, he was stalking her that afternoon. I only believe
that because the window is so short. Randy left and the
killer went in. I think he killed her and tore off that ring,
and left. Blood inside his car wouldn't hurt either. Can
we get a warrant for that?"

"Yes. I think I can get a judge—or two, or six—to sign for it."

"Let's see if he's smarter than we are." Ellie firmly believed she was on the right track. "Don't tip him off. I'm being serious, sir. Do not confront or question him."

"Like I would compromise a case."

He would. It was there in his face. She might too, in his place.

Luckily, she had Jason right with her, which was a good/bad thing in this instance. He said with vehemence, "Yeah, right. I'd do it. I'd have him backed up against a wall, my hands around his throat, but just listen to Ellie and not me. You represent justice. Let it do its thing. I wouldn't cry over his disappearance from this earth, but your wife might when you were arrested for murder even if she wanted the same vengeance. She's lost enough. We haven't proven a damn thing yet. I want to know we got the right bastard, not start all over again."

Great advice. And Metzger wanted *her* to always do the talking.

Jason was pretty good at it too, now and then.

Ellie agreed. "Okay, let's see if he has blood in his car or that ring in his possession. Either one will win this."

"He's far too smart to keep the ring."

"If smart killers didn't occasionally slip up, we wouldn't catch them. If Lambert hasn't slipped he'd still better concede we have reasonable cause. In our shoes, he'd recommend a full investigation." Ellie almost hated to ask it, but she did anyway. "Does he know where your family is right now? I can't think of any reason he'd need to harm them, but your wife would probably open the door for him just like Janet did if we are correct."

"Oh God, he does. I'll call my wife right away." Then

he gave an almost chilling smile that had nothing to do with humor. "That would be his final mistake if he showed up there. That woman has a .38 and she is one hell of a good shot."

Locke reached for his phone. "I'll get those warrants right now. I also think I'll cancel my lunch meeting with Michael. For some reason, I don't think I'm hungry any longer."

"You seem pretty convinced," Jason admitted as they left the parking lot. "I was a little blindsided. No wonder you insisted we talk to Locke again."

Ellie did know what she was doing. She looked resolute. "It was the sum of the parts. That missing ring Mrs. Lane described to us, the fact Hammett seemed convinced it wasn't a professional hit but rage was involved, that he had access to what was going on with where Randy might be . . . And think about it, Lambert wanted to know what we knew when we met the last time. He grilled us."

He had.

When he looked back on it, Jason was maybe not quite as convinced, but he was coming around. "When we arrive with a search warrant, he'll get what we know and don't know. Tracing that murder weapon is impossible for the marshal hits. No luck there. He'd have dumped it."

"We could try witnesses again. No one saw him running away, no one saw the murder, but maybe someone did see him near Janet's house. A nicely dressed man walking past might not seem like someone connected to a murder, but a picture of him could nudge their memory."

"Why would he ever murder Forsythe?"

"The suicide, if it was suicide, could be unrelated to Janet." Ellie stopped. "I don't think the undercover operation is all that secret any longer or there wouldn't be a dead operative and John Lane wouldn't have gone AWOL. The two marshals and Janet Locke however, I believe are linked. Think about it. That person wanted Randy."

"He seems to be a popular guy right now."

"That's fine if you are a rock star, but not if it means there's a bunch of hungry tigers out there that want to eat you alive. By the way, I want to pick up a slice of pizza for lunch."

He could have sworn he'd never get tired of it, but anything was possible. It was her pregnancy craving of choice and he was locked into it. At least it wasn't sushi. "Again?"

"You can't doubt this is your child, now can you? I'll eat it at my desk. I want those phone records right away, but even more so those warrants."

"I'm fairly sure Locke is on it. I want this wound up right and tight as soon as possible myself. What angle are we talking about, because right now this thing has more angles than one of those weird Picasso paintings. I've never thought that was art, by the way."

"Why am I not surprised? Though I have to admit I prefer a nice impressionist scene." Ellie looked out the window, but he could tell she was thinking, not seeing anything. "I wonder if somehow Forsythe figured out Lambert killed Janet and was foolish enough to try to blackmail him. Everyone says how smart he was even if they didn't like him, so maybe he knew about the investigation and decided to exchange immunity for keeping his mouth shut about Janet's murder."

"Ellie, how would he figure that out?"

"*We* did."

"We *think* so, and it was by a chance comment. A slip I hope he doesn't realize he made. Damn, I'm glad Locke was sitting right there and heard it too. Now we just have to find some sort of evidence. Our problem is Lambert is a lawyer, and no one would know how to cover their tracks like he would. Plastic bags over the seat of his car, leave the murder weapon without any prints on it behind, burning his clothes maybe, drop the bloody gloves in a public trash can . . . If anyone could cover their tracks, he could."

Ellie's eyes held a determined look when he glanced over. "I have two things to say to that. The first is that he already has made a mistake in front of two detectives and the victim's father. The second is that it might have been coldly calculated, but he was not cool and calm when he killed Janet Locke. It was savage, according to the autopsy opinion and the photographs I saw, and I doubt he thought of everything."

His phone rang and he had to pull over next to a barber shop when he saw the number. He'd switch over to hands-free, but he had a feeling they'd be changing directions anyway. "Got to get this."

Metzger said, "I just had a federal judge call a local judge and you now have a warrant to investigate one of their own. No one sounds happy, including me. That had better be one hell of a lead, Santiago."

It was tempting to point out the chief rarely sounded happy, but Jason managed to refrain. He was still astonished by his promotion.

"Locke thinks so. We just came from a meeting with him."

"He apparently does since he's throwing his weight around. Why is it when you and MacIntosh get involved in an investigation it always turns out to be my headache? You'd better find something solid. Keep Karsten in the loop."

End of call.

Jason switched off his phone and said sarcastically, "Good-bye, honey. I love you too."

"What did Metzger have to say?"

"We already have our warrants, thanks to Locke."

"That was lightning fast."

"Metzger basically said to not screw this up."

Ellie just lifted her brows. "I wasn't planning on it anyway, so that was wasted advice. Whoever committed the murder, I want them to go down for it. I guess lunch at my desk is now not an option."

"Let's go. You can eat your pizza in the car while the techs do their work."

Chapter 21

Midafternoon on a clear summer day and no bright sunshine in his future.

It was almost worse than jail to find out his court date was so many months away. Randy asked tautly, "Do they do this on purpose as some form of torture? Just try me, convict me, or acquit me, but don't make me wait. This is like an anvil over my head hanging by a thread. Let's just get it over with."

His lawyer had obviously heard the objection before. "They have to select the jury, there are other cases on the docket, and it will be high profile, so the court is being careful about how they handle it."

"I've cooperated."

"That's a different case. You and I are together on the murder and that's it. The federal case is out of my hands."

Randy stared at the computer screen and tried to stay calm. "They can't expect me to live like this for that long."

"The problem is they can. The government of the

United States needs you alive to testify, and I assume you want to stay alive, so they are in control."

He was bitter, no doubt about it. "I didn't kill anyone, much less Jan, and I haven't done anything except recognize some of my father's business associates. Do you understand how frustrating this is for me?"

"Oh, I do. I once represented a man who stabbed a coworker over twenty times and then went and used his ATM card. He got off. I was appalled. No charges. I couldn't believe it. When he was adamant about pleading not guilty, I urged him to think about asking for lesser charges but never dreamed he was right, and I was wrong. I thought he'd be convicted in five minutes. We have the finest court system in the world in my opinion, but there are hiccups here and there. That trial dragged on and on. My point is you'll get your day. And I will do my best."

Randy couldn't help but ask, "How did you feel about getting a guilty man off on a murder charge?"

His lawyer said quietly, "Like shit, if you want the truth. But if I got you off, I'd feel like I won the lottery. I'm not going to lie to you. This won't be an easy trial."

Lambert's car might give them needed evidence, but it wasn't there at the federal building. They had gotten a warrant for his home as well—thanks to Locke—and that was next. They'd stopped by to make sure they had all the official documents in hand because one slip and Lambert would have leverage.

"Lambert isn't on the grid." Jason slapped down the first piece of paper onto her desk. "Not answering his phone, and I'm going to bet not at his home either. No one can reach him."

She hadn't really imagined it would fly right by someone so closely connected to the U.S. Attorney's Office. "So he's running? That's evidence right there."

"Or postponing and cleaning house."

"Maybe. Shall we go? I got the phone records. She didn't call him or call the office. He didn't know about the engagement that way. Or the ring. We can at least bring him in."

"Grasso and I could handle this."

He was really starting to get on her nerves. *What?* No way. Ellie stood up and took out her badge and leaned forward. "Do you see this, Lieutenant? I'm an officer in the Homicide Division of the Milwaukee Police Department. This is my case and you are still my partner. Let's go."

"Dammit, Ellie, he's dangerous—"

"They all are. Let's go." She stalked out the door.

No quarter given, but they'd canvased that ground before. He followed, but stubbornly insisted on opening her car door and took the liberty of helping her in. In response to her glare he just said, "Protecting my kid. Cut me some slack. If you fell down on my watch, I'd never get past it. I'm looking out for me and I'm pretty good at that. If I can protect you and that baby in the cocoon, I will do whatever it takes."

She didn't want to, but independence was hard to give up. It was a lesson she was learning by a choice she'd made, but not necessarily an easy one. "I'm not going to fall down."

"Like I'd ever forgive myself if anything happened to either one of you." He didn't give either. "Please fasten your seat belt."

That she could do. For him and her child, and she was working through it all, but she certainly understood. He had no choice but to stand back, and she had no choice but to let him handle it his way.

She took in a breath and said tersely, "I was going to because I always do. You *do* realize I'll do anything to protect this baby also."

"Sure I do. Right back at you. I think you just made my point." He shut her door.

When he got in she mused out loud, "What is Lambert doing?"

"I'm betting he's off somewhere taking a dirt nap."

That set her back. "What?"

Jason deftly negotiated several lanes of traffic in a not strictly legal move to get on the road. "He's dead if I had to bet on it. In a grave or ready for one."

"Locke?"

"Who else? We fingered him. So he's dead. Yes, Locke. He wanted us to find the killer for a reason. I think my 'let justice prevail speech,' while you must admit was eloquent, fell on deaf ears."

"I don't have to admit anything except utter shock at hearing you just use the word 'eloquent.'"

He ignored that sarcastic observation. "Think about the sequence of events. Lambert knows what is going on now, but Locke knows more. I guess I should have said Lambert knew. Past tense. I bet they had that lunch after all as Lambert's last meal."

That would be a mess neither of them would want to tackle. She liked Locke, and the man had her respect.

Please no.

It *was* possible. She waited to respond as she sorted through it. "You do realize you are jumping to conclusions just because Lambert isn't answering his phone."

"We were there for Locke's true purpose, which was vigilante justice. We did it too. Never allowed to have access to the main investigation? A game changer there. He wanted us to succeed, don't get me wrong, but he doesn't care nearly as much about the rest of it. A man with a purpose who is as smart as Locke, and as angry, isn't going to let this go."

Ellie found though she was dismayed she couldn't really disagree. "We got the phone records, but I bet he looked at them first, saw there was no call, and immediately came to the conclusion we were right when we pinned down Lambert. She was taking a nap while Randy went out for food. Lambert knocked on the door; she never expected his obsession was so deep he'd kill her, so she opened it."

"You're the one who has been hung up on that all along."

"You're a male. A tall, strong male. Women are taught almost from the cradle to be careful about whom we trust, because we can't defend ourselves on an equal level. I maintain she knew whoever killed her."

"I agree Lambert is probably our guy, but beside the phone record and what he said in front of three witnesses, we have nothing solid going on. All he'd have to do is cast reasonable doubt by concocting a story saying he stopped by her house to return something she'd left in his car when they were dating, or something like that, and he saw the ring. That he never mentioned that to us would hold some clout, but we have just strong suspicion and no evidence right now, not to mention we can't find him."

"This puts us in a really bad position."

Jason didn't argue that. "Locke will know we know. Shit, when I got up this morning I just wanted to have a cup of coffee and a nice day. I skip the news because of crap like this."

"Get over yourself. We work homicide. There's no such thing as a nice day. Let me think about this. We don't really know Lambert is suddenly missing. For all we know he had a haircut scheduled. Tea with his grandmother on the to-do-today list."

But he wasn't in court. That she could check and had done it already. Lambert hadn't showed up for a scheduled hearing.

This was literally the last thing she wanted. "We are supposed to pursue cases assigned to us."

"Yes, we are. Let's hope we find Lambert sipping out of a porcelain cup with his grandma, but I'm going to guess he's long gone."

"I'm not agreeing or disagreeing what might have happened, but what are we going to do?"

"Try to find Lambert. I'd bet we never do. Locke has had time to think about it."

Ellie argued, "He has to know we'd know."

Jason said in response, "He has to know we'd *suspect*. We don't *know* a thing."

"How can we possibly pursue a federal attorney on a murder charge when I don't actually want to do it, and I'm talking Locke here, not Lambert."

"Coming face to face with your conscience is a look in the mirror none of us want to experience."

That actually *was* pretty eloquent.

"By the letter of the law," she pointed out, "we aren't allowed to."

Jason didn't argue, and arguing was his specialty. "That's where it gets dicey occasionally. Let's go search Lambert's house."

Lambert wasn't at home, wasn't at the courthouse, and he certainly hadn't used his passport, because they found it neatly tucked into a drawer when they searched his townhouse. The only thing even vaguely incriminating was a framed picture of him and Janet Locke on his dresser in the master bedroom. They were sitting in an outside café in the photograph, both smiling for the camera and lifting their drinks in a toast.

Jason liked being right, but he didn't like it this way. "The picture isn't even admissible evidence of a thing. He dated her and that is no secret. The fact he kept it means zero except maybe he was a sentimental guy."

"His car isn't in the garage. For all we know he could be in Minot." Ellie peeled off a glove and looked unhappy.

"Minot? Why North Dakota?"

"Seems like a good choice. I think their weather might be worse than ours. No one would want to go there to look for you. If I run, I'm going there. Except for all I know it's charming and has great real estate taxes."

"Ellie, it really seems to me he didn't take anything if he ran. We found his checkbook in his desk, but that doesn't mean much in this day and age, since no one really uses one anymore." He surveyed the living room again: leather couch, nice television, recliner, even a set of coasters on the coffee table. If Lambert had blood in his car, he definitely would have cleaned it up. Even his bed had been neatly made when they searched the bedroom.

"For all we know, he had a stash of money for just this occasion. The balance in the checkbook said $120.13. That seems a little low. We can trace his debit card and credit cards, but who knows."

"He's a public servant. We get shit compared to the private sector." Jason was with her, though—all possibilities needed to be considered. "Maybe he'd just paid his mortgage."

"Electric bill. I looked at the register. I don't think he planned on abruptly leaving town."

"His car is missing." Jason couldn't help but point it out. "Maybe he did just leave."

"Maybe he left because Locke confronted him, or worse yet, he isn't gone voluntarily."

This was off the wall, but only a little. Jason didn't even want to say it. "We mentioned Forsythe as a suspect before he was killed."

"No." Ellie reacted like he thought she might. "No."

He didn't want to play this card, but he had haunted his living room the night before this all started to snowball, thinking about it. "We told our suspicions about Forsythe to Grasso, who probably told Locke because he's overseeing this case. Fosythe died. That selfish asshole never killed himself. We both know it."

"That doesn't mean Locke killed him."

"We both like Locke. He's fair and straightforward as an attorney. But we both also understand more than ever his anguish in our current situation of expecting a child. He really might have done this. I believe in the guy's integrity, but I am worried about the father in him."

"You are worried about the father in *you*."

Fair enough. He acquiesced. "Fine. Where's Lambert then?"

"His parents live in Janesville. It's always the place to start. I never like to do it, but we have to make that call."

"I'll follow orders for once and let you do it."

She shot him a look. "Thanks a lot."

He wasn't positive it was the right time to say this, but he did anyway. "The sellers countered on our house. I just got a text." Using the word "our" was sticking his neck out, but he had a habit of doing that. "I'm going to take it."

"Congratulations."

She did smile. That was something positive in a less-than-positive situation. Then she added, "Let's find Lambert."

He had no confidence they ever would.

Two seconds later his phone rang. He said curtly, "Santiago."

"I just got a call from the state police. It looks like Michael Lambert is gone. His car was found sitting on a county road but not wrecked, just there abandoned. Not even a flat tire." It was Grasso.

"Signs of a struggle?"

"Not according to them. They were worried about foul play because the keys were still in it. They called central dispatch to ask if a vehicle had been reported stolen, and the information filtered over to me because of the name of the owner and the warrants. We are right now testing his vehicle for blood. I sent out a forensic team. If he did kill Janet Locke, we should be able to determine that. Where he is? Different story. That's your problem at the moment."

"That's an understatement," Jason muttered, thinking about their current dilemma. "Thanks. Can you text me the location?"

"Already done. Keep Karsten up on it. She's really all over this. She's definitely not my type as a woman, but so far I like her on a professional level."

"I heard your side," Ellie told him when he ended the call. "They've got his car. Let's go."

It wasn't too far outside of the city, in a small rural area bordered by trees and brush with a meandering creek, and the forensics team was still there wrapping it up, along with a tow truck. Heat shimmered up from the pavement.

"Blood in the vehicle," the state police officer said as they walked up and he offered his hand. "Officer

Kismeade. Since you are MPD homicide, I'm going to guess you aren't surprised."

"We aren't surprised, but will be certainly interested in the report from forensics." Ellie sounded her usual calm, collected self. "We are going to start looking around."

"We went over the area, but I always think another survey doesn't hurt. We found nothing. Not a button, not a weapon, and not even a viable footprint. Any trampled grass is probably from our search, because we thought maybe an impaired driver had parked and run, but then one quick call and his license number popped up with a warrant issued. Unfortunately Mr. Lambert appears to have vanished. He has a nice car. I wouldn't just leave it behind, so my input is either he's getting away from a situation that might hold him accountable, or someone found him accountable and put an end to that question."

Jason was inclined toward the latter, but that didn't mean he could prove it.

They walked the woods for an hour, but he knew they wouldn't find anything. Locke was far too intelligent—if that was what had happened.

Jason was more and more certain they'd come up against their most formidable opponent ever, and they were going to lose. It was one thing to track down a criminal without a law enforcement background, but something else altogether to fight someone on their own turf.

He watched his step as he walked through the long grass of the meadow closest to where they found the car, because he was definitely uninterested in stepping on a snake. "We won't solve this. I always think we will, but not this time. In short, we're screwed. Locke is going to win."

"We don't know that Lambert didn't just call a friend, claim he was having car trouble or something, got picked up, abandoned his car, and like John Lane, disappeared. It's been done before. If he had cash stored, it could be a possibility."

"I'm going to bet his parents haven't heard from him. No activity on his cell. Just tree frogs singing in the background."

"I thought that was crickets chirping, but I'm going to call that bet and raise you. I'm won over to your side and wager that they won't hear from him ever again, either way." Ellie looked somber. "The blood in his car is either Janet's or his."

"Or maybe both."

"Forensics will be able to give us an analysis. He's been gone only a day."

"Locke is too careful for that." He walked next to her back to the road and saw the tow truck was pulling away. "This is how it's going to play out. That's Janet's blood in the car, and Lambert *is* a goner, one way or the other. We'll search airline passenger lists and monitor his credit cards and nothing will show up like a car rental, or even a bus ticket. He won't even have bought a tricycle so he could motor his way out of our lovely state. No trace."

"That's a nice visual image. A murderer on a tricycle? Let's make that into an animated movie. You've found your true calling." Her tone was dry.

"I'm a pretty creative guy. So . . . ideas?"

"I absolutely hate to do this, but we need to check out where Locke has been since we walked out of his office. I'm hoping he can account for every single minute."

"I hate to agree as much you hate to do it, but I do."

Chapter 22

Another boring evening.

Agent Campbell was a formidable adversary.

Randy was allowed outside so he could at least get some measure of exercise, but they'd taken away his shoes and given him instead some slip-on footgear he would never have chosen in a thousand years, but the pair didn't have laces, so theoretically he couldn't hang himself. They'd also taken out the reading lamp in his bedroom, so he was stuck with the overhead light, and though they'd provided books and a game system so he could entertain himself, all questions were met with a stone wall.

Across the chessboard Campbell looked as stoic as ever.

Randy still tried. "Do you like what you do?"

Campbell's answer: "When this is all over, do you think you'll like what you do?"

Question for a question. Typical.

"Not sit in a prison cell. I'd planned on marrying Janet after I finished school, and maybe buying a nice little house to raise our kids. That dream is gone. Do you have kids?"

Campbell moved a rook and took off a bishop. "I don't think necessarily that dream is gone, I think it has changed. Life constantly throws us curveballs and you have to field them. Everyone is sorry about Janet Locke's murder, but your life isn't over. You're a young man. What is it you'd like to do?"

Question for a question. Two could play that game. "Did you think about law enforcement from the beginning?"

"You do realize I'm one move from taking off your queen."

He hadn't, and hastily moved Her Majesty out of harm's way. Playing chess with Campbell had proved to probably help his game, which was a bonus, and he enjoyed it, but he'd never even come close to winning. Their first game he'd been annihilated, though, so he was getting better and learning along the journey. At least he'd lasted close to a half an hour this time.

He persisted. "Did you?"

"No, I have a degree in medicine. Checkmate."

Campbell swept off his king, so bad move on his part. Randy persisted, "You're a doctor?"

No direct response from his opponent. "Another game?"

"Why did you decide to do something else?"

"We all need a calling, son. I'm much better at catching bad guys."

"I can hand you the person that killed that agent, Reid, that talked to the detectives."

That was his checkmate.

* * *

Ellie couldn't decide if she was elated or that they were just stopped at every turn. "He has in place an alibi we could never contest. Locke was standing before a judge and jury all afternoon when Lambert went off the charts. Not our guy. Locke has literally dozens of people who can account for his presence in that courtroom and had dinner with his aunt and uncle and armed his alarm for at home mode in the correct time frame for returning from their address."

"As neat and solid as a bulletproof vest." Jason took it in and regrouped as he sat down in the chair by her desk. He was good at that. Nothing stopped him for long. That was one of the reasons she liked working with him. He hit a brick wall, and then climbed over it. "All right then, we were wrong. I know this will astound you, but I've actually been wrong before."

"It astounds me to hear you admit it. That's about as good as you saying 'eloquent.'"

Sarcasm never bothered him. "So Lambert ran."

She wasn't as sure. "I don't know he did. We have one of two scenarios. He ran with the help of a friend or a kindly passerby he sold on the story of car trouble and persuaded them to drop him off somewhere, or else we need to consider somehow the connection to the Lane investigation is involved."

Neither one felt right, though. Jason said, "It's the timeline. Lambert had to be tipped off somehow. Maybe it is as simple as us meeting with Locke and not inviting him in for the conversation. I know if I'd murdered someone that I'd be nervous about that. Maybe he figured out he made the slipup about the ring."

That *was* possible. Lambert was an intelligent man. "Maybe."

"So pick up the phone and call his parents."

Ellie really wanted that cup of coffee she'd sworn off because she decided to be as much of an angel as possible during this pregnancy. "One step ahead of you as usual. I've already done that. They've heard nothing from their son."

"Why did I know that response was coming?"

"Because we both did. If he's running, he's not going to tell them, and if he's dead he can't tell them. They were extremely set aback at the notion he might be missing, as you would be as a parent, and quite confused as to my call since I said Milwaukee Homicide, because they asked me just what kind of detective after I identified myself."

"I bet they hung up from you and contacted Locke."

"I do too." Ellie didn't envy either one of them that conversation. "In their shoes I'd like to know why MPD was inquiring about my son and I wasn't evasive to any direct questions, but since we don't know anything conclusive, I didn't have much to say. All I wanted was an answer to the question 'Do you know where he is?'"

"And it appears you got a big, fat no."

"That's correct."

Jason shrugged. "It's still information. Unless they are talented liars, I think you'd have sensed from their tone if he was sitting there at the moment on their living room couch, munching on a chocolate chip cookie. So we still have nothing except that Lambert is gone off to parts unknown and he isn't driving his vehicle."

"That's a disheartening summary of the truth."

"I'm not sure where to go."

She'd been thinking about it. Ellie really didn't want to say it. She didn't want to do it at all.

"How do you feel about a trip up north?"

He got it at once. "To see Locke's *wife?*"

"Girls talk to their mothers. Maybe Janet told hers something about Lambert that might clue us in on where he's gone. That is if he did run."

"Do you think for a minute that interview would do us any good? She's a lawyer. She's not going to tell us anything. The minute she realizes why we are asking, she's going to clam up."

"I think she'll want to help us if we can pin this directly on Lambert, and in person might be the best way to handle it."

"Someone help us? In this case, that would be a miracle," he said with open cynicism. "Sign me up for your optimistic class. I could use a refresher course."

That point was hard to argue.

"I don't know. Let's go find out what she has to say."

"It's a decent drive there and back. You think this is worth it?"

"I do."

"Locke would know we'd suspect him if Lambert vanished. It is possible he kept that lunch appointment after all, killed Lambert, disposed of the body, and later moved his car to make it seem like his victim decided it was a smart move to leave town."

It was possible. Anything was possible.

He had to add, "Are we having a girl? I know you went to the doctor last week."

She turned to stare at him. "Where did *that* come from?"

"Girls talk to their mothers?"

"Well, they do. I've always talked to mine anyway."

"Ellie, come on."

She exhaled, knowing this conversation was coming eventually and now it was here. "I've asked to not be told. You are going to have to wait right along with me. I don't know if it is a girl or a boy. You can paint the nursery yellow or a soft green or something. Or I suppose you can ask the doctor yourself, but don't tell me. I want to be surprised."

"I've never painted a room in my life, but I'm willing to give it a try. *You* are going to have to define what you consider soft green, though. I have zero idea what that might be. I can be surprised too. I get you don't want to be pushed, and I also get we are both cautious, but if you think telling someone I love them comes easily for me, think again."

"I do know that," she confessed after a moment.

"Lukens would tell us we don't have a cookie-cutter life and should not buy a house in a nice friendly neighborhood, but instead live in a houseboat anchored on the Great Barrier Reef or something like that. Nope, not an option. Toss a ball to a dog and a shark eats him."

"Soft green paint aside, I'm sure you can understand how important it is for us to talk to Janet's mother face to face."

Jason was Jason. He said with equanimity, "Oh yeah, that'll be fun. Your daughter was murdered and we think maybe you plotted with your husband to murder her killer. That's going to fly really well."

"I never said that's what I think." What she thought was a variation on that theme. It was evolving, but it was there. Nathan Locke didn't do it. Hands down.

"But it *is* what you're thinking, right?"

"I need to see her face when we question her," Ellie informed him, because it was true. It seemed like if nothing else in her life went as planned, she could count on being able to read a witness. She would never compose a symphony or have the slightest idea how to run a Fortune 500 company, but one special talent she had was she could tell when someone was lying to her.

"Then you and I think alike."

"Well, that scares me."

"It should." He didn't blink.

"Can I sleep the whole way? The fatigue is much better, but with or without a baby, this case would make me tired. I'm almost trying not to solve it if that makes sense. If it was Forsythe and now he's gone, I think I can live with that. Where's Lambert? I have a very unwanted need to find out, and am afraid we're going to figure it out."

"We're supposed to, remember?"

"I think I have and I don't want to admit it even to myself."

Jason said, "I don't mind driving. Sleep on it."

"That's music to my ears."

Ellie drifted off so easily he almost envied her. Normally Jason would be on edge for hours, but he had a feeling her exhaustion took a different turn. It was an emotional reaction that did not address the homicide detective, but the woman, and she couldn't do much more than shut down now and then.

So he thought it over too.

If Locke called his wife and he set it up, she could easily make the drive to dispose of the body while he was in court. Between the two of them they could park the car and walk away.

Possible.

In any other partnership he'd been convinced he was the brains and not just the brawn, but not in this one. Her intuition was spot on. Ellie didn't work alone, but the thoughts seemed to flow through her.

She didn't just catch criminals, she dissected their psyche in her process, which was not his forte.

His angle was easier. He didn't care about why. He

cared about how. If he could explain that, he was satisfied.

He could envision Locke immediately calling his wife once they left his office, because who else would you call first, and she had time and motive to be an accessory to hunt down Lambert.

Ellie mumbled something in her sleep and he smiled, despite why they were headed north.

No car, and no answer to the knock on the door, so Ellie used her spare key.

The house looked perfectly normal—and deserted.

Woods and warm sunlight filtering through the leaves, the same familiar surroundings, the stone steps . . . and no one home.

Not a good sign. Ellie had woken up much more energized after her little respite right after they crossed the Wisconsin River bridge outside of Wausau. It was home territory and she was in place, but she hadn't expected this.

"They're gone?"

The house was clean, but silent. Jason tossed in his opinion. "Rapid departure with milk left I would still drink in the refrigerator. My standards are kind of low for dairy products, so who knows, but they left in a hurry. No suitcases, nothing personal to indicate they'd been here at all."

"You'd drink that milk?" At least they hadn't left her a mess. It was almost too neat.

"I might in a pinch."

"They packed up and left pretty abruptly then."

"I'm thinking you're dead right on that one. They even took the rat dog and her food."

Since she'd done them a favor, it was hard to process

how she felt about it. "I think they had a plan. Locke used us."

"From the beginning?"

"The minute they knew she was murdered they knew Lambert was the one. Had he been bothering her?" Ellie slowly surveyed her living room, just thinking out loud. Jason was right. No doggie bowl in sight. "Why didn't they tell us they suspected Lambert? Locke was pretty certain from the beginning it wasn't Randy Lane. I thought all along that conviction wasn't necessarily off, but maybe would not be how I would react to the situation."

"Because they wanted to kill whoever killed their daughter." Jason immediately chose her father's old worn chair and flopped down. "Here's a tip: Telling detectives you want to kill someone isn't wise."

"I'm not positive they killed him."

"But you aren't positive they didn't either."

"There are a lot of things I'm not positive about in this world. Whales beach themselves? To what purpose? I've never understood it and am still not positive why they do it, even though I've watched an entire documentary on it."

"I don't know about the whales either, but I think we've got a very real moral dilemma here. Lambert was an unstable dirtbag apparently. The minute we come up with solid evidence he might have committed the crime, he's gone, and probably because of us."

Ellie didn't argue. "I think Locke asked for us because he knew we'd figure it out eventually. He had more faith in us than I do, but we did our best. If I am responsible in any way for the murder of Michael Lambert, I don't feel culpable. I *know* Lambert killed Janet, because otherwise he just couldn't know about her ring unless he saw it on her finger, and there was no phone call.

Those two federal officers . . . they could be fallout from the federal case, but I think Lambert killed them as well to try to get to Randy. As for Forsythe, I now am back in the camp that maybe his death had nothing to do with our case."

"We'll let Campbell and his friends handle that one. I'm not losing sleep over Forsythe. Manner of death was undetermined, so we aren't officially involved anyway."

"How will we handle *our* case?"

They sat and looked at each other. Moral dilemma was exactly right. "I somehow don't think Karsten is going to let us just walk away with the explanation that we came to the conclusion that the murderer was Lambert but, oops, we've misplaced him. Why am I sure he's at the bottom of a lake somewhere? We could put forth our theory Locke and his wife are maybe behind it, but I don't know how we'd ever prove it, and I don't want to anyway."

"But if Lambert is running—"

"Then I want to track him down and shoot him like I would a rabid dog." Jason was not shy about his opinion. "I saw the pictures of Janet Locke's body."

Ellie didn't disagree. "Maybe someone took care of that for you."

"Say they did. Then what? Do we pursue it?"

She hated that idea. "I don't know. We are supposed to uphold the laws of this state. If someone killed him we are bound to find out if that is true. On the other hand, maybe it is a service to the people if we just don't push it. My stand is if we can't find evidence that he ran besides his abandoned car, we let it go. But let's try hard to find that. If he has disappeared voluntarily, I don't want him loose out there."

Jason didn't say anything for a minute, but then agreed. "Okay then. We look for Lambert because he is a decided person of interest in a homicide investigation and leave the rest of it alone."

"I think that will work for everyone."

"Are you going to tell Grasso? We know where Locke is. His wife left and I bet she has an alibi as tight as his. She full well knows we'll add this up. She's at home, grateful we pinpointed the killer, and taking care of Randy's little dog. That my solid guess."

"I might tell Grasso, but only if he asks. He's been in this since the beginning."

"I so fucking hate this." Jason really looked like he did hate it. "I don't care about being promoted in rank half as much as I hate the idea of not working with you. We solved this case. Well, no, you did. I came along and swept up the pieces."

"Where are you depositing those pieces?"

"In Locke's lap."

"He doesn't deserve it."

"Oh hell yes he does if he set us up."

I think we are about to agree to disagree."

Chapter 23

It was a pretty morning and the skies got even bluer.

"The murder charges have been dropped."

Randy about fell out of his chair. "What did you just say? I'm free?"

Special Agent Campbell nodded. "Essentially. You might still be called on to testify in court, but I'd say of your current list of problems, the biggest one has gone away. If the court needs more clarification we will be in touch."

That was absolutely not true. On his list of problems, Janet being gone was number one, but this was certainly number two. He wanted to fall to his knees and kiss the ground.

"I would ask why, but I know I'm innocent." He asked, "Are you serious? I can't believe this. I don't dare to believe it."

"Yes, I'm serious, but you aren't quite off the hook, son. There are two detectives outside that will give you a ride. I think you may have met them once or twice. You might want to thank them, by the way." Campbell almost smiled. "Your wound will heal up. None of us emerge from life without some battle scars."

He had, actually, efficiently checked them daily until the stitches dissolved completely, but knew Campbell wasn't talking about the physical damage. Randy figured not everyone had an experience where a federal agent was able to guard them, treat them, and also teach them how to play chess. He knew Campbell had quickly become a sort of father figure, mainly because his own father just wasn't there for him, but he liked the man.

"I'm still bleeding inside," he said quietly, "but I get what you're saying.

"They solved the case? Who killed Jan?"

Campbell said, "Just go. You can ask them all the questions you'd like to on your way home. I get the impression they have questions for you."

Home. His cheap apartment sounded like heaven. Randy was grateful on about a thousand levels, but mostly that Janet hadn't been ignored. He'd never unpacked and he had almost nothing, so he was ready to go. He tossed a few things into a bag and walked out the door. They were there. Tall blond guy and slender blond woman, and he wanted to hug them both.

MacIntosh headed him right off that track. "Hop in the car. We're driving you back to Milwaukee, but this isn't a dream trip."

"I don't have any dreams left, so you won't disappoint me."

"We want you to tell us about Michael Lambert."

He settled in and fastened his seat belt, which told him he valued his life more than he had in what felt like a lifetime. Santiago was driving this time and Randy was talking to MacIntosh.

Lambert. That was not his favorite name, but Randy had just been released from a possible life sentence behind bars. "He was a jerk and Jan figured it out fairly quickly. But an arrogant jerk can be a smart arrogant jerk and he really played her. Why?"

"Whatever you can tell us, we're listening."

All elation faded. He felt the blood drain from his face as he realized what was going on. "*He* killed her? Tell me he's sitting in a jail cell and enjoying it as much as I did."

MacIntosh said, "We don't know where he is and were hoping you might help us out."

It was difficult to figure out how to question Randy Lane and not give away they suspected anything about Locke and his wife. The phrase "obstruction of justice" came to Ellie's mind. This had to be handled perfectly, and perfection seemed to be an elusive mirage shimmering in the middle of a Wisconsin summer.

We want to find his body.

That didn't work.

"Can you think of where he might go?" Ellie tried to keep it neutral. "We really need anything you can offer us."

"Oh God." Randy bent over and put his head in his hands. Ellie was concerned he might pass out he'd gone so pale. "I so wish I didn't believe he killed her, but maybe he is capable of it. She broke up with him because he was borderline obsessed with her."

That border had been crossed.

"Give us a where." Jason was always straight to the point. "Anything."

"How would I know? We weren't exactly the best of friends. I'm trying . . . give me a second . . . that bastard. That *bastard*. He just wouldn't leave her alone. But why that? How could he?"

"That we can't explain. We can't explain why any violent crime happens. But we would certainly like to be able to ask him the question. Go through it for us. What did she say about their relationship? Obviously she'd mentioned it to you." Ellie could hear the distress in his hoarse voice, and she was sympathetic to it, but time was an issue. "Just talk me through it. You talk and we'll listen."

"Okay . . . okay." He caught his breath. "Let's start with him constantly calling her until she blocked him after they broke up. She thought he might be following her around too."

"Why?"

"She'd see him in odd places. Like running into him when she went out with her friends for a drink, or even putting gas in her car. It could be all coincidence, but she didn't think so."

"Did she get a restraining order?"

"No, she was too nice for that. It would impact his job. All she wanted was to forget the whole thing."

That made Ellie wince. "Was she afraid of him?"

"I don't think so actively." He paused. "Distrustful of him is better. All she said to me really was that he was nice looking and well mannered, but she had an uneasy feeling about him after a while, so she broke it off. He didn't take it well."

In Ellie's opinion, he didn't take it well *at all*. Jason felt the same way, she could tell, but other than sending her a meaningful sidelong glance, didn't say anything.

She asked it again. "Randy, any idea where he might be? We think he has a suspicion that maybe he's high profile in this case."

He shook his head and said bitterly, "He sure wouldn't

send me a postcard." But then he added slowly, "He has a property on a place called Long Lake. If he isn't at home, maybe he went there."

Long Lake? There were only about a thousand of those in Wisconsin and Minnesota, if she had to guess. "Can you give us a county or other source of location?"

"Yeah, I can." Randy was steadier now, his breathing slowing. "Up between Ashland and Cornucopia. It had been a camp at one time. Lambert inherited it from an uncle or an aunt, or someone in his family. He took Jan up there once to see it when he was trying to decide what to do with it. It has been closed for a few years. Maybe he went there. A bunch of unused cabins and stands of trees sounds to me like a good place to hide."

It was something.

But it could be nothing. She was fairly convinced Lambert was dead, just as Jason suggested. Still it was a lead. "Ever think of law enforcement as a career? Can you find it on a map?"

"No. She just mentioned it to me once because she said it was pretty secluded and she'd already been starting to get uncomfortable around him." Randy's voice was grim. "I was naturally never invited there. I know Lambert hates my guts. I bet if I'd been at Janet's house with her, we wouldn't be having this conversation because I wouldn't still be around. He must have been happy as hell when I was arrested."

Ellie didn't disagree. She really wasn't eager to take another tour of Wisconsin, especially all the way up to Lake Superior, not that it wasn't beautiful country, but that was quite a drive. She called Grasso anyway. "I need you to look up property tax records for Michael Lambert if you don't mind so we have an address."

"I'm at my desk right now, so no problem."

"I'm only interested in some property he owns up north. I'd also like for you to contact the local sheriff's office there and let them know we'll be up there looking around for a suspect that is likely armed and dangerous, so don't send some rookie deputy to meet us. It is not our jurisdiction, so he or she—I don't know who it is—makes that decision, but those two U.S. marshals were blindsided. They were seasoned officers."

"I'll do both those things." There was a pause. "Maybe I should go with Santiago instead."

It had occurred to her, and she had a feeling Jason would snap him up on that offer, but it wasn't like she'd put herself actively in harm's way. "We know full well what we're dealing with. Thanks for the offer. Down the line I might sit on the bench, but for now this is still my game. We're on our way."

"Just a thought."

"I appreciate it."

Jason said immediately when she hung up, "I didn't even need to hear his part of the conversation. You should have said yes."

"No, I'll just let you be my knight in shining armor."

"I'm going to have to babysit you in a very real sense of that word. Ellie, let's drop Randy off and pick up Grasso."

It never hurt to have more backup. Careful with her choice of words, she said, "Okay, fine, but I think Lambert is long gone."

"You know I agree, but he could be anywhere. In Vegas playing a slot machine for all we know."

"We have his abandoned car and even his house keys. As far as we know, he doesn't, or didn't, even know we suspected him in the least."

Unless he remembered that single damning description of the ring and decided that Locke's faith in them was well placed.

Lodgepole pines and small meadows. Jason had lived his entire life in Milwaukee except for his stint in the military, so this northern part of his home state wasn't all that familiar, but it was undeniably scenic. Lake Superior was lapping at the shores like a hungry creature, the water sparkling under a gleaming sun.

The camp had a faded sign with a canoe and a pine tree, and the lane was unkempt, and since it was dry, hard to tell if a car had been down it recently. Maybe if he was an Eagle Scout or something he could, but that was not part of his background. He also had no idea how to track a bear or a deer, and his first fishing experience had been with Ellie not that long ago. However, if you wanted to tangle with the enemy on foreign ground wearing combat boots, he could hold his own.

"This is a dead end."

"Nope." Ellie pointed upward as they bumped along. "A decent-sized vehicle broke off that overhanging branch and it is recent. Could be the sheriff."

"Let's see if his car is there, Ms. Sleuth."

"You better hope I am right."

It wasn't. A huddle of dark cabins, a general air of disrepair, and that Lambert had put it up for sale was no surprise. It was Grasso who said, "The lake proximity is nice, but that's about it. No wonder he didn't know what to do with it. If someone handed me this, I'd hand it right back."

No official vehicle was anywhere in sight.

Jason kind of liked it with the sun shining, but in the winter it would have to be downright desolate. Old but quaint if a bit dilapidated at the moment, with sagging roofs, and he wouldn't set a foot on any of the docks, but the trees were nice and the water rippled down below. "Let's look around."

Ferns had grown up along the paths and pines stood in solitary guardianship, and there was a musty smell of disuse. Jason had never gone to summer camp—that was not an option with his old man—but it was the ideal of a bygone age with small docks for each building and a beautiful view of the water. None of the cabins were locked, so they briefly opened doors and saw a repeated pattern of square rooms and a woodstove, and a small but functional dated minuscule kitchen setup. The cabins certainly needed some updating but were charming in an old-fashioned sense with slightly warped boards on the floor, bunk beds, and each had a view of the water.

First two cabins, not one footprint on the dusty floors.

The body was in the third cabin.

Lambert's glassy eyes were wide open and there was a bloody hole in his right temple. A gun lay on the floor next to his hand.

Ellie muttered uncharacteristically, "Well . . . shit."

Jason had to say, "Hey, not in front of the baby."

He deserved the look he received. Grasso was always the voice of reason. "Okay, I don't think there's any doubt he's dead, so we owe Randy Lane for this one. Let's get a top-notch forensics team on it, and I think I hear a car, so maybe that's local law enforcement."

The sheriff who arrived was a pragmatic man who took one look and called the coroner right away. His only comment was that it was a pretty decent place to commit suicide.

It wasn't suicide.

Just like Forsythe.

"Deserted old place like this, the owner might have just found a skeleton in a few months."

"No he wouldn't. That is the owner." Jason didn't have any choice but to at least say that much. "We can identify him. We've met him before."

"That's interesting. Why exactly are you folks up here? When Lieutenant Grasso said armed and dangerous, I decided to come myself to assist if I could. I'd say he was armed because I can see the gun right next to him, but it seems he was more dangerous to himself than anyone else."

Ellie took over. "We think he stepped on toes of the wrong people in a federal investigation. A tip came our way he might own this property. We wondered if he might be hiding out. He's an assistant district attorney. It's complicated. We'd really like a talented ME."

"Okay . . . all right, I agree with that. Here's a question, how'd he get here?" Sheriff Riggs was pretty sharp, a little weathered, maybe early sixties, but on it. "Any idea? There's no car but mine and yours. This is pretty secluded."

"Good question." Ellie was calm, but her tone was brittle. "Very good question."

"I have three homicide detectives right at this scene. It makes a man wonder if this isn't a murder."

She said, "It makes us wonder too."

Grasso was coming to a few conclusions too. Jason could see it in his expression. He said, "The investigation involves several agencies."

"Agencies?"

"Yes, agencies in the plural. Federal mostly, but we are definitely players."

Riggs let out a long breath. "I'm going to let you

handle it then with my hands off. Let me know what comes of all this. None of you seem happy about this situation, but also not surprised. Let me guess: We need to have him transported to your medical examiner. I'll send a deputy down with the body. Our coroner is going rule it a suicide, I know that already. It looks like one to me. I'm not positive you're on board with that. I'll stay here until Doc Carson arrives and we can let it go from there."

"Thanks for the help." Grasso shook his hand.

Jason muttered as they left, "*This* is a potential fan with not so fragrant debris behind it hitting a wall."

"From every way you look at it," Grasso agreed, hands in the pockets of his tailored slacks, a frown on his face. "I hate to break this news, but you two are great detectives and terrible actors. So you nailed Lambert as Locke's killer, he knew you now had a solid case, and Lambert came up here and killed himself. Case over, but I'm with the sheriff, how did he get here?"

Ellie looked at Jason. "That detail bothers us. No one tried to even hide that. Burden of evidence is on us. We have his car. Yet he got here somehow."

"Just like Forsythe. You put him forth as the possible killer and suddenly he commits suicide. You decide Lambert did it instead and actually have some proof instead of just a suspect, same thing happens. Lambert decides to check out. Or it looks like it anyway."

"That detail bothers us a lot."

"How much?"

"How much does it bother *you*?"

Grasso said contemplatively, "I'm still trying to process it."

Jason felt the same way. "We have hours to hash it out as we drive back to Milwaukee."

Grasso wasn't shy. "I don't need hours. I'm thinking someone might have brought Lambert here and killed him. I just don't know who. It wasn't Locke. He'd have to be a magician with a transporter device to pull it off. Someone else did it. Conspiracy to commit murder is the closest we could get for him. It was his wife."

Jason thought so too.

Grasso went on. "The cabins were wide open, so no forced entry is immaterial. All three of us know what might have happened."

"'Might' is the most important word. We can't prove anything." Ellie was prosaic about it, walking next to them both under the moving leaves. "Oh, we could try. Go with the idea we're right and drag up charges against grieving parents who are smart enough never to leave evidence. Good luck with that. I can't see a win here for either side. I want to see the tox report. If he was drugged, we have a case."

"If Randy hadn't happened to remember about this place and tell us, the sheriff is correct, there could have been a skeleton there months from now when—and if—someone decided to look around." Jason was just thinking out loud. It was a hot day, but at least the breeze was cooling things down. "We'd maybe look down the line when we went through Lambert's finances, but it wouldn't be so soon. That he owned the property wouldn't necessarily mean anything to us without Randy's description of it. We might have just labeled him a fugitive."

"That's really true. A decent attorney would rip any circumstantial case to shreds, and I bet Locke knows a lot of decent attorneys."

Ellie was right again. If anyone would have contacts, he would be the one. "Maybe the autopsy could make a case. Even if the ME comes back with homicide to contradict the suicide, I don't know it would fly. It could be anyone. Lambert was involved with the federal investigation."

Grasso was a pragmatic man. "I guess let's wait and see if our ME agrees with the coroner up here."

Jason had a feeling the case was open and closed now.

Chapter 24

Long two days. If Ellie didn't see the inside of a car again anytime soon, that would be fine with her. They'd stopped in Wausau to stay the night on their way back south. She'd declined the restaurant and eaten a sandwich in the room, and gone straight to bed after catching up on emails.

Jason muttered as they walked into the federal building, "This won't be fun."

She agreed.

Locke was in his office at his desk, cool and composed as ever, but Ellie knew for sure he understood the purpose of their visit. "Hello, Detectives. Have a seat and close the door, please."

Jason took care of the door, Ellie sat down. She wasn't interested in playing a game. "Lambert is dead."

"So I've heard. I am understandably not sorry."

"We didn't think you would be." She looked him straight in the eye. "In fact, we aren't all that sorry either, considering this case, but it is our job to decipher what might have happened. Lo and behold, we have another inconclusive crime scene."

"I've argued some cases with inconclusive evidence. It is never an easy undertaking." His face was expressionless, and that spoke to Ellie more than anything. "Why do I have a feeling there's an accusation coming my way?"

She kept her tone very even. "I don't have the slightest idea how you did it. Very clean. But we are really good at what we do, and you surely knew we'd figure it out. Isn't that why you asked for us to investigate?"

Locke didn't dissemble. "But then you have to cross the street to my side and need to prove it. That is our territory."

"I don't want to prove it. But I should try, shouldn't I? Isn't that the letter of the law?"

Locke spread his hands. "If you are asking for my opinion, I'll give it. I believe there is law and then there is justice. One is delivered by man and one is delivered by a force we have yet to define, though we really have been trying for thousands of years. That is merely an observation. You hand them to me with proof, and I see they are punished."

"We are the hunters and you are the warriors?"

"I think that is very well put." Locke didn't look tired as much as resigned. "Maybe this world shouldn't need either of us, but it does. I wish my daughter still needed me."

No words for that one. Jason didn't comment either, though she sensed he wanted to say something.

She opted for, "Randy said your wife can keep his little dog if she wants her, otherwise he'll take her back and place her somewhere else. I don't get the impression he's going to stay in Milwaukee."

Locke rested his elbows on his desk. "You have done a lot for my family, so I will tell you this. The arrest warrants are starting to come through, including one for his older brother Robert for the murder of Reid. Don't ask me what the investigators found, but it was enough for a judge to agree. I believe Randy's mother and his youngest brother have gone off to parts unknown. An excellent choice, because that ship is sinking and neither one of them was at the helm. His father's assets have been seized, and his passport confiscated. For what it's worth, I always thought Randy Lane loved my daughter and that Lambert just wanted to own her. Please tell Randy, Detective MacIntosh, that we'll keep the dog and it will have a good home."

That was an exceptionally effective way to say the conversation was over.

"I'll write up the report." Ellie said it quietly, sitting behind her desk. "You handle Karsten. Deal?"

Both Grasso and Jason said in unison, "Deal."

Then they both looked annoyed with each other. Oh, this transition was going to go smoothly. Not.

The box had been there in plain sight right next to her keyboard when they'd gotten back to the station. Ellie worried it might be a gift from Bryce, because while her name was printed on a label there was no return address, so she had no desire to open it in front of Jason. She'd made up her mind that if all went smoothly with this house purchase, she'd end her lease and really see how it went if they moved in together. At least this time she wasn't moving into someone else's house, but would truly be starting new and fresh. She knew he'd want her to bring her furniture and pictures, and she could just let him take care of the outside touches of that beloved yard he wanted so badly.

That third bedroom could be a den with his obnoxiously large television and old comfy couch. They were both very used to having their own space. She'd put her desk in the nursery for now.

Thinking ahead. Nothing ventured and then nothing was gained. They could try it.

She said firmly, "One of you go talk to Karsten, the other one go talk to Hammett, unless you're dying to write this report instead."

Jason turned to Grasso. "Don't we outrank her? Can she order us around?"

Grasso looked amused. "No wonder you get shot all the time, you live dangerously, Santiago. You handle Karsten because I'm well aware of how you feel about the Underworld, but if you'd rather—"

"No, no. Karsten scares me too, but I'd rather take another bullet than go down there if I have another choice." He left in a hurry, walking down the hall in long strides.

Grasso lingered a moment, leaning a hip on her desk. "If Hammett says homicide is her manner-of-death opinion on Lambert, does it determine what are we going to do?"

It wasn't like she hadn't turned that over and over in her mind. "I'm not sure what we could possibly prove."

"I'm also disinclined to push it."

At least they were on common ground. "We are not the maestros, we are the orchestra. We play the music, but we don't direct it. I say we'd ask Metzger if it comes back that way, and I'm going to guess he doesn't want us to ask at all because then he'd have to make a difficult decision."

Grasso gave her a level look. "We'll make good partners. At least we understand each other. I'll go talk to the ME."

He left and she looked at that unopened box.

Neither of them had particularly noticed it, but she

had. It looked like nothing besides just an ordinary small box, but *she* hadn't left it there. Someone had paid her a visit.

Inside was a ring, but it certainly wasn't from Bryce.

Opal. Garnets. It was absolutely beautiful. Ellie almost made the mistake of picking it up—her forefinger actually touched it—but then saw the note beneath it.

It read in plain printed type: *It was in his pocket. He was carrying it like a trophy.*